PRAISE FOR JENNY HALE

"Jenny Hale writes touching, beautiful stories."—***New York Times* Bestselling Author RaeAnne Thayne**

"A festive addition to the Holiday romance genre with a subtle poignancy that sets it apart."—***Kirkus Reviews*** on *The Noel Bridge*

"I can always count on Jenny Hale to sweep me away with her heartwarming romantic tales."—**Bestselling Author Denise Hunter** on *Butterfly Sisters*

One of "19 Dreamy Summer Romances to Whisk you Away" in ***Oprah Magazine*** on *The Summer House*

One of "24 Dreamy Books about Romance" in ***Oprah Daily*** on *The Summer House*

"Touching, fun-filled, and redolent with salt air and the fragrance of summer, this seaside tale is a perfect volume for most romance collections."—***Library Journal*** on *The Summer House*

"Hale's impeccably executed contemporary romance is the perfect gift for readers who love sweetly romantic love stories imbued with all the warmth and joy of the holiday season."—***Booklist*** on *Christmas Wishes and Mistletoe Kisses*

"A great summer beach read."—**PopSugar** on *Summer at Firefly Beach*

"This sweet small-town romance will leave readers feeling warm all the way through."—**Publishers Weekly** on *It Started with Christmas*

ALSO BY JENNY HALE

Where Are You Now

Out of the Blue

The Golden Hour

The Magic of Sea Glass

Butterfly Sisters

The Memory Keeper

The Summer Hideaway

Ten Christmases Without You

The Noel Bridge

Meet Me at Christmas

The Christmas Letters

The Broken Hearts Beach Club

The Broken Hearts Beach Club

JENNY HALE

USA TODAY BESTSELLING AUTHOR

HARPETH ROAD
PRESS
Nashville

HARPETH ROAD PRESS

Published by Harpeth Road Press (USA)
P.O. Box 158184
Nashville, TN 37215

Paperback: 978-1-963483-58-1
eBook: 978-1-963483-57-4
Library of Congress Control Number: 2026906810

The Broken Hearts Beach Club: A Heartwarming Women's Fiction Novel

Cover Design by Kristen Ingebretson
Cover Images © Shutterstock

Harpeth Road Press, April 2026

ONE

As Emily Jacobs entered The Brewing Bloom, a bustling coffee-shop-slash-floral-boutique in her neighborhood of Inglewood, Tennessee, she struggled to focus through the fog of distress that had been plaguing her for the last three days. Today, she was supposed to be offering emotional support to her friend, Blair Andrews, but given the news that had blindsided her, she was bound to fail miserably. Once she got talking, her own emotions would surely spill out.

She'd had so many plans for the warmer months, but in the span of a few minutes, they'd all dissolved into thin air—gone just like the rest of her future.

Six years ago, she and her fiancé, Will, had chosen this area for their future home. It offered a quieter, residential feel with a sense of community, while still being close to Nashville, where Will was getting a foothold in songwriting circles after scoring a publishing deal. She'd fallen in love with its charming, historic neighborhoods, tree-lined streets, and blend of lifelong residents and transplants.

The previous year, his first published song had made

enough for them to make the down payment on a bungalow that sat between two oak trees on a quiet street. They'd planned for the renovations to be finished just in time for their wedding in August. Because of that, she hadn't renewed the lease on her apartment, and all she'd thought about since was sinking into a king-sized bed in her gorgeous new house and falling asleep without the constant buzz of traffic she'd become accustomed to.

Like everywhere in the city these days, however, Inglewood wasn't as quiet anymore. And today, neither was her mind. With a lump lodged in her throat, she scanned the busy seating area for a table that would accommodate three.

The coffee shop was lively, with a line of at least eight patrons snaking along the wall toward the register. Two women chatted merrily as they waited. They seemed so relaxed and carefree, one of them throwing her head back and laughing at something the other said. At the counter, the barista greeted a customer, wrinkling her nose in conversation. None of them had a clue about the battle raging in Emily's mind.

A couple got up from a small table by the window, next to a shelf of silver buckets filled with twine-tied bundles of peonies, lilacs, and lavender. Only two seats, but it was the lone option. Emily loped over to it, quickly dropping her bag in the empty chair and sitting in the other. She scanned the place for familiar faces, but Sienna and Blair hadn't arrived yet.

Out the window, heat rose from the sidewalk, giving the air a wavy appearance. A pair of women ambled through the haze, pushing strollers with one hand and holding ice cream cones from the shop down the street in the other. The Southern summer had come in like a lion.

Summer was Emily's favorite time of year. She'd

packed up her second-grade classroom and put her blonde hair into a ponytail, where it would stay for the next two and a half months during her school's summer break. This year, she and Will had planned to use her time off to put the final touches on their kitchen renovations while they began to move their things to the new house. Over the last few weeks, in anticipation, she'd shopped for paint swatches for the cabinets that would bring in muted pops of color—olive green, deep beige, bright white... She'd imagined a mason jar of daisies on their wooden table, and an oatmeal-colored runner along the distressed hardwood in front of the sink. Ever since they'd bought the home, she'd been taking tiny steps toward building the perfect place for a growing family. She wanted to have kids as soon as possible—she couldn't wait to start their life together.

Tears pricked her eyes, and she quickly blinked them away. She'd been so good about putting on a brave face, but her emotions welled up knowing she was about to see the two women she confided in. She'd tell them. She always told them everything. But there hadn't been a good time yet, and now wasn't good either.

"Ah, you got a table."

Sienna Duvall's voice sounded as if it were at the end of a long tunnel. Emily forced herself out of her thoughts and smiled at her friend.

"Nice job." A friendly kiss plucked Emily's cheek and Sienna gave her a squeeze. Her dark hair with golden highlights smelled like jasmine and citrus. When Sienna pulled away, she put her hands on the hips of her fashionable trousers, looking around. "Is Blair here yet?"

But Sienna didn't wait for an answer.

"Excuse me," she said to someone at a nearby table.

"Are you using this chair?" She waggled a finger at it, her gold bangles jingling.

The patron shook his head and gestured toward the empty seat.

Sienna slid it over to their table, then plopped down. "I have some *incredible* news. Have you ordered yet?"

Emily dragged herself out of her state of heaviness and focused on Sienna's dark eyes. "No, I haven't." She forced another smile.

"Wait." Her friend leaned in, inspecting Emily's face. Sienna noticed right away. She always did. "What's wrong?"

"It's okay," Emily said, fluttering her hands in the air. If she tried to explain, she'd blubber right there in the coffee shop and make a scene. "Just a tough day. Man the fort. I'll get us coffees and then you can tell me your news." She hoisted herself out of her chair. "What do you want?"

Sienna squinted at her with suspicious curiosity, but she didn't ask anything more. "Decaf latte, oat milk, no foam. *Decaf,*" she repeated.

"Got it." Emily turned away before her friend could inquire any further. She jumped in line at the back of the shop, glad to have a minute to collect herself.

A few seconds was all she got, though, as Blair entered and stepped up next to her.

"Hey."

"How are you?" Emily asked, putting on a brave face.

"Good." Blair waved across the room to Sienna.

If they were up for awards for the worst life event, Blair would win. As a social media influencer, she'd made an incredible living video blogging. She was approachable; she could shoot those bright, airy videos that made everyone else feel as if they were living in a cave; and she was as beautiful inside as she was outside. For nine months, she'd documented her pregnancy online—the stunning nursery she was creating, the preparatory shopping trips, little onesies she was buying in anticipation, and first-time-mom hacks she was devouring. Her ad revenue was through the roof—baby-equipment companies, clothing shops, custom diaper bags all wanted a place in her feed.

Then, on one horrific day, everything fell apart. She lost the baby in her ninth month. She hadn't posted a video in the six weeks since.

When Blair lost the baby, Emily and Sienna formed a support group for her, meeting her for coffee regularly. They spent most of the time talking about nothing—just everyday happenings. Blair told them the normalcy of their conversation reminded her of what it was like to feel human.

"I'm better than usual, actually," Blair continued. "My hormones are evening out. The night sweats seem to have finally subsided."

Blair and Emily moved a few paces in line.

"And I have fewer mood swings, but I still can't shake the bad days..." She rubbed her temples. "Sorry. By now you were probably hoping to hear 'fine.'"

"No, I want to hear how you really are," Emily said.

"I don't know if the coffee line is where you want me to unload anyway." Blair rolled her head on her shoulders. "I wish I could feel like myself again. Look at everyone. They're laughing and chatting. I wonder if I'll ever be like that?"

Emily opened her mouth to answer, when Blair threw her hand to her head and groaned.

"Listen to me. I'm such a downer."

"You've been through a traumatic event. You *are*

allowed to be a downer with your best friends. We're here for you."

"You two make me feel like sunshine for a little bit. You're the only ones who can get me laughing these days. It's good for my soul."

They shuffled forward as the group in front of them finished up.

Blair took a breath, her petite chest rising under her gauzy ivory sundress. The color, against her long honey-brown hair, brought out her tan skin and pink lips. "What's new with you?" she asked.

"Also not a question to answer in the coffee line," Emily said, pushing the dread back down where she'd tried to keep it since arriving. Today was about bringing Blair that all-important sunshine. "I'll tell you later."

Blair offered an interested once-over and then frowned.

Emily changed the subject. "Sienna's got news. *Incredible* news, apparently."

"Oh? I could use some good news! What is it?"

"I'm not sure. I told her to hang on until I got back with her coffee."

They stepped up to the barista, put in their orders, and stood among the other waiting customers. Blair pointed at their table. Sienna was wiping the surface with a napkin and straightening the chairs.

"That's just like her," Emily said with a punch of humor and fondness for her old friend.

The three women had known each other since college. Emily had been the first to move to Nashville, chasing Will's dream. Blair, whose husband, Rocko, was friends with Will, followed soon after, once she'd seen Emily's new bungalow. The two couples became inseparable. Then Emily and Blair lured Sienna to Music City with their endless talk of the booming housing market. A year later, Sienna was living in a condo in The Gulch with glass walls overlooking the city skyline, drinking cosmos with the young and privileged, and caught up in a whirlwind relationship with her now-husband, Tyson.

When their order was ready, Emily handed Blair her coffee, grabbed hers and Sienna's, and they made their way back to the table.

"If I wasn't saving this spot for us, I'd have joined you in line," Sienna said when they reached her. "We could've had a full therapy session while we waited, as long as it took." She eyed Emily with a concerned look, obviously still trying to figure out what had upset her.

"I know, right? It's swarming with people today." Emily handed Sienna her coffee, moved her handbag, and sat down.

"Decaf, right?" Sienna asked, holding up her cup.

"Yep." Blair took the chair across from Emily and grasped her cup with two delicate hands.

"So tell us your news." Emily immediately diverted the attention from herself to Sienna. "I told Blair you'd used the word 'incredible.'"

"Wait. First, how are you doing, Blair?" Sienna brushed Blair's hair behind her ear and put a manicured hand on her friend's shoulder.

"Decent enough, but I'd love some good news."

Sienna blinked rapidly in a show of drama. "Okay. You won't believe it."

"Do tell," Emily urged her.

"Remember the three-million-dollar listing I got?"

"Yes..." Emily said.

Sienna was an up-and-coming real estate agent. Her friendly personality, no-nonsense approach, and intelligence gave her an instant trustworthiness. So much so that she'd already jumped ranks faster than anyone at her brokerage, taking on some pretty incredible properties.

Blair leaned forward, poised to hear the news.

Sienna set her cup down slowly, prolonging the drama. "I sold it."

"That's fantastic," Emily said. "Holy moly."

That one sale probably made her just as much as, if not more than, Emily made in a year teaching school.

"Isn't it?" But Sienna's lined lips were spread in a tight smile. Then her eyes suddenly and unexpectedly brimmed with tears.

"What's the matter?" Emily asked, blindsided by her complete one-eighty.

Sienna tipped back her head, her long lashes bobbing as she blinked away the emotion. "I'm so sorry. I'm just really happy," she said. But the catch in her throat told a different story.

Was there something in the air? It seemed all three of them needed a shoulder today.

Blair took Sienna's hand. "You can tell us, Sienna. What happened?"

"I really can't tell you yet." She angrily wiped her tears with her free hand, smudging her perfect makeup. "Why am I *crying*? I don't cry."

Sienna was a pro at hiding her emotions. Her poker face was world-class. She hadn't shown disappointment when someone had outbid her client, and she'd lost the sale she'd hoped would pay for her and Tyson's honeymoon. No tears fell when they'd all watched *Titanic* together. And when they'd surprised Emily for her twenty-seventh birthday, Sienna had walked her up to the spa stone-faced—Emily'd had no idea.

Emily had never seen Sienna like this before. She eyed Blair to question if she seemed to have any idea. Blair's head was cocked to the side, her stare locked on Sienna with a strange expression.

"Yeah, you never cry. That's not like you," Blair said, her voice soft. "Your face is puffier than it usually is too."

Sienna rolled her eyes as she dragged her red fingernails under them. "Great."

What was Blair getting at? She and Sienna were in some sort of silent deadlock.

"Someone want to fill me in?" Emily asked.

"I don't know," Blair said. "Sienna, want to fill her in?"

"I don't want to." Sienna sniffled, looking around before fluffing her hair.

"It could just be me..." Blair said. "But if I'm right, it's okay to tell us. I'll be fine."

Sienna snatched a napkin from the holder on the edge of the table and dabbed her tears. "I'm pregnant."

"I knew it," Blair said.

Emily threw her hands over her mouth to stifle her gasp. Sienna and Tyson loved their freedom, and the fact that their life was unrestricted and void of emotional vulnerability. Sienna's independence was the core of who she was. It was nothing for her to go on a 6:00 a.m. run before she spent an hour at the gym and then schmoozed with people all day. A typical night involved cocktails and extravagant dinners with clients. She lived in a high-rise apartment, seven stories in the air. Her furniture was modern, with lots of clean lines and sharp edges. Her life was the opposite of childproof.

"What did Tyson say?" Emily asked.

"He doesn't know yet."

"You told *us* before you told your husband?" Blair asked, her head tilted.

"You think he'll want to sell the condo and buy some God-awful single-family new construction in a neighborhood called Maplewood or Pine Ridge? He's going to panic." She put her fist to her lips as if she were stifling nausea. "I don't know what this will do to our marriage. I don't even know if I'll be a good mom."

"You might surprise yourself," Blair said. The way she assessed Sienna, it was as if she were pondering the cruelty of why Sienna would have been given such a gift when a baby was all Blair had ever wanted.

"We don't even have a dog," Sienna said. "Tyson didn't want one. But it's a good thing because we ended up finding our apartment, which I love. And there's no way I could truck up and down six flights of stairs to let a dog out. He and I work too much anyway. Neither one of us would ever be home to take care of it."

"Well, a baby won't need to pee outside," Emily offered brightly.

Sienna huffed. "But a baby will need a whole lot more... And I work for a living. What will I do?"

"You can still work," Emily offered.

"How will I fit a child into our lifestyle? I'm going to fail this baby."

Emily wanted to tell her that her life would take shape around the child, and she'd love that little ball of joy, but not having any kids of her own, she wasn't anywhere near an expert. A flash of fear overtook her as her personal issue took hold of her mind again, but she quickly pushed it away.

"What are you going to do?" Emily asked.

"I don't know yet." Sienna hung her head. "I've thought about the options, and I can't fathom doing anything other than keeping it. I just don't know how Tyson is going to react."

Blair squeezed Sienna's hand. "I'll help you. It'll be okay."

Sienna's shoulders fell, and she addressed Blair. "I sound like such an ungrateful jerk. I'm supposed to be lifting you up." She took a long, slow drink from her cup.

"I'm not the only one in the world with struggles. It's okay to have your own. I've got your back," Blair said.

Emily leaned across the table and gave Sienna's arm an affectionate squeeze. "When will you tell Tyson?"

"I don't know. He's not going to be thrilled. And I need time to get my mind around us having a baby before I say anything to him." She looked down at her cup.

"We're here for you," Emily said.

As the coffee shop buzzed with activity, the three of them sat in turmoil. Were they headed toward some kind of crossroads in their adult lives? A singular moment where things would change forever? In a strange way, it felt as if they were.

TWO

ONE WEEK LATER

Emily stood at the bottom of the walking trail at Radnor Lake State Park, bent at the waist and stretched, grabbing hold of one ankle, and welcoming the pull on her leg muscles. She righted herself and shifted her weight into a side lunge.

The sun was already blazing, casting its warm glow over the grass. A morning hike had been Blair's idea. Her holistic health practitioner had suggested she lay off the caffeine and get outside more, so this week's meet-up had been relocated from The Brewing Bloom.

"Morning," Sienna said, coming up beside Emily. She was wearing a fashionable pair of aviators and a matching shirt and shorts set.

"Good morning," Emily said.

Sienna held out her arms and began doing circles with them. "I'm glad we skipped the coffee today. Yesterday, when I got one with Tyson, it turned my stomach out of nowhere. I had to fake that they'd made it with dairy instead of oat milk. He insisted on taking it back to the barista, but I convinced him not to bother."

"You still haven't told him?" Emily asked.

"No. I don't know how long I can keep this up, though. And once he knows, it'll feel real, and I'll have to deal with it. What if he doesn't want the baby? What if he doesn't want us? The mere thought is heartbreaking. I've still got a few months to figure it out before I show."

A few months was longer than Emily had to fix her problem...

"What's that face?" Sienna asked.

"What face?"

Sienna eyed Emily. "You have the same weird look you did when we were at the coffee shop last week."

"I saw it too," Blair said, crossing the grass toward them. "And you'd admitted in line that something was going on, but you wouldn't say what it was."

Given how close Blair's husband was to Will, she couldn't believe she hadn't gotten wind of everything from Rocko. She was just going to have to come out with it. Better the news came from her than Will. Her friends had both confided in her. Now it was Emily's turn to drop her own bomb.

Blair put an arm around her shoulders. "You can tell us."

Emily took in a deep breath, her heart fluttering. "Will broke off the engagement."

The words floated on the air toward her friends; their reactions slow to emerge. Then their shocked expressions caused her breath to go shallow, and she understood what Sienna had meant by her comment a minute ago: Now they knew, it felt *real*.

"*What?*" Blair's mouth dropped open. "When?"

"A few days before our last coffee meeting."

"Why didn't you say anything before now?" Blair asked.

"We had enough to worry about without me dumping my problems on top of everything else."

Blair chewed her lip. "Rocko hasn't said anything. You'd think Will would've told him."

Emily shrugged, blinking away more tears.

"I can't believe this." Blair looked down at the ground, pacing. "Did you see it coming at all?"

Emily shook her head. "He left a note saying our differences were troubling him. I didn't even know we had any. But, apparently, the differences were that he thought it best to date the girl he'd met at the gym, and I guess he supposed I wouldn't think the same."

Sienna gasped.

"I have a month to get the house ready for sale. Even though it's mostly ready. Our things are still in boxes. I'd kept it all empty for the kitchen remodel." She swallowed against the lump forming in her throat. A tear slipped down her cheek, and she wiped it away.

"Where is he now?" Sienna asked.

"At his apartment, I guess—but his lease was up last week, so I'm not really sure." She didn't want to think about him shacking up with his little something from the gym. "He's left everything we bought together at the house. We're going to divvy it up at some point."

"There's no way Rocko knows," Blair said. "I'm certain. Even if it's escaped his attention to tell me, which it wouldn't, he'd have offered for Will to stay at our house, and I haven't seen him—not once."

"How are you coping?" Sienna asked.

"My chest feels like I have a boulder on it." Emily's voice broke. "I have all the wedding plans to cancel, and I'll have to let everyone know. It's mortifying."

"Oh my gosh, Em." Blair gave her a hug and then Sienna joined in.

Trying not to make a scene with a total breakdown, Emily cleared her throat. "Let's walk."

The three of them quietly began to stride down the paved pathway.

"Look at us," Sienna said as they paced along the trail leading around the bright-blue lake. "We're all three brokenhearted for our own reasons. What a summer."

"It's unbelievable," Blair said.

They fell into silence.

Emily turned her attention to the golden rays of sunshine on her face, the laughter of small children in the field, and the chirping of the birds. She stepped in and out of shady spots on the path, trying to focus on her breathing instead of everything on her mind. When they'd gotten far enough for the children's voices to fade away, a warm breeze rustled the leaves in the trees, which was a welcome sound, since no one was talking.

They strolled over the Spillway Bridge to the Lake Trail when Sienna stopped.

Blair and Emily did too.

"I wasn't expecting Emily's news today, and I'd planned to share something good, but now I'm not sure any of us are in the mood for it."

Emily looked over at her friend. "What is it?"

"It's fine if you all don't feel up to it."

Emily and Blair faced her.

"You know *the musician* client I have?" Sienna always added emphasis on "the musician" when she spoke of the mystery man she sold houses for. Under a strict nondisclosure agreement, she wasn't allowed to tell them who he was, but given his real estate budget, he had to be incredibly famous. Recently, he'd hired her to find a two-million-dollar house for his mother.

"Yeah?" Emily and Blair said in unison.

"I pulled a few strings and got his mom the house she wanted. To thank me, he offered me his private beach house along the Gulf Coast. It's free all summer, since his wife surprised him with an impromptu trip to Mykonos."

"Careful," Blair warned, her tone lightening the mood considerably. "We'll look up which country music star is in Mykonos and figure out who he is!"

They were always trying to guess.

Sienna made a face. "I've said too much. *Don't* try to look up who it is. I'd like to keep selling him houses, and I'd prefer not getting wrapped up in a lawsuit, thank you very much."

"I'm just saying, if I get on Instagram and see photos, I can't help that..." Blair giggled.

Emily couldn't wrap her head around an impromptu trip to somewhere that fabulous. A trip like that would've taken her years of saving and preparation.

Sienna held back her dark hair to keep the breeze from having its way with it. "Originally, I thought we could all take our significant others. But after your news, Em, it should be a girls' trip," she said as they started walking again.

"It's fine if Rocko and Tyson go," Emily said. "I love them both."

"I wouldn't want to make you the odd one out," Sienna said. "We should go, just the girls. It might be the therapy we all need—our own beach club for the brokenhearted."

Blair's face filled with life. "My holistic health guy did say I should be outside more," she said.

Sienna linked arms with Emily and then Blair. "Let's

take our weekly meet-ups on the road. We'll be The Broken Hearts Beach Club."

"It might do me some good," Blair said. "I'll run it by Rocko. He's got a few days off from building the apartment complex they're working on while they wait for permits, and he wanted to have a boys' weekend to go fishing. That might work out perfectly."

"Blair and I can work remotely," Sienna said, "and, Emily, you're off for the summer. We could always do Monday through Friday with the girls and then the husbands can come for the weekend or something."

"That's an idea," Blair said. "I'm in."

Emily considered the alternative: sitting alone in her apartment or the house she'd thought would one day be filled with the patter of tiny feet, happy family moments, and love between her and Will. Running away from her problems did sound enticing. She'd have some work to do to deal with the cancellation of the wedding, but she could do that anywhere.

Emily filled her lungs with warm air and let it out slowly. "The turquoise waters of the Gulf Coast, secluded from the world? Definitely count me in."

"It's open all summer. When would you all want to go?" Sienna asked.

"I can go whenever," Emily replied, pushing her shoulders back defiantly. "I have no one to answer to anymore." She dared not admit, however, that she'd gladly give up the freedom for the love of the man she'd lost.

"What about the sale of the house? Do you need to move things out to get it ready to sell?" Blair asked as they rounded the bend, the sapphire lake sparkling in the sunlight.

"Will can move the boxes to my apartment if he wants

to sell the house right now. Why should I make things easier for *him*?"

"Truth." Blair pumped her hands in the air.

"Let's talk to the hubbies and see what they say," Sienna said. "Tyson will be fine with whatever."

"I'll let you both know this afternoon." Blair leaned on the wooden railing overlooking the lake. "I could use some seclusion with just you girls. It would be therapeutic."

"I think so too." Emily tipped her head toward the sunshine. Maybe there'd be a silver lining in all this pain. She'd get to spend time with the people she cared about most. It could be a fresh start.

AFTER HER HIKE and a run to the grocery store, Emily stepped onto the front porch and opened the door to the quaint, single-story home with a gabled roof. She was tired from the trail they'd chosen to walk, but she wanted to get some boxes out of the way that she didn't trust Will with. She'd packed her grandmother's dishes in one of them and had keepsakes from her childhood in another. It wouldn't take her long to just stack the boxes against the wall in the garage.

The door creaked as she closed it behind her. She slipped her sneakers off her sore feet and padded across the original hardwood she'd refused to cover with large rugs so she could admire its charm.

The house was too quiet. Normally, Will was there chatting about plans or strumming a new song he'd written. She peered at the empty corner where his guitars had been, the hole he'd ripped in her heart breaking open again.

She went through the living room and into the kitchen,

dropping her two bags of food on the counter because it was too hot to leave them in the car. The open shelving where she'd previously stacked the plates and matching coffee mugs they'd gotten as early wedding gifts was empty. She'd already packed all the dishes for the remodel, but since they were going to sell the house, she'd taped up the boxes and pushed them into the hallway.

The room looked stark. Over the last week or so she'd worked there, but she hadn't *lived* there. She hadn't really had a life since she'd come home to find a note on the table, where it still sat—just a single envelope with her name on the front in Will's handwriting.

"WHAT IS THIS?" she'd asked him on the phone through her tears. She'd come to the house, ready to get started on more renovations after long hours spent finishing her end-of-year paperwork at school.

"I'm sorry, Em. I didn't want to hurt you." He'd sounded distant, not the same Will she'd spent her evenings with, cuddled under a blanket in front of the TV after work.

"Well, it's too late for that," she'd spat at him. "You left me a note?"

He'd told her it had been a mistake to commit to marrying so young. He wasn't ready.

Funny, he'd seemed very ready until recently. She'd combed through their last few months together, mentally bulleting the red flags she hadn't noticed before: the faint rose scent wafting around him that she'd caught a couple of times, wondering where it was coming from; the few days he'd said he'd be late to work on the house because he had songwriter meet-ups, but he'd come in smelling like a grill, his cheeks rosy; the expensive lunches she'd found on the credit card that he'd brushed off, saying he got hungry. None of those things had been the end of the world at the time, but since the note they'd occupied her mind all day, every day. Her imagination ran rampant with scenarios about what had really been going on. How could Will have even gotten to a point where he was looking around for someone else?

Emily had sighed a breath of relief when they'd gotten engaged. She loved being with someone who got her, the one person she could be entirely herself with. She was glad there was no more dating in her future. She relished the little moments with him—slips of time she couldn't have with anyone else, like sharing a sink when they washed up after dinner or hearing him hum as he plucked his guitar on the couch while she put dishes away. Married life was what she was built for.

Planning a future as Mrs. William Jacobs had been easy. Once they got their house updated the way they'd planned, she'd expected to build their little family. She taught school during the day, then drove to their house and took long strolls through their neighborhood when the weather was nice, imagining all the years they'd make that same walk together, pushing strollers and tossing footballs with their kids. Will had occasionally gone with her. But he hadn't joined her on those walks in quite a while. Perhaps the very monotony that made her so relaxed had been what had eventually broken them? Maybe he hadn't been quite as invested in their dream as she was.

The worst part about the situation was that the only way to make the pain subside was to have the Will she'd promised to marry in her life. But even if he changed his mind, she'd never be able to take him back, knowing what he'd done. She hoped he was happy with the mess he'd made.

AFTER GETTING the house in order, Emily went to her apartment and put away her groceries for one. Her phone rang. With a deep breath, she rolled her head and answered.

"Hey, it's Sienna."

"Hey." Emily put her phone on speaker and slid a half-sized carton of eggs into the fridge.

"Sooo, what are you doing tomorrow?"

Emily righted herself. "Depends. Are we hiking or drinking coffee?"

Sienna chuckled. "Neither. We're driving. Rocko told Blair to go whenever she wanted. Both he and Tyson are fine meeting up with us for the weekend. I don't have any showings this week. How do things look for you?"

Emily stared at the groceries she'd just bought. In her old life, she'd have wanted to run things by Will, take her time, make a packing list so she didn't forget anything, but right now all she wanted to do was get out of town because it reminded her of everything she'd lost.

"I'm wide open. What time do you want to leave?"

Sienna squealed on the other end of the line. "It's a long drive. I'll pick you up tomorrow at seven."

"I'll be ready."

For the first time in her life, Emily didn't care to make a single plan. She'd put the house key under the mat and told Will he could come and go with the agent as he pleased. She had her whole summer ahead of her, and it was time to start finding out who she was now.

THREE

Monday morning, Sienna pulled up outside Emily's apartment in the royal-blue Maserati she'd bought after one of her larger home sales because she'd "needed a decent mode of transportation to show millionaire clients prospective homes." She leaned out the window.

"Morning, Sunshine!" she called from behind a large pair of black sunglasses and a floppy hat.

Blair waved from the passenger seat.

"Morning." Emily lugged her bags and the Yeti cooler Will had bought her for Christmas last year to the car and opened the trunk.

"What's in the cooler?" Sienna asked.

"Eggs, cheese, cold cuts, lemonade, and a bunch of fruit. I didn't want it to go bad."

"Well, it might anyway. I'm planning on living on cocktails and seafood."

Emily shut the trunk, climbed into the backseat, and cocked an eyebrow. "Cocktails?"

Sienna sighed. "Well, I'll have a mocktail. But you know

what I mean." She threw her hands in the air. "It's our girls' trip!"

They all laughed, and Emily delighted in the relaxed atmosphere. She needed this trip more than anything. While she couldn't run from her problems forever, she could give herself a break and have some quality time with her best friends. They'd stood by her for everything since college and they'd stand by her now. She fastened her seatbelt as Blair leaned her thin forearm out the window. Then Sienna drove away.

Emily rubbed her empty ring finger where her engagement ring had been. She'd set it on the table and told Will to take it the night he'd shown up at their house to pack his things, not knowing she'd be there. She'd tried to get him to talk to her then, but he'd brushed her off, saying he "wasn't ready." How could he be ready to write her a breakup note but not ready to explain why? Her finger felt too light, not natural. A piece of her was missing, but the ring wasn't even the half of it.

She turned around to watch her apartment fading into the distance, along with the future she'd planned. She was so thankful for Sienna and Blair. They were the only constants in her upended world. Even though they all had their own battles at the moment, they could bask in the sunshine, breathe in the salty air, and let their troubles fade away for a little while.

Emily forced the thoughts out of her mind and breathed in the summer air. The warm breeze whipped through the backseat, blowing the runaway strands from her ponytail against her face. She closed her eyes and let out a long breath, allowing relaxation to set in.

SEVEN HOURS, two coffees, a lunch on the road, and a handful of bathroom breaks later, they arrived in Santa Rosa Beach. The boardwalk was humming with people, the shops' bright wares drawing them in.

"I'm dying for the bathroom again," Sienna said, parking and throwing open the door. She rushed ahead, running into a café with a striped awning and white bistro tables outside.

Blair laughed. "I can't imagine what she'll be like when she has the weight of a baby on her bladder." She nodded toward the beach shop next door. "Let's shop. She'll find us."

The bells on the door jingled as they went into the quaint seaside store. Emily ran her hand along the rainbow of pastel sweatshirts with beachy slogans printed on the front.

Blair pulled a yellow T-shirt from a nearby rack and held it up to herself. "Is this my color?"

"You could pull it off," Emily replied, sliding on a new pair of sunglasses and inspecting her reflection in a small mirror. She returned them to the display.

Blair hung the shirt back on the rack, and they meandered through the shelves of trinkets—coffee mugs with "Santa Rosa Beach" in swirling font, picture frames full of sand, baskets of seashells and starfish, refrigerator magnets with slogans like "Vitamin Sea" and "Good Vibes Only."

"Oh, books." Emily paced over to the wall of reading material. She bent down and grabbed a brightly colored rom-com, flipping it over to inspect the description on the back. Deciding against it, she returned it to its spot and selected another.

Blair flipped through one of the magazines.

"Thank goodness," Sienna said, breezing toward them.

"I didn't think I was going to make it. That last bottle of water did me in. What's that?" She hooked a finger over the top of Emily's book selection and pulled it down to view the cover. "Looks good."

Emily handed it to her and then picked up another—this one, a biography about a famous sea captain.

"Y'all doing okay?" a young blonde said from the other side of a short shelf of folded beach towels as she fished out new stock from a basket beside her.

Emily nodded brightly.

"Let me know if I can help with anything."

"Which of these local magazines do you recommend?" Blair asked the shopkeeper.

The girl pursed her lips as she eyed the wall. She draped a towel on the edge of the basket and came around to them. "If it were me, I'd get this one." She took a magazine off the shelf and handed it to Blair. "We just got them in today. It has a new article about Patrick Owens I plan to read." She leaned in dramatically, her eyes wide. "He's *so* hot."

"Who's that?" Sienna asked.

"A local. He's real mysterious. He's opening a new restaurant, and we've had New York magazines asking the locals if we know anything about it. They couldn't get him on the phone—he doesn't talk to a lot of people. Sometimes I see him at the fish market, but he rarely speaks to anyone."

Sienna made a face. "Gripping. Sounds like a real blast to read about."

The girl laughed. "I didn't sell it very well, did I?"

Sienna shook her head.

"No one could believe he actually sat for an interview—it's been the buzz in town." She grabbed a copy. "Now I've talked my own self into it." She rolled up the magazine and folded it under her arm. "I swear I spend half my paycheck in the very store that pays me."

"Thanks for your help," Sienna said.

"No problem." She set the magazine on top of a stack of towels and went back to folding.

"I'll pass for now," Blair said.

"How about you?" Sienna asked Emily. "Getting anything?"

Emily shook her head. "Nah. I already packed a book, so I should wait to see what the other shops have before I buy a second."

Blair led them back out to the car.

"Off we go to the beach house! Who's ready to live like the rich and famous?" Sienna said, starting the engine of the Maserati.

"Me!" Blair and Emily said in unison.

Sienna pulled out of the parking lot and put down the windows. The warm, salty air blew against their skin as they drove down the main drag, palm trees lining their way.

***

SIENNA'S CAR came to a halt outside a large, meticulously landscaped property with an iron gate. She leaned through the open window and punched in the code. With silent smoothness, the gate opened. They drove through, the gates closing behind them as they rounded the paved drive that was lined with beds of Japanese blueberry trees and purple muhly. Palms dotted a manicured yard of St. Augustine grass.

The mansion came into view—its white siding, deep wraparound balconies, and Bahama shutters made it look like something out of a magazine. Nestled along the Gulf, the sprawling estate had floor-to-ceiling windows facing a private beach and turquoise water. Emily could already imagine the feel of the golden sunsets on her face as she sat outside each evening.

Blair looked over at Emily as they got out of the car, her green eyes wide in astonishment.

"This is incredible," Emily said, using a hand to shade her view of a private boardwalk leading directly to the beach and an infinity-edged pool that spilled seamlessly onto the horizon.

"I'd say so." Blair pulled her bags from the trunk, her attention moving from the house to the beach and then back to the house.

"Perks of my job," Sienna said with a laugh.

"You really can't tell us who owns this house?" Blair asked.

"Sorry. Confidential." Sienna pretended to zip her lips.

"I think it's Luke Bryan's," Emily offered.

Blair pursed her lips and put her hands on her hips. "Mmm. I could see that. It kind of has Kenny Chesney vibes. Imagine a blue chair on the beach out back."

Sienna rolled her eyes. "Guess all you want. I'm not telling and risking the best client of my career." She air-zipped her lips again with two fingers.

Emily slipped the cooler strap onto her shoulder and grabbed her two suitcases. They hoisted their bags up the staircase to the double front doors, where Sienna typed in a second code and let them in.

Emily tipped up her head to view the vaulted wood-beamed ceilings. Then, she took in the white-oak floors as they made their way through the house. A soft, neutral color palette accented by shades of blue and turquoise comple-mented the natural textures that dotted the rooms. They entered the spacious kitchen. Emily set her handbag on the marble countertop, dropped the rest of her things onto the floor, and then unloaded the cooler's contents into the fridge. When she'd finished, she went into the open, sunlit great room with only a double-sided fireplace separating the two spaces.

"Is this an elevator?" Blair said, punching a button on the wall next to a glass sliding door.

"Yep." Sienna opened one of the French doors leading to the balcony, sending a breeze through the gauzy floor-to-ceiling curtains. "It also has a home theater and a wine cellar," she said.

"Wine cellar? Could be the McGraws' residence," Blair said, looking around. "I could see them having a wine cellar."

Sienna laughed.

"I feel relaxed already." Blair pushed the button. When the doors opened, she stepped inside. She waved from the interior of the elevator, her bags at her feet.

Emily picked up her two suitcases and joined Blair. Sienna followed. The door slid shut, and they were whisked to the second floor where they stepped out onto the balcony that overlooked the great room. They walked down the hallway, following Sienna's map to the primary suites: private rooms, each with their own view of the Gulf.

"I'll take this one." Blair ran through one of the open doors and fell onto the bed.

"Do you have a preference?" Emily waggled a finger between the other two open doors.

"You can have that one," Sienna said, pointing to another extravagant room closest to Blair. "Let's all take a dip in the pool once we've unpacked," she called on her way to the third bedroom.

"Sounds good to me!" Blair called from her fluffy bed.

Emily took her bags into her room and set them against the wall. A king-sized bed full of throw pillows and a crisp white duvet was opposite a set of French doors with a view of the private beach through the glass. She unzipped her suitcase, opened it, and fished out her bikini, laying the two-piece on the bed. Then she gathered up her toiletries and took them into the en-suite bathroom—a spa-like room with marble tile, a freestanding tub with Jacuzzi jets and built-in seats, and a chandelier made of sea glass in the center.

Twisting a gold knob next to a set of matching bottles of bubble bath and hand soap, she turned on the water at the faucet, testing the stream until it ran warm. She splashed her face and dried it on a soft towel hanging beside the sink.

"You coming?" Sienna called.

"Be down in a minute," Emily replied. She went back into the bedroom and opened the doors to her private balcony. A chair sat at the edge with an endless view of the water. Putting her hands in the pockets of her shorts, she leaned over and admired the stripes of light turquoise that blended into a deep teal, then a dark blue. The waves lapped calmly on the secluded white-sand beach.

She might actually forget the world here. At least, she hoped so.

WITH HER HAIR LOOSE, her pink bikini on, and her white mesh cover-up draped over, Emily took the stairs down to the pool to join Blair and Sienna. Blair was already on one of the loungers, taking in the remaining sun of the day, and Sienna was in the water, swimming to the edge that overlooked the beach.

"It's incredible here," Sienna said after spinning around to face Emily, her arms making ripples through the water.

"It really is." Emily dipped her toe in the cold pool, a shiver climbing her leg.

Sienna's phone pinged and she swam over to check it. With a dripping hand, she turned the sound off. "Always work," she said. "But I can't sell any houses from this pool right now, so I'll get it later."

A seagull squawked overhead, and the sound, coupled with the shush of the surf, was better than any tonic. A breeze rustled through the palm trees at the edge of the patio and the sunlight wrapped Emily in a cocoon of warmth. She closed her eyes, the backs of her eyelids orange with the brightness of the day. She and Will had been so busy planning a life for themselves that they hadn't taken time for little moments like this. Had that been their demise? Similar questions had plagued her over the last few days. Should they have taken more walks together, made more time for each other? Was that what he was doing with his new girlfriend? She opened her eyes and took a purposeful step into the water to try to shock the thoughts out of her brain. She couldn't fix things—they were too far gone. So she'd better get on with moving through it.

Blair sat up and took off her sunglasses. "I need to admit something."

Sienna and Emily turned.

"I keep thinking how perfect a place this would be to post about on socials, but I haven't posted anything since..." She took in a tight breath.

Emily left the step and went over to sit at the end of the lounger.

Blair's plump lips turned downward. "My private messages are overflowing, and emails have piled up. I've got at least seven hundred already. The subject lines are asking if I'm okay, wondering if something happened to me."

Emily rubbed her back. "Your fans are worried about you, that's all."

"I know. I just can't face them. Do you know how many times I'll have to relive what happened?"

Emily nodded, unsure of the best thing to say in that moment.

"And I lost my sponsors." She waved her hands in the air. "A couple are threatening legal action." She looked away quickly, blinking. "I'm sorry! Look at me, letting reality seep in already. I'll just be quiet."

Sienna swam over to their side of the pool and got out.

"I did wonder what happened," Emily said, fiddling with the edge of the striped towel under Blair. "I wasn't sure if you were explaining yourself behind the scenes or avoiding the issue of telling people altogether."

"I just stopped cold—*that's* what happened. I didn't hold up my end of the contracts, and all those businesses pulled their sponsorships and ads." She set her sunglasses onto the towel and looked Emily in the eye. "I didn't want to document it because then I'd have to re-experience the pain every time I opened my social media, when I want the memory of losing the baby to disappear just like I did." A tear slipped down her cheek. "I had my dream job, but now I can't bear to do it. I feel lost... I'm sorry to dump it on you two."

"I worry about my job as well," Sienna said. She wrapped herself in a towel and stood next to them, water dripping onto the white concrete. "I adore real estate. And I've gotten used to my lifestyle. What if, when the baby comes, I can't rush out on a client's whim? Then what?

Even if Tyson doesn't freak out, I don't know what my future will look like, and it terrifies me."

Emily swallowed the lump in her throat. "None of us know."

"We were supposed to be healing and relaxing here," Blair said. "We've not even been at the beach an hour and look at us. How can we get on with life when we're all still dealing with our problems? They're not going to go away."

"What did you call us the other day, Sienna?" Emily asked. "The Broken Hearts Beach Club? That's definitely us."

"Indeed," Sienna said with a sniffle.

The three of them were a sight to behold.

"I'll pour us all a glass of lemonade." Sienna dried off and threw on the delicate black cover-up that was draped on the chair under the umbrella. "Then we'll make a toast to The Broken Hearts Beach Club."

FOUR

Before they could toast to their sad little club, chimes rang inside the mansion.

Blair's brows pulled together. "Is that the doorbell?"

"I think so," Sienna said. "I'd better get it. Be right back."

Blair used the edge of the towel to dab her eyes, but then brightened. "What if it's the famous person and they've stopped by to say hello. We'll finally know who it is. We should go see."

Emily grinned. "I doubt it's the musician. Didn't Sienna say they were in Mykonos?"

"Oh yeah." Blair lay back against the lounger. "Probably maintenance or groundskeepers or something. Who do rich people employ?"

But a few minutes went by, and Sienna didn't return. Then the shadow of a man on his phone passed the glass door to the great room. Emily stood up and went inside, with Blair following.

In the kitchen the counters were littered with insulated cooler bags, baskets of fresh vegetables, and cooking supplies. The tall, broad-shouldered man with gold stubble and a striking jawline glanced over. His attention lingered on Emily as he talked quietly into his phone. She smiled, but he turned away.

"What's all this?" Emily whispered to Sienna, waggling a finger at the items on the counter.

"He's the musician's personal chef. He's supposed to be cooking dinner for him and his family this week," Sienna whispered. "They forgot to tell him they weren't going to be here."

Just then, the man finished his call and joined them. Emily smiled again. He noticed her once more, a slight curiosity brimming in those brooding blue eyes. He turned to address Sienna, the movement revealing the bottom edge of a tattoo on his round bicep peeking out from under his short sleeve.

"The owner expresses his deep apologies for the interruption," he said. "I'll just leave the week's groceries with you all. Dinner's yours if you'd like it. I can bring the rest by tomorrow."

"What was on the menu for tonight?" Blair asked.

"A starter of heirloom tomato and burrata salad with basil oil and sea salt, a main course of fried snapper with citrus herb butter, and a side of grilled sweet corn tossed with cotija, lime, and smoked paprika. For dessert, I planned key lime tarts with coconut crust and hand-whipped cream."

"I'm salivating," Sienna said as Blair peeked into one of the containers.

He didn't laugh, but he offered a strained smile. "Well, enjoy."

"Wait a minute," Blair said, snapping one of the lids back into place. "None of it's cooked."

He pursed his lips. "Correct. I cook the clients' food on-site."

Blair waved a hand between the three of them. "We don't know how to make any of that, do we?"

Emily and Sienna shook their heads.

"Leaving it would be a waste of food," Blair said.

"She's right," Sienna agreed. "You're welcome to take it back with you."

"The boss paid for the whole week already, and he said to leave it here. You can dump it if you want to."

Blair piped up. "There are children starving at this very hour. I can't in good conscience throw all this away."

He frowned, clearly considering this.

"Have you already been paid to cook as well?" Emily asked. "If not, maybe we could all chip in for the cost and have you cook for us, since you'd planned on doing that this week anyway."

He searched her face and then his shoulders fell. "I've been paid, yes."

"Perfect." Sienna gave him a loaded grin. "Then cook us this fabulous food."

Expressionless, he went over to the counter and began unpacking his supplies.

When it was clear the chef was only there to do his job and not to entertain them with small talk, they each poured themselves a lemonade and went back out to the pool.

"I think he was trying to get out of working this week," Blair said under her breath as they sat at the poolside table under a large blue-and-white striped umbrella. "Should we have let him go?"

"I'm sure it's weird for him to stay, since he doesn't know us," Emily added, uncertain why, given his frosty introduction, she'd stuck up for him. He could've at least been friendly.

"It's weirder for us," Blair said, craning her neck to get a glimpse of him through the French doors. "Did you see the way he looked at us? We don't know him from Adam. Did he actually call the musician? He could be a murderer."

Sienna laughed. "A murdering chef who works for my biggest client. Plus, the voice coming through his phone sounded just like *the musician*. And he's too attractive to be a murderer."

Blair's mouth opened slightly. "That's the perfect cover-up." She looked in at him again and shivered dramatically, then moved to the lounger. "The sky looks gray over there." She pointed to the horizon. "I'd better get my sun now. Looks like a storm's on the way."

Sienna slipped off her cover-up and draped it on the back of the chair again. "I heard most of the storms here are quick. It'll rush up on us, but I'll bet it'll be in and out in less than an hour. And the sun doesn't set for ages. It'll be light until after eight." She stepped into the pool, rolled onto her back, and floated across the water as a seagull squawked overhead.

The quiet shush of the Gulf and the coastal breeze lulled Emily into a state of calm. She leaned back in the chair and tipped her face toward the sunshine, relishing the quiet of her mind. All her problems suddenly seemed far away. Until then, her mind had been full of thoughts about where she would live once the house was sold, if she couldn't get her apartment back, whether she wanted to stay in Nashville where she was bound to run into Will, or if she should leave the area. But after being at the beach house for a while, it was as if there was some sort of tropical shield keeping all those questions at bay. She welcomed it. The vacation was finally kicking in.

After a while, she stood up. "I'm going in to get my novel. Does anyone need anything?"

Blair rattled the ice in her glass. "I could do with another lemonade, if you don't mind. I'd rather not bother the murderer."

Emily laughed. "Okay." She took Blair's glass and went inside.

Her vision adjusted to the interior light to find the chef working between a couple of bowls, marinating the snapper. The scent of butter and herbs wafted toward her, making her stomach growl. She set the empty glass on the edge of the counter, then went past him and up to her room where she dug her book from the pocket of her suitcase. Tucking the book under her arm, she returned to the kitchen to refill Blair's glass.

The chef glanced at her when she opened the fridge to retrieve the lemonade. She set her novel on the counter, careful not to trespass on his workspace. While he mixed herbs in a small bowl, Blair's murderer comment floated into Emily's mind, and she had to fight off a giggle.

His strong hands worked gently, meticulously, his attention focused. Having him in the house with them was awkward when they didn't even know his name. Especially if there was a possibility that he'd be cooking for them all week. Emily's years of teaching had taught her how to break the ice with quiet children, and she was sure that if she could just get him talking, the tension would fade away.

"My name's Emily," she said as she closed the refrigerator. "Emily Jacobs."

He nodded, continuing his prep work, dicing tomatoes with a large knife.

While they were at the beach, and the dress code was certainly more relaxed, he seemed less like a fancy butler-type and more like a regular guy she might see casting a fishing rod off the side of a pier with a can of beer in his other hand. His skin was tanned, and the gold flecks in the hair at his temples and the small sun lines around his eyes made him look distinguished. Nothing about him was fussy. She wondered what he looked like when he laughed. He couldn't be this serious all the time, could he?

She set the bottle of lemonade and glass onto the counter beside his bowl. "And you are?"

Those stormy eyes found hers. "Patrick Owens."

Her mind pinged with recognition. She offered her most friendly smile, but he'd already resumed his chopping. Then everything came back to her: The girl selling the magazine to them had said the New York chef was hot, mysterious, shopped at the fish market. Yep, that had to be the same guy. But didn't he own a restaurant? He was a personal chef too?

"It's nice to meet you, Patrick." She unscrewed the cap on the bottle of lemonade. "So do you only work for the rich and famous?"

His hands slowed, but his attention remained on the pile of vegetables on the cutting board.

Emily pretended to be interested in his cooking gadgets, but his career choice aside, she really wondered why he was so standoffish. The shop girl who'd shown them the magazine had said he didn't talk, but certainly he'd want to make a good impression for his client, right?

The insignia on a plastic measurement-conversion chart caught her eye. She picked it up and ran a finger over a gold seal on the bottom. Embossed in the center was a matte-gold emblem, flanked by small lettering:

JSOC – Culinary Detachment

"Is this from the military?"

"Navy."

"You were a chef in the navy?"

"Yeah."

The center emblem depicted a bald eagle clutching arrows and lightning bolts, perched over a globe, and surrounded by Latin words.

She read them aloud. "*Silentium Est Fidelitas.* What does that mean?"

"Silence is loyalty." He plucked the card from her hand. "Silence is also my preference. If I'm distracted, I might burn your snapper." While he still wasn't terribly forthcoming, his tone had softened a little. "Dinner will be ready in about a half an hour."

"Okay," she said, returning the lemonade to the refrigerator. She picked up Blair's drink and her novel and headed outside.

"Thank you," Blair said as Emily handed over the full glass. "I was starting to wonder if I needed to go inside and check the closets for you." She sent a dramatic look through the window.

Emily grinned. "His name is Patrick Owens."

Blair perked up. "Oh. Isn't that the guy from the article in the magazine?"

Emily nodded. "I knew right away after he said it."

Blair's eyebrows bounced. "Oh, now I want to go back and buy it. I wonder how he ended up as the musician's personal chef. Doesn't he run a fancy restaurant or something?"

Emily shrugged. "Did the girl at the shop say he's opening one?"

Blair eyed Sienna, but Sienna just shook her head.

"What did he say to you when you were in there?" Sienna asked from the water.

"He was in the navy," Emily replied.

Sienna fanned out her arms and pushed herself over to the edge of the pool. She placed her elbows on the pavement and set her chin on her forearms. "What else did he say?"

"That was it."

Blair rattled the ice around in her lemonade. "It took all that time just to find out that little bit of information? He's a ball of fun."

"He's working," Emily said. "I didn't want to bother him too much."

She placed her novel on the table. A warm, salty gust of air blew, sending Sienna's cover-up to the pavement. Emily put it back on the chair, and they settled into a moment of quiet. Blair took a sip from her glass, set it beside her, then leaned back and closed her eyes. Sienna pushed away from the edge and did another lap around the pool. But they didn't have peace for long before Patrick stuck his head out the door.

"Someone's phone is ringing off the hook upstairs. Just wanted to let you know."

"I'll check." Emily went into the house just in time to hear the phone ring one final time. She went upstairs and into her room, where her phone lay, lit up, on her bed.

Three missed calls from Will.

Reality slithered through her. *What does he want?* With a deep breath, she dialed his number and put the phone to her ear.

"The real estate agent needs your house key so she can put it in the front-door lockbox," Will said without a hello.

Emily tensed at the sound of his voice. It had a quality she hadn't heard before, except when she'd called him about the breakup. "I put it under the mat."

"What about the extra one? We also need one for the real estate office so she can have it for inspections, staging, and any emergencies."

"Well, I'm not in the state, and I have it with me so I can get back in to get my boxes when I get home."

"Can you overnight it?"

She sucked in another deep breath. "Give her *your* key."

"I need mine to work on packing and organizing all my stuff in the garage. I'd already brought all my tools and things over, remember?"

A pinch took hold of her shoulder. "That's *your* problem," she clipped instead.

"I know you're still furious with me, but you don't need to be difficult."

She gritted her teeth. "*I'm* being difficult? You called me on my vacation to ask me to solve your problems. Problems you've brought on entirely by yourself. Use your own key." She hung up, silenced the phone, and threw it back on the bed.

Emily stood there, staring at the dark screen, her lip quivering, tears brimming. She'd acted the way he deserved, but she didn't want any of it. She wanted her happy life back. Her worries about selling the house, canceling the wedding, and figuring out the rest of her life flooded her, spreading through her limbs in a warm, thick panic. She focused on her breathing to get herself together enough to rejoin her friends, then went into the bathroom and checked her face. From the outside, no one could tell that her heart was shattered. She washed her hands and patted her cheeks with cool water.

When she came downstairs, Patrick glanced at her curiously.

"It won't ring again," she said, trying to keep her voice from wobbling. Before she burst into tears, she went outside and sucked in the warm air to calm herself once more. Blair and Sienna were in the pool. Emily slipped off her cover-up and waded into the cool water. With every step, her friends in front of her and the sun on her shoulders, she silently released her pent-up feelings into the air.

She would not allow Will to ruin this moment. He'd ruined enough already.

FIVE

Once they'd all dried off and thrown on some fresh clothes, they settled at the dinner table inside. Emily had finally calmed down enough after her call from Will to be present in the moment, and she decided she'd do her very best to keep him from stealing any more of her happiness. She scooted up to the table, immersing herself in the atmosphere of gorgeous food and good friends in paradise.

"This looks incredible," she said to Patrick as he placed the starter of heirloom tomato and burrata salad in front of her.

The corners of his mouth turned up subtly. "Thank you."

His voice was careful, soft, deep. She couldn't imagine him in the armed forces, given how reserved and nonthreatening he was. Instead of being full of command, it seemed as if he'd dart away at the first opportunity. Perhaps his quiet nature was why he was no longer in the navy?

The sun went behind a cloud, darkening the room. He noticed, and immediately pulled a lighter from his pocket and lit the candles in the center of the table. An orange glow illuminated their places, making it feel cozy and intimate.

"He's not so bad," Blair whispered in Emily's ear when Patrick had gone back into the kitchen to retrieve a bottle of wine. "He was quick with lighting the tapers. I need to teach Rocko that trick."

Emily chuckled.

Sienna leaned across the table. "We'll definitely have to get that magazine. I'm so curious. Or I could just try to start a conversation."

"I wouldn't," Emily replied. "He literally told me he actually *likes* silence."

Sienna made a face. "Weird."

"For you," Emily said with a laugh.

"Are you sticking up for him?" Sienna teased, thoughts behind those brown eyes of hers. "He is attractive. Could be a good rebound..."

Emily shot her a look.

"Seriously," Sienna insisted.

Emily's expression tightened, and she glanced at the doorway to the kitchen. "I am in no place to entertain any thoughts apart from this girls' week. I have enough to juggle, thank you very much."

They hushed when Patrick came back with the bottle of wine and the final plate of salad. He set the plate in front of Sienna and then popped the cork out of the sauvignon blanc. As he reached around the water goblet to fill Emily's glass, a clap of thunder exploded outside. Patrick jumped, the wine spilling onto her plate and into her lap. Instinctively, she pushed back and sprung to her feet, the liquid dripping a little on the hardwood floor.

Patrick flinched. He gathered himself quickly, setting

down the bottle and snatching a cloth napkin. "I'm so sorry." He reached out to blot her, then obviously thought better of it and handed her the napkin.

"It's okay." Her shorts were soaking.

"I'll get you a new salad." His words came out in almost a growl. Then he disappeared into the kitchen.

Another roll of thunder rippled above them, as dishes clanged behind the closed doors.

Sienna leaned across the table and made a face, glancing at the kitchen. "What was that?"

"I guess the thunder startled him," Emily replied, dabbing at her wine-soaked shorts, unsuccessfully trying to remove the ice-cold wetness. "I'll be right back."

She ran upstairs, slipped off her wet shorts, threw them over the edge of the tub, and put on a different pair. When she returned, the floor and table were clean, and she had a full glass of wine and a fresh salad, along with a steaming plate of snapper.

As if the heavens opened up, a swooshing sound outside drew her attention to the French doors. Only a slip of blue Gulf was visible through the haze of pouring rain.

Emily sat down, stabbed a forkful of the salad, and took a bite, focusing on the food to avoid thinking about the rain and the fact that she and her friends had yet to really get to talk. The crisp, fresh flavors exploded in her mouth. The sweet, juicy tomatoes complemented the creamy, rich, buttery burrata cheese.

She swallowed. "This is the best salad I've had in a while. Wow."

"I might agree with you on that," Blair said, taking a bite.

Sienna sipped her water.

"You don't like the fish?" Emily asked quietly.

Sienna's phone pinged on the table beside her. She checked the message and then clicked it off. "The smell of the oil is turning my stomach. And I'm not sure I can have it because it might contain mercury." Sienna made a face. "I'm worried because the only foods that smell good to me right now are pizza and burgers. In our family, this baby had better like the finer things in life or he or she will be in trouble."

Blair laughed. "I figured your baby would come out of the womb yearning for white truffles and sashimi."

"It had better!" Sienna pushed a few leaves around her plate.

"When do you think you'll tell Tyson?" Blair asked.

"Maybe when he gets here this weekend. But when I do, I'm going to have to promise him that, one, I won't make him get an SUV, and two, I won't ask him to sell the condo." For the first time since Emily had known Sienna, she saw a tiny spark of fear in her eyes.

Patrick came in, his muscular arm lined with the sides for the main course. He also set butter and a few condiments in front of them.

Another clap of thunder rang out, but his hands were steady this time.

"There's a ton of food left, so if you want seconds of anything, just let me know," he said. "Once everyone's full, I'll box up the leftovers and put them in the fridge."

"How many clients do you have in the area?" Sienna asked him.

His gaze flickered over to her. "A lot."

Sienna was bent on getting him to talk, but if anyone was going to facilitate a conversation with him, Emily would be the most diplomatic of the three. She could gauge his reactions and keep things light.

"Why don't *you* have some dinner too?"

Sienna and Blair swapped interested looks, but Emily ignored them.

His brows pulled together. "I'm fine, thank you."

"We don't mind," Blair offered. "If there's plenty, have some. It's the least we can do, considering you had to cook for three strangers tonight."

"Thank you again for the offer, but I'll pass."

Blair's chin lifted. "Why? Is there something in the food?" She looked at Emily as if to say, *I told you he was a murderer.*

Sienna snorted and covered her mouth with her napkin, pretending to cough.

Patrick wasn't in on the joke, and he stared at them suspiciously.

"Please," Sienna said after recovering. "We don't bite."

"And we won't ask you to talk," Emily said. But as soon as the suggestion left her lips, she reconsidered, the offer sounding more awkward than it had in her head.

But instead of a perplexed response, he seemed surprised and self-conscious. "I don't make a habit of dining with my clients."

"Right," Emily said, "but you're going to be hanging out with us all week. And if your clients are the kind of people who own houses like this, we aren't your typical clients. I'm an elementary-school teacher. I usually eat a bagged salad out of Tupperware, or I have lunch with my kids. School pizza is an acquired taste, for sure."

The corners of his mouth rose slightly.

"And Sienna over there is a real estate agent. She got to

stay here as a gift from the owner. Blair works in social media."

"We really don't mind if you want to take a load off," Blair said. "Eat. The longer you stay, the less chance you have of loading your truck in that." She pointed to the sheets of rain coming down outside.

Emily got up. "I'll make you a plate."

"Please—"

He tried to stop her, but she went into the kitchen anyway.

He followed. "Why are you and your friends so persistent?"

She picked up a plate and dished a pile of sweet corn onto it. "It's uncomfortable to have a stranger cooking our meals. We don't usually have people waiting on us. I'd like to know you better so the atmosphere is less formal. And Blair thinks you could be a murderer," she added, playfully baiting him.

He flinched instead of laughing.

Her skin flushed. "You're not a murderer, are you?"

He shook his head subtly, but her joke had landed flat.

She scrutinized him. His eyes didn't look like a criminal's eyes. Instead, she could almost see fear in them, which made no sense, given how strong and masculine he was.

She added a piece of snapper to the plate and held it out. "Is this enough?"

"Yeah. Thanks."

She handed him his dinner and led him back to the table.

"Where's Blair?" she asked, taking her seat.

"She got a call from Rocko. Sorry, I have to dip for a second too. I've got a family who's found the perfect listing, but there's already a contingency offer on it, so we'll need to move fast. They've texted me twice now. I should send them the MLS information." Sienna pushed away from the table. "Give me ten minutes."

Emily settled in opposite Patrick and cut a piece of her snapper. They worked on their plates until the silence ate at her.

"So have you always lived in Florida?" she asked.

"No, I'm originally from North Carolina. Raleigh."

She smiled. "I grew up in Virginia. Not too far away."

He stabbed a piece of fish with his fork.

"What brought you to this gorgeous area?" she asked.

"I wanted to escape to paradise. This is as close as I could find."

"It's definitely a different way of life, isn't it? So calm and relaxing. Although, I'll bet it's not the same for you, since you have to work and live your regular life."

He shrugged. "Nothing's really paradise. But I have some family nearby, so that helps."

His comment about paradise resonated with Emily more than he knew. "How long have you been here?"

"Five years in this location, but I've been in Florida for over a decade. I was in Jacksonville before this."

Emily picked up her wine. "The Naval Air Station's in Jacksonville, right? Is that why you were there?"

He nodded.

While he was short with his answers, there was something about him that made her feel as if there was more to that hardened exterior, and if she could just crack it, she'd see a different side of him. She hadn't determined exactly why she wanted to see any side of him particularly, but the curiosity was enough to drive her.

"Sorry," Blair said, coming back to sit at the table.

Patrick stood up. "I forgot dinner rolls. Want anything?"

"No, thanks. I'm okay," Emily said.

"I'm fine, thank you," Blair said, scooting her chair into place.

After he left, Emily dug into her snapper once more. "Everything good with Rocko?"

"Yeah, he wanted to make sure we got here okay." She took a drink of wine. "He's excited to come on Friday night. He couldn't get anyone else's schedules to line up for fishing anyway. Now, they'll all be jealous." She stabbed the salad with her fork. "He ran into Will and Lanie at the gym."

Emily's hands stilled.

Lanie.

"I didn't know her name until now." When she'd been able to pry out of Will that he'd called things off because he'd met someone at the gym, she'd stopped him there, not caring to hear any more. She swallowed the grief that wanted to overflow. "That's...awkward."

"I'm so sorry, Em. What a complete jerk he is."

"I still can't believe he wrecked our future marriage over this."

"It's due to his own problems. He's obviously dealing with something," Blair said.

Patrick returned with a plate containing four rolls and sat down. He brought a breath of fresh air with him. Even though he wasn't the most talkative person on the planet, the fact that he didn't know anything about Emily or her current situation was nice. A clean slate.

"You okay?" he asked her.

"Yes, why?" She blinked a little too much, worried her emotions had seeped through to the outside.

"I overheard. It's none of my business. Sorry."

Blair leaned on the table, addressing Patrick. "Will is Emily's ex-fiancé and my husband's good friend."

"Ah." He eyed Emily but then turned his attention back to his plate.

"Apparently, he's a real idiot. Who knew?" Blair raised her hands in the air. "But the real downer is that he's ruined our monthly dinner nights."

"All done!" Sienna swished across the room and slid into her chair next to Patrick. "Normally, I wouldn't jump so quickly, but this is a big client." She looked back and forth between Blair and Emily. "What did I miss?"

"Nothing you don't already know," Emily said, ready to change the subject. "Except that Patrick has been in Florida for over a decade. He used to live in Jacksonville."

"Oh wow." Sienna's eyebrows bobbed at Emily.

The table fell into an awkward silence, the one-sided conversation between the women and Patrick dwindling.

"Did you say for dessert you had key lime tarts?" Sienna asked. "I'd love to try one."

Patrick immediately pushed away from the table, as if he couldn't wait to end the exchange. He served them dessert, and then he cleaned, packed up, and loaded his vehicle without finishing his plate. By then, the rain had stopped, leaving a steamy residue in its wake.

"Thank you for dinner," Emily said from the grand front door.

"You're welcome." He hoisted one of the coolers into the back of his Ford F-150 SuperCrew.

She slipped her hands into her pockets, not sure what to say to smooth things over. Why had he even mentioned that he'd heard her and Blair's conversation? He could've easily played dumb. But instead he'd asked how she was. Mr. I-Prefer-Silence. His curiosity about the situation had her brain in a muddle.

He got in his truck, started the engine, and put down the window. "I'll be back tomorrow at six."

"Sounds good."

Without another look, he drove away, down the long winding path to the main road.

Patrick had been an unexpected addition to their little getaway, and she wondered how, exactly, he would fit into The Broken Hearts Beach Club. Only time would tell.

SIX

Freshened up and ready to have some girl time, the three women walked through the bar at the end of the road. The rain had long evaporated in the heavy heat, and it seemed that everyone had picked up with business as usual. A band strummed an island melody outside under string lights and flickering tiki torches for a full crowd of restaurant-goers.

"I don't see a single open barstool," Blair said, gesturing toward the crowded area.

Sienna made a face. "Maybe we can grab seats on the deck."

Emily led them through the lively atmosphere, her spirits lifting with every step.

"Three for drinks, please," Sienna said to the woman behind the outdoor hostess podium.

"Of course." The hostess showed them to a table at the edge of the jam-packed dining area.

Blair took a deep breath and audibly exhaled. "No wonder everyone's out. Can you feel the atmosphere? It's electric. I could stay here all night."

Emily agreed. "Just let us know if you get sleepy, Sienna."

"I'm fine." Sienna perused the menu. "I'm trying not to let this pregnancy get a hold of me. I'll push through."

"I'm not sure you'll have a choice," Blair said. "I was dog-tired in my first trimester. Your body is responding to two now."

"Yeah, I know," Sienna relented. "I'm reminded every time my stomach lurches at the smell of foods that I used to adore."

A waitress came over and took their drink orders. Sienna got a virgin piña colada, and Blair and Emily ordered margaritas.

"I hate to break the news to you," Blair said once the waitress had gone. "A baby is going to change *everything*. Nothing will be the same. You'll sleep when you can, eat in the two minutes you have a moment, your hormones will be all whacked out... I read enough getting ready for it to know."

"I don't want to sound awful and ungrateful, but I like my life. While I love the idea of a baby, I worry about how much change is going to happen and whether Tyson and I can successfully make the adjustment. I want things to be stable for this child."

Blair leaned on her hands, her elbows on the table, and smiled at her friend. "When you see that little face that looks just like you and Tyson, I'll bet you won't care one bit what changes." Suddenly, her eyes brimmed with tears. She cleared her throat and peered down at her menu. "Sorry. You can't take me anywhere."

"You're safe with us," Sienna said.

Blair dragged a finger under her eye. "Why did I have to try to have a baby? If I'd have just ignored the feeling, I wouldn't be in this boat right now. I'm the odd one out, actually *planning* to start a family."

"I never said anything, but I'd wanted to try for a baby this summer," Emily admitted. "Can you imagine if we'd have gotten pregnant before Will decided he wanted a different life? I don't think I'd be able to juggle it all."

"Things worked out for the best then?" Sienna asked.

Emily nodded. "I wonder, though, whether I'll ever have that family I'd hoped for. I've been out of the singles game so long that I don't know how to date anyone. And I don't really want to. Talk about exhausting."

Sienna giggled. "You don't have to get in the game already! It hasn't even been two weeks since you and Will split up."

"I know. I don't plan to jump into dating, believe me. But I'm an organizer. I like to have things all worked out. I thought I had, and now I'm starting at square one."

The waitress brought their cocktails as the band kicked into a lively tune. "Anything to eat?"

"Just drinks tonight," Sienna replied.

The waitress slipped her free hand into the wide pocket of her apron and retrieved a few cocktail napkins. She set them on the table and placed their drinks on top of each one. "Okay. Let me know if you decide to order some apps. We've got a calamari sampler to die for."

"A few of these, and I might take you up on that," Blair said, raising her drink and winking. "Once I'm in good spirits, I'll be down in front of the band, dancing."

When the waitress left, Emily put her arm around her friend. "You don't need a margarita to get you into a good mood. You have us."

Blair cooed, "You're right. Where would I be without you two?" She lifted her glass. "To us."

They raised their glasses and clinked them together.

"Oh." Sienna put down her drink, licking her lips. "I taste rum. It's not virgin." She scooted the glass over to Emily. "Take a sip and see what you think."

Emily stirred the frozen concoction with the straw and tried it. "Yes. I taste the rum." She looked around the buzzing crowd for the waitress.

Sienna leaned back in her chair, the coastal breeze blowing her hair behind her shoulders. "You all can have it if you want. I don't have to have a drink. Even though it tastes *divine*."

"No. If you ordered a mocktail, you should have one," Emily said, trying and failing again at locating the waitress. She got up and took the cocktail off the table. "I'll ask the bartender. Be right back."

Emily weaved through the crowded dining area and reached the bar. Every seat was full, the bartender busy on the other side. Emily hung back, trying to figure out where she could squeeze in without infringing on someone else's personal space. She stepped around the edge of the bar, making her way to where the bartender was, but by the time she got over there, the man had moved to where she'd been, completely oblivious to her attempts to get his attention.

Then someone at the far edge got up, so she darted over and took the seat, setting the cocktail in front of her. But when she sat down, she accidentally bumped the back of the person beside her. The man twisted around from the friend he was talking to, and she sucked in a breath of surprise.

"Hi," she said, staring Patrick in the face.

He looked over her head and without a hello, he asked, "Where are your friends?"

She pointed toward the crowd outside.

The lines between his eyes deepened.

"The waitress got Sienna's drink wrong. I thought it would be faster to get her another one at the bar, but I'm second-guessing that decision now."

Patrick eyed the cocktail and pursed his lips. He leaned on the bar. "Alex."

The bartender turned around and came over.

"This lady needs a drink," he said.

Emily explained the situation, and the bartender nodded, then took two more orders, lined up silver cups on the bar, and began flipping bottles of liquor and syrup upside down, filling each one. He pulled a third glass and filled it with ice.

"Thank you," Emily said to Patrick.

"No problem." He was relaxed, his shoulders loose, that storm in him calmed.

"You gonna introduce me?" his friend said.

"Mark, this is Emily. She's a...client."

Mark gave her a once-over. "Was this tonight's client—the one you were talking about?"

The tranquil demeanor he'd had left in a hurry. "Yeah," he said under his breath.

Mark's eyebrows bobbed once before Patrick blocked Emily's view of him. "So the drink. That all you need?"

"What did you tell Mark about me?" she asked, ignoring his question.

"I just mentioned the misunderstanding with the schedule and how I ended up cooking for you and your friends."

Normally, she'd have believed that answer, but his voice was low, directed at her, as if he didn't want Mark to hear. But she knew better than to think he'd go into a lengthy conversation now. In fact, he looked as if he couldn't wait for her to leave.

The bartender set the drink in front of her. "No charge. And you can keep the cocktail as well."

She thanked him, took the drinks, and hopped off the barstool. After lingering a second to see if Patrick would turn around, she said to his back, "I'll see you later."

He awkwardly glanced over his shoulder. "See ya."

Emily opened her mouth to tell him thank you again, but he'd already turned toward Mark and resumed his conversation.

When she got back to the table, she handed Sienna her mocktail and told her and Blair what they'd missed, as well as Patrick's cryptic answer regarding his mention of her.

"Was he talking bad about you to his friend?" Sienna asked, scanning the bar for him. "Jerk."

"He's so hard to read. Maybe it was as simple as what he said," Emily offered. Given Sienna's personality, she'd march over there and ask. "Don't let whatever he said impact our night."

"You're right," Sienna said, taking a drink from her glass.

As they settled into their conversation, Emily's mind returned to the encounter. What had Patrick told Mark about her? And why did not knowing bother her so much? Across the sea of tables, he got up to leave, tossing some cash on the bar. Before he turned to go, he caught her eye.

She quickly turned her attention back to her friends.

SEVEN

"How did you sleep last night?" Blair asked, climbing onto an iron-and-wood chair-style stool at the kitchen island.

"Like a baby." Emily poured her friend a cup of coffee and took a seat next to her. She didn't mention waking a couple of times because she hadn't slept well since she and Will had broken up. "The bedding was so luxurious."

"I know. I video-called Rocko to show him how soft the sheets were so he could look forward to snuggling up in them when he gets here." She giggled.

A hollow pang pelted Emily. She could go on normally, but out of nowhere, hopelessness from the loss of her old life would swarm her like bees. "I love how you two call each other all the time. Will never called me like that. Should it have been a sign?"

"Everyone's different," Blair said, leaning against the chair back of the barstool. "And phone calls don't necessarily make a marriage."

"Yeah but connecting with one another does."

Blair took a drink from her mug, heaviness in her pause. "Rocko and I aren't all roses either," she said, her honesty lingering heavily in the air. "We haven't been great since I lost the baby."

"Really?" In all their coffee dates, Blair had never mentioned this.

"Yeah. He bounced back, but I'm still struggling. Every time he wants to get close to me physically, I can't do it."

"I'm so sorry. I had no idea you were dealing with that."

"We used to be so flirty, unable to keep our hands off one another. Now, when he touches me, I flinch. And if I let him, all I can think about is how I could end up pregnant again, and I don't know if I could survive losing another baby."

"There are ways to ensure you won't get pregnant unless you're ready," Emily offered.

Blair traced a vein of marbling on the slick countertop and then picked up her mug. "I know, but there's also the loss of the baby that hangs over the moment, spoiling it."

"Have you talked to him about it?"

Blair stared into the steaming dark liquid in her mug. "Of course. We talk about it all the time. I'm in therapy. But nothing seems to help. I know he needs intimacy, but I'm not in the right place to give him that."

"Has he said how he feels?"

"He's supportive, but I think it's putting a strain on him. I know he wonders if he'll ever get his wife back."

"Morning." Sienna came in, her attention on her phone. "I just talked to Tyson. He misses me and can't wait to get here. I thought I was the one who was supposed to get all hormonal. He doesn't even know about the baby yet and he's got couvade syndrome."

"What is that?" Emily asked with a huff of laughter.

"It's a condition where the father experiences similar symptoms to pregnancy," Blair said.

Emily's mouth dropped open. "That's a thing?"

Blair laughed and nodded, but her attention moved back to Sienna when her phone beeped. "Is he texting again already?" She batted her eyelashes playfully.

"No. It's just weather alerts. A system's forming off the coast." Sienna set down her phone on the counter. "It's still pretty far out to sea, though, so hopefully it won't bring too much rain. That coffee smells divine. I wish I could have a cup."

"I can make you a decaf," Emily offered. "I brought some."

"Don't trouble yourself. I'll have juice." Sienna patted Emily's shoulder and then air-kissed Blair.

Blair brightened as if their earlier conversation had never happened. Had she been putting on a brave face for all of them? Maybe she hadn't recovered as much as it seemed.

Sienna reached into the fridge and grabbed the decanter of orange juice. "It better not get cloudy. I'm trying to get a tan while I still have my figure."

"Maybe I should take a few sunny photos just in case the weather turns," Blair said. "I don't know if I'll do anything with them... I've been trying to decide how to get back online."

"Preserving the moment is actually a great idea," Sienna said, pouring the juice. "Why don't we all get dolled up and pose for a few photos of the three of us to remember the trip? All our lives are about to change irrevocably. It'll be the last time I'm thin, the last time Emily isn't in the dating scene, and from the sound of it, this could possibly be the last time Blair is offline before she jumps back into the lion's den of social media."

"I like that idea," Blair said.

"This could also be a good exercise for you," Sienna continued, rounding the island and pulling out the barstool on the other side of Blair. "Focus on your talents, something you haven't been able to do in a while."

"You direct us, Blair," Emily said. "What should we wear?"

"Hm." She tapped her lip, a sparkle in her eye. "Let's go with casual elegance. Maybe a sundress or something." She pushed her coffee mug away. "I'm kind of excited about this. Let's go."

They went upstairs and got ready. When they reconvened back in the kitchen, Blair and Sienna wore striped flowy dresses, while Emily had opted for flowers.

"Blair, you look like a magazine model with your oversized sun hat and glasses," Emily said.

Blair gave a little spin.

Sienna sighed. "I'm jealous. I want a hat like that. But only if it makes me look as pretty as Blair."

Waving off their compliments, Blair ushered them outside near the infinity pool, with her tripod tucked under one arm. She pursed her lips, as if taking stock of the surroundings. She put down her equipment, dragged the table over a few feet, and then lined up the chairs.

"Let's start under the umbrella," she said, setting up the tripod and getting the camera lined up. "The light is perfect with the pool behind us." She squinted at the view. "Em, can you go in and make us fancy-looking drinks? Slice one of the oranges and add a few of the sprigs of mint Patrick left."

"Yes, ma'am."

Emily went inside and opened the cabinets to browse the stemware for the trendiest cocktail glasses. There were plenty of options: martini glasses with shells etched into the stems, wine goblets of all sorts, champagne flutes with beaded edges... She settled on three flutes that had little glass starfish along the bottom. Once she'd filled them with orange juice and lemonade, she prepared the garnishes.

Sienna was working on tipping the umbrella just slightly when Emily came out, balancing the three glasses.

"These are awesome." Blair took over, scooting each drink into place. "Now, Sienna, you sit here because your hair is the darkest, so we want the most sun on you. Plus, the light will shine off your gold strands and you'll look stunning." She wagged a finger at the other chair. "Emily, sit there, but lean in toward Sienna."

Emily followed her lead while Blair set the timer on the camera. She called out various poses, and the camera snapped stills of them. As they became more comfortable being photographed, they relaxed, offering their best model poses. Sienna leaned in front of Emily and made an impromptu and ridiculous sexy stance with one shoulder forward and her sultry lips on the rim of her drink just as the camera snapped. Emily fell into a fit of giggles, the camera still going off.

"You might not want to keep these," Emily teased.

"Why?" Sienna protested playfully before posing for a few more in similar fashion. "You don't think they're *spicy?*" Her eyebrows bobbed.

Blair giggled.

Emily made a face. "It looked like you were making out with your glass." She laughed again as the camera snapped, once more catching them in their candid moment. "Blair, you need to be in the photos to keep us under control." She beckoned Blair over.

"I beg to differ. I'm enough, aren't I?" Sienna said, licking her glass again to their guffaws.

Blair reset the timer and then jumped into the picture before it went off, bouncing into her seat, tipping it backward. Emily and Sienna lunged on either side, attempting to steady the chair, all of them tumbling to the floor as the camera went off. They doubled over, guffawing and gasping for air.

"Something tells me these might not be social media worthy," Sienna said, wiping tears of laughter as they helped each other up.

"That's fine," Blair said, righting her chair. "This is more fun than getting that perfectly curated shot anyway." She giggled and then sobered out of nowhere. "I really don't have a clue how I'm going to start posting again. After all this time, do I just jump back in with beach and pool photos? What will I say?"

"Tell them you took a mental health break," Emily said.

"She's got a point," Sienna added. "And that would make you look current and health conscious. Everyone's worried about their mental state these days. You can make taking me time cool."

"But everyone will ask where the baby is. I was going to do a big announcement, and I posted a ton of teasers about the gender. Then I went silent." She tipped her head back toward the sun. "I don't even know if I want to be an influencer anymore. I don't have any ambition, really. All my excitement was wrapped up in being a mom, and now I feel like an empty shell of myself." She sat up.

Emily handed her one of the juice glasses.

"Sorry *again*," Blair said, taking a drink and swallowing. "I ruin every moment." She shook her head. "I know you both have your own issues to deal with."

Sienna stood up and stomped her foot. "Stop apologizing every time you open up." She waved her arms between the three of them. "I don't know how many times we need to tell you that this is the place to do it. Yes, we have our own crap. But we want to support your crap too."

Blair cracked a smile. "Thank you."

Sienna plopped back in her chair. "This is a free space for crap."

They stared at each other, the mood lightening.

"Let's go down to the beach," Emily suggested. "Maybe we can take a few photos there."

They gathered up the tripod and supplies, put their drinks in the fridge, and went down to the soft, powdery sand. The pearly coast stretched out before them, leading to an expanse of bright turquoise-and-cobalt-blue striped water. The waves rolled softly onto the shore.

Blair buried the bottom of the tripod legs in the sand to keep it from blowing over and fiddled with the timer on the camera. "I set it for five minutes. Let's just do our thing and see what it captures." She lifted the hem of her dress and padded down to the water.

Emily followed, along with Sienna. The salty spray bubbled over Emily's toes, her predicaments seeming so far from here. She breathed in a cleansing breath of briny air.

Blair bent down and ran her fingers through the water. "You can see all the way to the bottom." She fished out a white shell and held it up to show them. "My first memento." With a grin, she slipped it into her pocket.

Wind rippled the bottoms of their dresses as they walked back up the beach and sat down in the sand. They fell into a comfortable silence. The only sounds were the quiet shushing of the tide and the occasional squawk of a seagull.

There wasn't another house visible in either direction, the smooth sand reaching for each end of the shoreline. The sun beat down on them, and Emily was glad that whatever storm had been on Sienna's phone was far enough offshore to be nonexistent. It was as if this perfect day were meant for the three of them—a balm for their souls.

Sienna was the first to break the hush. "Look." She pointed to the horizon where a white sailboat was almost out of view.

The breeze coming off the water cooled Emily's hot skin. "This place sure does make you feel like life might turn out okay, doesn't it?"

Sienna leaned back in the sand. "It does." Then, right away, she sat up. "I've got an idea."

"That's scary," Blair teased.

"Seriously." Sienna looked out over the ebbing surface of the Gulf. "What if we took a few hours each day where we *purposely* steered clear of our regular lives? We could fill the time with all sorts of adventures—boat rides, shopping, long hours reading..."

Emily raised her hand. "I'm in."

Blair tipped her head and made eye contact from under her hat. "That's the best idea I've heard in a while. But what if we took it a step further and one of us plans each day? The outing can be a surprise."

"I love that," Emily said with an excited gasp. "Should we start today?"

"I'll take today," Sienna said. "I already have an idea. I spotted it on the way into town." She got up and brushed the sand from her dress. "I'll see if I can get us in."

Emily and Blair stood as well. Blair went over to the camera and peered at the image it had caught. They gathered around as she shielded the screen from the sun. The three of them, from the back, were sitting side by side on the beach, looking out on the water.

"That looks more posed than the shots we *tried* to do," Sienna said with a laugh.

Blair shut off the camera and folded up the tripod. "It's a keeper, for sure."

When they got back inside, Emily checked her phone and slumped in dread. All the calm she'd worked for dissipated in an instant. She shouldn't have looked at it.

"What's wrong?" Blair asked.

"I have two missed calls and a text from Will saying I need to call him ASAP."

Sienna gave a quiet scoff.

"He says I need to sign a form. It could be something for the real estate agent. I'll be right back." With a sigh, Emily went out by the pool and dialed his number. Her shoulders tensed the minute he answered. "I need to sign something?" she asked, turning toward the coastal breeze, yearning for the tranquility it offered.

"I've been trying to get a hold of you. Where have you been?"

"None of your business."

Her comment had clearly startled him. The tick of silence gave her strength. She'd never been combative; it wasn't in her nature. But that's how upset she was—so wounded that she wasn't acting herself, and she was glad he'd noticed.

"The property disclosure statement has to have both our signatures before the agent shows the house," he said, his voice clipped. "We had to disclose anything wrong with the property. I took the liberty of listing out all the things."

My hero. She gritted her teeth. Heaven forbid he'd have to do a little work. This was his mess after all. She tucked a wayward lock of hair behind her ear.

"I mentioned the loose shingles and the drip under the sink in the kitchen. Can you think of anything else?"

She took in a long breath of warm, briny air and fixated on the rolling waves at the shore. He didn't need to call her for this. It could've easily been done with a text. He'd already listed everything that was wrong with the house—he knew that. Was he purposely trying to keep tabs on her? How dare he. He'd lost the right to know anything about what she was doing.

How had they come to this? He hadn't even had the decency to sit down with her and tell her how he'd strayed so far from what they'd promised one another. What had become so irrevocably broken between them that she hadn't been able to see it coming?

"No," she replied. One word was all she could muster without her lips trembling from the absolute anger she felt toward him for wrecking their perfect life.

"Okay, can you sign it? I have to go. It should be in your email."

"Sure." She got off the phone and stretched her arms out to release the pinch in her shoulders. Then she opened her email, signed the form, and sent it off. With that one task, a deluge of wedding cancellation tasks came flooding back. She needed to call the florist, the photographer, the caterer, the bakery, the seamstress... Had Will called any of his side of the wedding party? Suddenly, it all locked in her chest like a boulder of panic.

"What did *he* want?" Sienna asked when Emily went back inside.

"Real estate requirements," she replied.

"I'm surprised he didn't reach out to me to sell the house." Sienna winked at Emily, evidently trying to lighten the atmosphere. "Who did he get anyway?"

"I don't know. I don't care, to be honest."

"Have you let your landlord know so he'll keep your apartment?"

"I need to, but I know he had another couple looking at it. I think they plan to move in."

"Where are you going to live then?" Sienna asked, retrieving their drinks from the fridge and handing them to Blair and Emily.

The sun went behind a cloud, the room darkening in response.

"Honestly, I have no idea. I thought maybe I should go home and live with my parents in Virginia for a while, but I've signed my contract to teach next year, so I can't really do that."

Blair offered an empathetic frown. "You're welcome to stay with me until you find somewhere."

"Thank you. I'll figure something out." She didn't want to be a burden.

A text pinged from Will that just said, "Thanks." Emily cleared it from her screen. "Enough of this negativity." She slipped her phone into her pocket.

"So, Sienna," Blair said. "What are we doing today?"

Sienna grinned. "Something inside." She lifted her head to the view through the large window. "The clouds are moving in. Just in case we get a shower, we'd better drive."

Rain or shine, Emily was glad for their decision to leave their lives for a while. Whatever they were doing, it had to be better than what she had to face back home.

EIGHT

They headed for Sienna's undisclosed location. On the way, they came to a stoplight next to a brand-new building.

"Wow, that's some sexy construction," Sienna said, sliding down her sunglasses and peering past Emily at the sleek structure that was nearly all glass and exposed beams.

A sign out front read, "Future home of The Low Tide Supper Club, a culinary evolution of Main Course."

"That looks like it's going to be fancy," Emily said. "I'll bet the musician will go there."

"Probably," Sienna said, squinting at the building.

"I don't know," Blair said from the backseat. "Does Luke Bryan like that sort of thing?"

Sienna turned around. "You're trying to catch me, and I'm not telling you who owns that house!"

The light turned green.

"Sienna's answer was 'probably,'" Emily said. "So, what musician would probably go to that restaurant? What about that guy with the really gorgeous wife?"

"I know who you're talking about." Blair snapped her fingers. "He might. Hard to say."

"Maybe all three of us could come back next year and see if we can catch him there," Emily suggested. "Would he say hi if we were with you, Sienna?"

"I have no idea," Sienna said with a laugh.

They pulled into a parking spot and got out of the car.

"Surprise!" Sienna waved her arms in front of a lavender storefront with lacy curtains and a neon ice-cream-cone-shaped sign by the door with the name Tropical Treat.

The place was brimming with tourists. Through the large window, pink-skinned vacationers filled the tables. They dipped their spoons into decadent bowls of confections—vanilla ice cream with whole pieces of cake on top and drizzled with chocolate, or milkshakes the size of milk cartons.

"We're doing a sundae flight," Sienna said.

Emily wrinkled her nose. "Flying ice cream?"

Blair let out a chuckle.

"I really need to get you into the Nashville bar scene," Sienna said, shaking her head. "A flight is a sampler of small-portioned drinks. But we're doing sundaes instead of alcohol." With a dramatic flourish, she opened the door and ushered them into the pastel-colored interior that smelled of sprinkles and sugar.

"Oh, let's grab that." Blair slid onto a shiny booth that had opened just as they walked in. "I'll hold our seats. I'm game for whatever. Surprise me."

Emily and Sienna went to order.

"We have to pick five flavors," Sienna said, peering up at the chalkboard menu with eight rows of options. "Any standing out for you?"

Emily studied the choices. "The Beach Bonfire S'mores looks good. 'Toasted marshmallow ice cream with ribbons of melted chocolate and crushed graham cracker pieces, just like a summer night by the fire,'" she read.

"That does sound delicious." Sienna pointed to the middle column. "How about Coconut Cabana Crunch? 'Toasted coconut ice cream with macadamia nuts, white chocolate chips, and a caramel drizzle.'"

Emily nodded enthusiastically. "We only get five? We might need two flights." She read the next on her list: "We have to get Sunset Sorbet Swirl. 'A dreamy mix of mango, raspberry, and peach sorbet in a creamy vanilla base, swirling like a summer sunset.'"

When it was their turn, they settled on their last two: Strawberry Picnic Shortcake and Boardwalk Breeze. They put in their order, and one of the Tropical Treat crew got to work on their selections, pulling out a miniature teal-and-yellow surfboard with divots to hold the mini sundae glasses. With precision, she placed each glass into its spot and then with scoops, ladles, squirt bottles, and finally a spray of whipped cream, she handed over the flight, along with a handwritten explanation card, a pile of napkins, and three long-handled spoons.

Sienna took it to the booth Blair was holding for them and placed it in the middle of the table.

"I have to get a photo of this," Blair said, wide-eyed. "It's adorable."

Emily and Sienna stepped aside so Blair could capture the purple-striped wall and bright-green-and-pink flowering plants in the background. Then, they sat down and each took one of the spoons.

Blair waved them together. "Get close. I want a photo of you two."

Sienna and Emily posed for the shot.

Emily took that second to commit the moment to

memory. "This trip really does feel like a turning point," she said. It was a line dividing who she thought she'd be and who she would become. "Thank goodness for you two. I couldn't have managed without you."

"Of course." Blair set her phone on the booth seat beside her. "Back at ya."

Sienna leaned on the table. "Truly. This trip couldn't have come at a more opportune time. I needed to get used to the idea of this baby before I told Tyson. And I couldn't have done it without the support of you two."

"How do you feel about motherhood, really?" Emily asked.

"I never saw myself with children, but the idea is growing on me. Having a family feels more natural every day. I just hope Tyson will feel the same with time." She shook her head. "He said before that he doesn't want kids and, until now, I was fine with that. But now, I'm not. I'm changing the game, and he doesn't have a say."

"Just be honest with him," Blair said. "He might come around."

Sienna blinked away tears. "And if he doesn't? I'll be forced to trade the happiness I chose for myself for an unknown. I have no idea what kind of mother I'll be, and, for that matter, what kind of father Tyson will be. If he doesn't want to be a father, what will his involvement with this baby be?"

"Those are big questions," Emily said. "And they're only answered by Tyson."

Sienna picked up her spoon. "I've already broken the rules of our little game. We were supposed to purposely leave our baggage behind during our outings, remember?"

"It's okay," Emily said. "But we should get on with it before our ice cream melts."

Blair raised her spoon. "Cheers."

They each dug into the first sundae—Beach Bonfire S'mores—and filled their spoons, tapping them together and then, in unison, had a taste.

The vanilla flavor of the airy marshmallow and the rich, creamy ice cream, combined with the honey crunch of the graham crackers and drizzle of chocolate, tickled Emily's senses. "I rate the s'mores one a five out of five."

"Same," Blair said, going back for another spoonful.

Just then, a stream of light hit her face as the door opened, and a little boy of about five with freckles and sandy-brown hair ran in, laughing. He came to a halt at the counter, barely able to see over it on his tiptoes.

The Tropical Treat server leaned in to make eye contact with the adorable boy. "Well, hello, Winston. How are you today?"

"Good," he said, wrinkling his nose.

Emily was just about to comment on how cute he was when a man stepped up behind the boy and picked him up to view the choices.

"Can you see better now?" he asked, his navy tattoo peeking out from under his sleeve as he steadied the boy.

"Yes!" Winston giggled.

"We're glad you stopped by," the attendant said. "I know you've been busy." She gave Patrick a smitten smile.

"Winston's been helping me on-site today, and this is his treat for all his hard work." That familiar voice sailed toward Emily.

"How's it all coming along? I've been seeing the advertisements."

"Good," he said in his usual short but polite tone. He said to Winston, "What sounds good to ya?"

The boy eyed the pictures along the wall. "That one. I remember it. The Wave Whipper," he replied.

"The Wave Whipper? You can't eat all that," Patrick teased, tickling his sides and making the boy shriek with laughter and dart away.

Emily struggled to take her eyes off him. He was a completely different person with that little boy than the man she'd met. He was relaxed, happy. The sight of it intoxicated her with interest.

Patrick laughed. "I guess we'll have two Wave Whippers to go, please." He pulled out his credit card and paid for their order.

"Can we go to the beach, Uncle Patrick?" the boy asked, tugging on the hem of Patrick's T-shirt.

"Not today, bud. I've got a little more work to do."

Winston pouted. "Can't we finish later?"

"It'll get too late, and I have more work tonight. Your mom's class will be done soon anyway. But if you want to, you can shoot basketballs again while I finish up."

The boy brightened. "Okay."

"I promise we'll go this weekend."

Emily was riveted. She'd never been one way with one person and then completely different with another. But Patrick was cold to her and so warm and lovely to this little boy. Why? It was as if someone had turned on a light inside him, a light she hadn't been able to reach. She didn't need to reach it—who was she to him? But the difference in him with this boy was enough to pique her curiosity about him to immense levels.

"What are the odds we'd see him here?" Sienna whispered.

But Emily barely heard her.

The worker handed Patrick two large cups with domed

lids full of whipped cream, a long spoon coming through the center. "Thank you." He turned around and stopped in his tracks when he met Emily's stare.

She offered a little wave.

With a reserved smile—a stark contrast to the one he'd given the boy—he nodded and then took Winston's hand and moved swiftly toward the exit. "Ready to have some ice cream and then shoot basketballs?" Patrick asked, his entire attention back on the boy as he pushed open the door.

"Rude," Sienna said. "He's going to cook for us tonight. The least he could do is come over and say hello. He clearly saw you, Em."

"Maybe since he was with the little boy, he decided not to mix work and pleasure," Emily said, although she, too, would've liked him to say hello. Had she done or said something that had made him so standoffish? Could that be what he'd told his friend Mark about? She racked her brain for anything he might have taken offense to, but she came up empty. After seeing him with Winston, she had to wonder, though.

"It is kind of a weird situation," Blair added. "He isn't even really working for us, but he's been roped into it. He probably isn't sure whether to treat us like customers or strangers."

Perhaps Blair was right; that could very well be the reason for his cold reception. Maybe he didn't enjoy chatting with tourists. After all, the area seemed like a small town in a lot of ways, and surely every summer the residents were overrun by all the vacationers.

"Hello-o." Sienna's hand waved in front of Emily's view of the door. "Earth to Emily."

She yanked her attention back to the table.

"You got the hots for Mr. Grumpy?" Sienna asked, the corner of her mouth twitching upward.

"What?" Her face heated. "No, of course not. I was just still wondering why he wasn't friendlier with us." She sunk her spoon into the second flavor. "What's this one?"

"Changing the subject... Subtle." Sienna snorted.

"I'm not. I'm focusing on us."

"Fair enough." Blair tapped the handwritten paper. "This one's Sunset Sorbet Swirl."

Emily took a bite, ignoring Sienna's appraising stare. She should be focused on her two friends and not the chef. They had her back no matter what, and this was their time. Concentrating on that, she fell into conversation with the two people who mattered most.

NINE

By that evening, the sky was a menacing gray, as if all the clouds of the world had banded together in a flat-out refusal of the sun's appearance. A blanket of dark, looming cloud cover rested above them, not moving, just hanging there as if they wanted to open up and unleash a massive storm at any moment.

"I think this is more than a daily shower," Sienna said, scrolling the weather app on her phone. "This says the storm's intensified offshore, and it's pushing rain this way."

"Let me see?" Blair leaned over. "Oh gosh, we're in the red." She swiped the screen. "It looks like the rain keeps going through tomorrow."

Sienna grumbled, picked up the remote, and flopped down on the sofa. "Maybe we should eat in here and watch a movie tonight to take our mind off the fact that we get one shot at a millionaire's beach vacation, and it rains."

The door chimed.

"I'll get it." Emily stood up and went through the lofty corridor to the entrance.

She opened the door to find Patrick holding cooler bags full of ingredients.

"Hi," he said, coming in with his usual lack of sociability.

"Hello." She smiled even though he'd already passed her and was heading down the hallway. "What's for dinner?" she asked, stepping in stride next to him.

"Grilled red Chilean sea bass, truffle parmesan grits, and brown-butter peach cobbler with bourbon vanilla gelato for dessert."

"That sounds incredible," Emily said. When he didn't respond, she added, "I think we might eat in the living room and watch a movie if you want to join us."

He made eye contact but didn't say yes or no.

The hard line of his face was softer tonight, but he still wasn't terribly talkative, so Emily left him and went back into the living room with Blair and Sienna.

"I guess he's the quiet type," Blair whispered, eyeing Patrick from across the open space as Emily sat beside her.

Emily shrugged.

Sienna glanced at him, but then turned her focus to the remote, clicking on the television. The wall-sized screen lit up with a symphonic hum.

From the kitchen, Patrick's phone rang. He wiped his hands on a towel and answered it quickly.

"What should we watch?" Sienna yawned as she clicked through the channels, stopping on a few chick flicks and then scrolling past them.

Blair suggested something, but Emily had sharpened her hearing curiously. Patrick's brows were pulled together, his jaw set as he mumbled quietly into his phone. She pretended to get comfortable, scooting infinitesimally closer to his conversation.

"No more PR, okay... Hasn't there been enough press already...? When I hired you, I thought you would take care —" He turned around, his back to her. A few minutes later, he got off the phone, washed his hands, and resumed his food prep.

PR? Press? They'd convinced him to cook for them without any knowledge of the demands of his career. And he'd done it. He could've stuck to the musician's suggestion to leave the food for them that first day, but instead he'd shown up for dinner with quiet resolve. In his unique way, it seemed to Emily that saying yes to them was an act of kindness.

The room darkened. Through the windows, the usually quiet Gulf smashed against the sand, its gemstone hues and light fizz now an angry ashen spray. A red warning beach flag down shore flapped in the wind. Blair got up and turned on the lamps, a glow filling the room.

Patrick seemed unaffected, seasoning the sea bass with some sort of dry rub.

"Maybe there's a good drama on," Blair offered. "Or a mystery—something that'll have us riveted so we don't have to consider that the storm is coming in pretty fast." She made a face.

Sienna stopped on the national news, where the storm was being reported. That was enough to give them all pause.

"We're currently seeing the outer bands of Tropical Storm Claudette moving across the Gulf and beginning to affect parts of the Florida Panhandle. While the storm's center remains well offshore, we are already beginning to see outer rain bands moving into the area, bringing heavy precipitation, gusty winds, and the potential for localized flooding, especially in low-lying and coastal neighborhoods.

"Stay with us for continuous updates and download our weather app for real-time alerts. We'll be here around the clock tracking the storm and letting you know what to expect, hour by hour."

The outside umbrella, secured and strapped, rattled against its holder.

"Think we should bring anything in from the back patio?" Emily asked. "It's getting really windy already, and with all these windows, I'd hate for it all to start flying through the air."

"Maybe we should stack the chairs at least," Blair said.

"The house has staff," Patrick called over. "I'm guessing they'll be here any second." He went back to cooking.

Just as Patrick had predicted, in a matter of minutes, men in coveralls carted the furniture off the patio, covered the pool, and secured the fire pit. They were in and out in a flash.

Blair's phone went off. "It's Rocko. He might have seen the weather report. I'll be back." She put the phone to her ear as she left the room. "Hello?"

"This weather is killing me," Sienna said with another yawn.

A loud sizzle came from the kitchen as Patrick flipped the sea bass in the hot pan. He turned around and began cleaning his knives.

Sienna tugged on the waistband of her dress. "I'm going to change into a tracksuit. This dress is tighter than it used to be, and I'm dying for something with a little give." She handed Emily the remote.

Emily clicked through a few channels just as a loud clap of thunder shook the house.

"Agh!" Patrick shrieked.

Emily jumped to her feet just in time to see him grabbing a towel and wrapping it around his hand.

"Are you okay?" She walked over to the kitchen.

"I'm fine," he snapped before loping over to his things and pulling out a first aid kit. He took it to the sink, unwrapped his hand, and ran it under water, grimacing as the stream hit a large gash on his palm.

"You jumped yesterday when it thundered," she noted.

He pulled out a gauze pad and medical tape as another rumble barreled through the sky. "Can you take the fish off the burner for me?"

She turned off the heat and moved the pan of sizzling fish to the back of the stove.

He ripped a piece of tape with his teeth and wrapped it around his injury.

"So you get jumpy during storms?"

"I was just surprised. Twice."

"You seemed different at the ice-cream shop today," she ventured.

He washed his knife, then dried it with a towel and slid it into a leather holder, his attention turned inward.

"Who's the little boy you were with?"

He began cleaning another knife. "Winston. My sister's kid."

"They're the ones who live in town?"

"Yeah."

"That's lucky your sister lives near you."

His attention fluttered to her and then away. "Yeah."

"You're good with kids." From witnessing only the one interaction, she didn't know that for sure, but she was hoping he'd either refute it or agree—something to keep the conversation going and maybe soften his edge.

But he didn't answer.

"Sorry I'm so talkative," she said. "It's the elementary-school teacher in me. I chat all day. And it's a good way to make friends."

Interest flickered across his face before he snapped the leather knife holder shut and turned away to pack it into his bag. He pulled out three plates.

"Why don't you like to talk?" she asked.

"I don't need to. And it's overrated."

She considered the magazine feature they'd heard about on the way into town. Wouldn't the fact that he'd been in a feature article say otherwise? But she decided not to bring it up. "Why is it overrated?" she asked instead.

"We'll share a few thoughts, chuckle at each other's jokes because we're supposed to, and then we'll go back to our regular day, and everything will be exactly the same."

"I saw how you interacted with Winston. Why do you talk so freely with him then?"

His brows pulled together. "Because he's a kid."

"And that's different?"

"He has no motives."

"I have no motive," she said. "I just want to make small talk since you're cooking dinner for me every night."

"But at the end of this you'll go back home, continue on with your life, and none of it will matter. Winston *is* my life —every day and night."

His comment warmed her. "Fair enough." She sighed. "I'll let you get back to it."

She went into the living room, picked up the remote, and scrolled through the movies, ready to shut out the real world, but she struggled to leave the conversation. He was with that guy Mark at the bar, and he knew the bartender by name, so he *was* social. Just not with her or her friends...

When Blair and Sienna returned, Patrick served their plates in the living room and then slipped out while they were eating. He didn't even say goodbye.

TEN

At first, given the dark room, Emily thought she'd woken too early, but a check of her phone informed her that it was after eight *and* Will had tried to call an hour ago. She stretched and peered across the room to the window. The storm clouds that had blanketed the sky last night hadn't budged. And on top of that, now they were unleashing a torrential downpour.

Last night, she'd silenced her phone to get some sleep, but she didn't feel rested this morning. Her shoulders ached, and she wasn't sure if the pain was due to the rain or the subconscious stress about her life. While this trip had succeeded in diverting her attention occasionally, it hadn't been able to erase the pain completely. And while she was ignoring all the work to be done regarding canceling the wedding until after her vacation, she couldn't eliminate the stress of it weighing on her.

Pushing the covers off her legs, she climbed out of bed and padded into the bathroom. With a turn of the tap, the water squealed quietly from the spigot. She splashed her face and then lathered with lavender soap. The sweet scent calmed her nerves.

She didn't want to jump right into a phone call with Will first thing. What did he even want at this early hour? But if it was about the house, she'd better call. In the end, getting rid of their joint asset as quickly as possible was in her best interest.

With a deep breath, she rinsed her face and dried it on a fluffy towel. Then she went back into the bedroom, dialed Will's number, and put her phone on speaker. He picked up right away.

"Morning," she said. Although, no greeting seemed to fit the conversation anymore. Even "Morning" was friendlier than she wanted.

"I decided to wait until I was sure..." he said.

Will's dramatic pause annoyed her, but so did everything he did now. She rubbed her temples. All of a sudden he liked to wait for things? The memory of their engagement floated back into her mind. *I didn't want to wait*, he'd said as he'd proposed in the middle of the street, even though they'd had dinner reservations in ten minutes' time. He'd produced an oval diamond set in platinum and slid it onto her finger—a perfect fit. Stunned and overjoyed, she'd wrapped her arms around him and kissed him right there. Cars were honking in celebration, the drivers clapping and hooting out their open windows.

She focused on the grain in the hardwood floor to get the image out of her head.

"I want to buy the house with... We want to buy the house together." His words seemed unsure, nervous.

He *should* be nervous.

His request hit her like a sledgehammer. He wanted to buy the house with *her*. The house Emily had found online?

The one they'd gone to look at together right away because it was so "them"?

The agent had left them alone in the house to think it over and Will took her hands and spun her around in the empty living room.

"What do you think?" he'd asked, pulling her close.

She giggled, looking up at his smirk. "I love it."

"Can you see us here?" He gave her another spin.

He'd said "us."

"Definitely."

He pulled her in and nuzzled her neck, sending a fleet of goosebumps racing down her arms and making her laugh.

"Since we both own the house," Will said, his voice yanking her from the memory, "you'd need to sign a quit-claim deed. We're going to refinance in my name, which would remove you from any liability, but we can do a cash-out option so you can have a little equity. And I could give you some time to get all your stuff before we move in..."

She'd stopped listening. Will was buying their house with this woman? They were that serious already? Everything she'd worked for in life was being jerked out from under her, and she had no say in the matter. She couldn't make Will love her, and she couldn't get back the years she had lost. Her chin wobbled.

"So if we send over the document by email, will you sign it?" he asked.

She grabbed her shoulders and squeezed to release the tension. "We can talk about this later," was all she could get out.

"Emily—"

Before she lost it completely, she hung up on him. She fell back into bed, buried her face in the pillow, and sobbed. Warm, salty tears puddled on her pillow, her back heaving, all the emotion she'd been holding inside finally breaking free from her stronghold. Why had he done this to her?

After longer than she'd wanted to cry over Will, she got up and went into the bathroom. Flicking on the light revealed her swollen red eyes. Her cheeks looked like the windows of her bedroom right now—streaked and void of color. She unrolled some toilet paper, balled it up, and blew her nose. Then she spent the next few minutes getting herself together before heading downstairs.

"Good grief," Blair said when Emily got to the kitchen. "What happened to you?"

Emily cleared her throat and took a seat at the bar next to Blair.

"Your eyes are so puffy they're almost shut. Here." Sienna slid a cup of coffee toward her. "You need this more than Blair does." She came over to Emily and put a hand on her shoulder. "What's wrong?"

With a groan, Emily told them about the call.

"I'm so sorry, Em." Blair wrapped her arms around Emily and gave her a squeeze.

Sienna rolled her eyes. "He's a selfish jerk. How did we not see it sooner?"

Emily took a long drink, letting the nutty, rich flavor settle on her tongue. "Believe me, I've been asking myself the same question. I agreed to *marry* him. If anyone should've seen it, it's me. But I didn't have a clue..."

"It's terrifying actually," Blair said. "You did nothing wrong, and Will strayed." Her face paled.

"You okay?" Sienna asked, pouring another cup of coffee.

"This isn't anything to do with your situation, Em, but it just hit me: What if Rocko looks somewhere else because I can't give him what he needs?"

"Rocko isn't Will," Emily said.

Sienna slid a second mug over to Blair.

"Since losing the baby, I'm in my head all the time, worried about what might happen with every choice I make," Blair said. "It's got me paralyzed. But at the same time, I'd die without Rocko. He doesn't really understand, but he's supportive. He was the first one to cheer me on when I wanted to start the influencer thing, while my family cautioned me. I knew it was a crazy idea, and the chances of anything coming of it were relatively low, but he had my back from day one. He still does."

Sienna sat down on the barstool beside Emily. "Now you two have *me* worried. Tyson isn't my rock like Rocko. And, to be honest, I wouldn't know if he had a chick in the city. We're like two ships passing in the night. But we don't worry about one another because we've always wanted the same thing—basically a single lifestyle minus the dating. We can come and go as we please. And now, I'm going to change that. I'm not sure we're ready for this."

"I'm living proof that we can never be ready for the things that get thrown at us," Emily said. "But it's how we deal with the unexpected that matters."

She wasn't sure yet how she planned to deal with it, but the first step was to sign that form to transfer the house so she could start the next chapter of her life.

"You're right." Blair took her coffee and twisted around on the barstool. "Focus on the positive. And my counselor says I need to develop emotional intimacy before I'll feel totally comfortable with the physical. Rocko has been trying. He's been bringing home fresh flowers because he knows I like them. And he spends an hour each night talking to me. That should say something, right?"

"Absolutely," Sienna said. "But now I'm more nervous

than I was to begin with. Tyson and I have a long way to go."

"Talk to him about it," Emily suggested.

"I'll call him tonight and just feel him out."

Blair leaned on her elbow, a dreamy look on her face. "It all seemed so easy when we were young. I used to put my bedsheet on my head and pretend to get married. I'd cradle my baby dolls and make-believe they were my kids. I never imagined any other future for myself."

"Me too," Emily said. "I had tons of dolls. It's a wonder I didn't start a daycare center."

"Well, you did become a teacher," Blair said. She leaned around Emily. "Sienna, what did your playtime look like as a girl?"

"I dressed up Barbies in their little business attire and created scenarios about how they were headed off to make millions in their pink convertibles."

Blair laughed. "That sounds about right. We had no idea then what we'd all face as adults…"

Sienna blew out a loud breath of air. "We're not even through breakfast, and I think we all need an escape from our regular lives already. It's got to be this dreadful weather." She shot an angry look at the gray view. "Who wants to plan the outing today?"

Blair raised her hand. "I'll do it."

"Perfect." Sienna got up and walked around the bar. "Given that my waistline is expanding anyway, I'm planning on carbs this morning. I found ingredients for pancakes. Anyone up for some?"

Emily's eyes widened. "I could definitely go for some pancakes. And I packed syrup."

"The morning's getting brighter already!" Blair cheered.

AS RAIN PATTERED against the windows, the women retreated to their rooms. Over the last hour, while getting dressed, combing her hair, and putting on her makeup, Emily had picked apart every moment of her and Will's life together, trying to figure out the warning signs she'd missed. It was true they'd gotten busy with work and remodeling plans, and they hadn't been as romantic as they used to be, but was preoccupation grounds for *this*? Why didn't he ever say something? She'd have dropped everything to have a date night. She'd have reorganized her time immediately to allow a candlelit dinner or a pizza in. The question she kept coming back to, which she didn't want to ask herself: Was she not enough? Could this Lanie give him something she couldn't?

Who was this woman? What were her likes and dislikes? Did Lanie have anything in common with her?

Emily grabbed her phone, opened her email, and stared at the signature form until the image blurred. A part of her didn't want to give Will the satisfaction of her compliance. He and Lanie were stealing her life, and she was handing it over with a single signature. His behavior was so erratic. One minute they were remodeling the kitchen, then he was selling the house, and now he's buying it? This was the same guy who took two weeks to change a burned-out lightbulb.

The night of their engagement came back to her and her stomach plummeted. He had been excited. That was the only time he acted spontaneously.

A knock on the door interrupted her ruminating.

"Come in."

Blair poked her head inside. "Hey, I found a cool place for our outing today. Wanna go in a few minutes?"

"Yeah, I can come down right now." She closed the screen without signing. Her future could wait a few more hours.

But as she took each step down the sprawling staircase, a quiet yearning to hold out as long as possible whispered to her. Maybe Will would realize he'd made a terrible mistake and ask her to come back. He'd break it off with Lanie, then they could go to couples' counseling and spend the rest of their lives rekindling their romance.

Scenarios whirled in her mind as she dashed through the rain and climbed into Sienna's car. Blair put on the navigation. Music played, and Blair and Sienna made small talk in the front, but it only sounded like a faint hum behind the weight of hope for something Emily knew would never come to pass. Why did she hope to rekindle something with someone who didn't think enough of her to try? Until now, she'd never seen Will as the spineless type, and even though she didn't want to believe he was, the notion was pretty obvious. How had she managed to get wrapped up in a life with someone like that?

It was a ding to her ego. Maybe this whole mess could've been avoided if she'd taken more time to actually get to know him on a deeper level. She'd been so excited about the wedding and then house shopping and renovations and eventually planning for children that she hadn't spent enough time digging into who Will was as a person. Maybe *he* didn't even really know. He'd rarely expressed strong interests in things; he'd always just gone along with whatever she planned.

She hadn't really unpacked his core values. Where did he see himself in ten years? Twenty? How did he view his role in the family? Was he planning to be involved—would he go to school PTA meetings and father-child days? What were his views on discipline and education? She could go on and on with questions she didn't have answers to. And with every one, the fact that she might have brought this on herself by not knowing these answers pinched her chest.

"Here we are," Sienna said as they pulled up in front of a small light-blue cottage.

Inside was an art studio just big enough for a long table full of containers with shards of brightly colored glass. While they each took a seat in front of an empty framed platform, a woman explained that they'd be using an adapted mosaic technique to create pictures with glass pieces.

"We have bins along the side here," she said, waving a hand by the windows, "where you can cut your own pieces of glass..."

"We can take out our aggression with the glass cutters," Sienna whispered, shaking her umbrella and setting it next to her chair. She side-eyed Emily.

"We also have beads, seashells, and other materials that you might want to use to enhance your design," the woman continued. "When you have the design just the way you'd like it, we pour resin on top to keep it all in place, and you can either pick up the finished piece tomorrow or have it mailed to you."

They thanked her and turned their attention to their platforms.

"You were quiet on the way here," Sienna said. "Wanna dish?"

"Nothing new," Emily replied. "I'm glad we're here. I'm excited to focus on something entertaining and mind-consuming." She forced herself into a bright smile, wanting nothing more than to leave her thoughts behind.

"What are you going to make?" Blair asked Emily as she floated her phone through the air, taking a video.

"I'm not sure yet. Maybe stripes of turquoise and navy like the water at the beach?"

"That's a good idea," Sienna said, fishing out a few pieces of ice-blue glass. "I might do an abstract."

"These peachy pink pieces are pretty," Blair said, standing up to peer into the bowl. "I might do an abstract design as well—maybe in this color and cream." She snapped a photo inside the bowl.

Emily got up and went to the far wall with an empty supply cup. She filled it with pearls, pink seashell pieces, and sparkly beads. When she had enough to create her project, she took them back to the table and began to line the interior bottom platform of her frame with them, arranging each piece to appear like the white Gulf Coast sand. From there, she added turquoise and dark blue and then some of the ice-blue Sienna had chosen for a sandbar effect.

As she placed each piece of glass, Emily considered where she'd put this little masterpiece when she got home. *Home*—where did she want to live? She didn't have to be close to Nashville for Will's writing anymore. She could get an apartment somewhere outside the city—maybe in Spring Hill or Franklin, where she could visit the farmers' markets and spend long afternoons walking through the parks. She didn't need anything fancy, just a place where she could recover. Her current apartment was small, but outside Nashville she might be able to afford a larger place.

The bedroom suite in the house was hers, so she'd get to take that with her, and Will would probably let her have the kitchen table, which was larger than the bistro set she had now. She could get some new place mats and add cushions to the chairs. It might take her a while to furnish a larger living room, but she could buy things a little at a time so she wouldn't have to put anything on the credit card. And this design could be her first piece of artwork.

Emily forced herself to believe that starting over could be therapeutic. And that perhaps she could learn from this. She refocused on lining up the colored sea-glass shards on her frame.

Sienna had created a beautiful starburst of oranges and yellows, and Blair's creation looked like a peach-and-pearl-colored baby-blanket pattern. Maybe Blair and Sienna should switch, Emily thought. But she didn't mention it. They were too happy, chatting and giggling as they selected their pieces. Their lighthearted chatter lifted Emily's spirits. Who knew what the future held? If she could ever crawl out of the shock of the situation, the sky was the limit.

ELEVEN

That evening, after Emily woke up from a nap, the rain was still falling; a heavy mist of heat and salt hovering over the patio. The Gulf was barely visible through the thick gray haze.

"I ran out in this awful rain for you all." Sienna threw a handful of magazines, three new novels, and a deck of playing cards on the coffee table. "If we're stuck inside, we'll need something to do... And I had to get out of the house. I'm going stir-crazy already."

Sienna plopped down on the sofa next to Emily and Blair while Blair scrolled through her phone. Just as Emily was reaching for one of the novels to read the back, Blair let out a loud exhale.

"Oh my gosh."

Emily looked over. "What?"

"The latest conspiracy theory is that I ran off with all the endorsement money to live in the wild with Rocko and the baby. Since Rocko's in construction, he's built us an off-grid mansion."

Emily couldn't hold in her laugh. "The *latest?*"

Blair folded her thin legs underneath her. "There are a ton of conspiracy theories online about what happened to me; I've just been ignoring them all."

Sienna scooted closer, interest sparkling in her eye. "What are the others?"

Blair clicked off her phone and set it on the coffee table. "Well, there's the one that I've had triplets, and I starved myself so I could look thinner during my pregnancy, and now we're all in the hospital fighting for our lives."

Sienna's mouth hung open.

"How awful," Emily said.

Blair nodded. "Another one floating around is that I had a nervous breakdown, I've turned on everyone, become impossible to live with, and refuse to get any help, so Rocko's raising the baby."

Emily gasped.

"People are crazy," Sienna said, making a face as she crossed her legs on the sofa.

"What's crazier," Emily added, "is that as much as you share about you and Rocko online, they have no idea who you really are."

Blair shook her head. "Someone always has something to say, you know? It didn't bother me before, but now, every time someone takes a jab, it's as if they're poking that raw part of me that's still healing from losing the baby."

"I'd be furious. Don't you want to set the record straight?" Sienna asked.

"Who cares what they think?" Blair said. But the sadness on her face gave away how the lies affected her.

Sienna squinted hatefully at Blair's phone. "They're so busy blaming you for the silence. I'll bet it would shut them up *really* quickly to find out what you've been dealing with."

Blair shrugged. "I'm not out to prove any points to anyone. I thought my core fans were kinder, that's all. And seeing how some of them are reacting makes me question if I want to ever resume posting. I thought I'd created this wonderful community, but have I?"

"I'm sure they're not all like that," Emily said. "And your *true* fans might really want to know. They're probably worried about you."

"Yeah." Blair let out a long exhale. "I waffle back and forth with whether I want to continue. I do have to manage my paid endorsements. That's what I was doing in my room a while ago—reaching out to the companies to let them know what happened. The ones who responded have been very understanding. But even still, how do I ever get back online after the trauma and then all the hate?"

"I think you'll know when the time is right," Emily said.

"I have gotten some really good footage of our trip so far." Blair brightened. "If I break up the content into bite-sized pieces, I'll have enough for a good two weeks."

Sienna pulled a fashionable large-weave cotton blanket from the arm of the sofa and draped it over her legs. "Posting about us during a beach rainstorm might be a light-hearted way to get back into it."

Blair laughed. "I am going to have to address the elephant..."

"Maybe you could post an unrelated video with a quick explanation in the comments," Emily suggested. "Just say that you've had a family tragedy, and you prefer to keep the details private until you're ready to share them—if ever."

"I should talk more with Rocko about how to manage it. He'll have some wild idea none of us have thought of."

"You do need to talk to Rocko," Emily said. "And, Sienna, you also need to break the news to Tyson."

"It feels so easy, sitting here," Sienna said. "I tried once, but I chickened out. And at home we're in the busy swing of things, and life gets in the way. I end up falling into bed exhausted. I should probably tell him when he comes. But I don't want to ruin our trip together, you know?"

"Ruin?" Emily said. "His son or daughter is on the way. You might find he's more open to that than you think."

"It'll be good when they get here," Blair said.

"I don't want to spend the whole trip talking about our issues, though." Sienna shook her head. "This is our vacation. Our problems will still be there when we get home."

"I agree," Blair said. "We need the weekend to be a chance to have some couple time with our guys." She turned to Emily. "Sorry, Em. Are you going to be okay once they get here?"

"I'll be fine," Emily said. "This might be a really great opportunity for both of you. Tyson wants to take off work, which he never does, and Rocko's fishing trip fell through. It's perfect timing. I could get some quiet moments in— believe me, I'm very happy to spend my days away from Will and his drama back at home."

"We won't leave you out, Emily, we promise," Sienna said.

Blair leaned in. "Agreed."

Sienna clapped her hands happily. "This rest of the week, though, it's just us girls. Rain or shine, we'll make the most of it."

The doorbell chimed, echoing throughout the large house.

Sienna threw the blanket off her legs. "I'll bet that's our chef. Right on time." She folded the blanket, then went to let Patrick in. "I'm starving."

A minute later, Patrick shuffled through the open

living area with armfuls of bags as he had before. But tonight he'd brought a little something extra: Winston was on his heels.

Emily got up and walked through the living area and into the kitchen while Blair called the boy over to say hello.

"Sorry." Patrick eyed Winston across the room, but didn't elaborate.

"What are you sorry for?" Emily asked.

"I don't usually bring my nephew to my clients' homes, but I had no way around it."

Winston ran across the room, returning to his uncle.

Emily greeted the boy. "I'm Emily."

"I'm Winston. I'm six."

She adored him already. "I hear you're helping your uncle this evening."

"Yeah, my mom's finishing up a meeting for her class. She couldn't leave early because it's supposed to storm, and this was their last chance to get together."

"Oh?" Emily grinned at him, finding his animated chattering endearing. "What class is she taking?"

"She's taking a couple of them. She's studying to be a nurse."

"Wow. That's pretty cool." Emily pulled out one of the barstools. "Want to sit up here and watch your Uncle Patrick make our dinner?"

Winston climbed onto the barstool while Emily held it steady. Taking advantage of the rotating seat, he began to spin himself around, pushing off the counter.

"Uncle Patrick and I are coming up with ideas for how to pay for Mom's college," he said as he spun.

Patrick pouted fondly at him and shook his head, seemingly trying to indicate that the subject of finances wasn't something to share.

But Winston continued. "He might try a long-term rental or something."

"A long-term rental? You know about those?" Emily asked with a chuckle.

"Not really, but Uncle Patrick said it to Mom. His restaurant uses up a lot of his savings, but he'll make them back ten... What was it, Uncle Patrick? Oh! Ten*fold*." He wrinkled his nose. "What even is tenfold?"

"It means 'a lot,'" Patrick said. "But let's talk about something else. We don't want to bore Emily."

Winston pouted in thought. "I play basketball," he said.

Emily nodded to show her interest. "You do?"

"Yeah. And since the tables aren't up in the restaurant yet, Uncle Patrick lets me shoot hoops in the main dining room."

"What restaurant?" she asked.

"What's it gonna be called again, Uncle Patrick?"

He took the last dish out of his bag. "It's called The Low Tide Supper Club."

Sienna perked up from the living room. "Isn't that the one we passed earlier?" she called over.

"I think so," Emily said. She turned back to Patrick. "We actually drove past it. The building is beautiful."

He continued to prepare dinner, but a softness shone around his eyes. It was clear he was proud of it.

Sienna and Blair clicked on the TV in the living room and began talking quietly, the moment gone. Neither were super impressed with Patrick's cordiality so Emily could see why they didn't feel inclined to get up and make conversation.

"So you're a personal chef *and* you own an up-and-coming restaurant?" Emily pressed.

"Mm hm." But Patrick didn't add anything. Instead, he

pushed the covered dishes toward her. "I cooked earlier so I could heat dinner up quickly, given the weather," he said with an inconspicuous nod toward Winston. "I've got steak and shrimp tonight."

"Mom's only got a few more classes, and then she'll be done," Winston said, continuing with their previous conversation. His little chest puffed out with a breath. "Then I won't have to cook with Uncle Patrick as much."

"Hey, I thought you liked cooking with me." Patrick wrinkled his nose playfully.

"Yeah, but you do it a *lot*." Winston nodded, his little eyebrows raised.

Emily laughed. His candor warmed her.

Patrick glanced over at them as he took the lids off the food—baked potatoes, steak, salad, and shrimp in some sort of delicious-looking creamy sauce with parsley and herbs.

"How long has your mom been taking classes, Winston?" Emily asked, going to the cabinet to get a glass so she could offer him some lemonade.

"Since before my dad died."

Her breath caught.

"She stopped for a while after that. But now she's taking some again."

"Oh. I see."

"Hey, bud," Patrick cut in, "why don't you help me tear this lettuce. Come over here and wash your hands."

Winston clambered down and ran around to the other side of the island. Patrick turned on the water and lifted him up. The boy pumped the soap into his hands and lathered, his feet dangling above the floor as he hung from Patrick's strong arms. With a rinse and a dry on the towel, he went back to the barstool. Patrick set a bowl of lettuce in front of him.

"Half the size of my hand, right?" Winston asked, pulling out a large lettuce leaf.

"Yep."

Emily poured a glass half-full with lemonade and set it beside the boy. "You've done this before," she said.

"Yeah, I help Uncle Patrick cook when he makes dinner for me and Mom."

"That's very helpful," she said, her heart squeezing. She'd love nothing more than to hear the little feet of children as she cooked dinner—something that had been in her near future and now seemed impossible.

"It's so fun." Winston's eyebrows bobbed. "Just not all day."

"He was at the restaurant today and then had to come with me tonight, so he's ready to get home, I'm sure. It's definitely an adventure," Patrick said as he tossed mixed veggies in a bowl.

Winston brightened. "We go on lots of adventures together." He put both hands around his glass and tipped up his lemonade.

"Oh really?" Emily pulled up a stool next to Winston. "Like what?"

"We like to hike Timpoochee Trail and look for wild animals. I try to find a dog, though, whenever we go."

Emily chuckled. "A *wild* dog?"

"Dogs aren't wild," Winston said with a giggle. "Uncle Patrick says if we find one, he'll take care of it for me so I can keep it." He grabbed a handful of lettuce.

Patrick slid the potatoes into the oven to warm. Then he went over to Winston and inspected the lettuce. His unique scent of cotton and musk floated toward her.

Emily got up and went back around to the sink. "Dogs are a lot of work. A dog would keep your uncle busy."

"Mm hm, but Uncle Patrick could do it. He can do anything."

Patrick ruffled Winston's hair and went back to unloading the grill.

She washed her hands and dried them on a towel before going back to her stool. "May I help you?"

"Sure." Winston scooted the bowl between them.

Emily sat back down and grabbed a lettuce leaf. "Could you show me how?"

"Like this," Winston said, demonstrating by placing a leaf in the palm of his little hand and tearing it.

Patrick had set up a tabletop grill and was warming the steaks. As Emily prepared the lettuce, she stole glances at Patrick, noticing now how he and Winston had the same sandy-brown hair and jawline. Did Patrick look like Winston as a kid? He was so stoic; she couldn't imagine him as a child. Was he as serious and quiet as he was now? The glimpses she got of him when he interacted with Winston made her interested in knowing more.

He seemed to notice her looking and heat rose through her face. A gentle fondness shone in the curve of his lips.

"Thanks for letting Winston help. His summer camp was closed today, due to the weather, which is why he's been working with me all day," Patrick said, drawing her out of her introspection. "My sister, Julia, called me last minute in a panic."

"I don't mind at all," Emily said. "He's been a big help. He can come anytime."

Winston flashed a giant smile before taking another long drink of lemonade.

She turned around to share in Winston's cuteness with her friends, and both of them were smirking, their attention moving between her and Patrick. She discreetly waved them off.

"YOU SURE ARE chatty whenever Patrick comes on the scene," Sienna said as she stabbed a bite of steak and threw a wink to Blair.

Emily shook her head. "Don't start. I'm no different. I'm just as chatty with you all."

The pelting rain blurred the view of the churning Gulf even more than it had earlier. They could hardly tell they were on the coast at all. With the wind picking up, Patrick had served them quickly. Emily offered for him to leave everything and pick up his things after the storm died down. He promised to come back tomorrow, and then he and Winston were gone in a flash. His grill and bags still littered the kitchen.

"He's handsome," Blair said, fueling the fire. "Easy to flirt with, I'd imagine."

Emily wound her napkin around her finger in her lap, her cheeks heating up again. "I don't need or want to flirt with anyone right now. I'm tapped out emotionally."

"Fair enough," Blair said with a sigh. She leaned back in her chair and turned her attention to the television that was still squawking with red-blotched weather maps and hourly forecasts for the area.

"I know the owners gave me the whole summer here if I want it, but I do have to get home to show houses," Sienna said. "I was hoping for a week of sunshine." She lifted an eyebrow. "I doubt I'll be able to come back. It's quite a drive, and even if I flew, it wouldn't be the same without you two.

Should we try to come again before the summer's over, or would it be too much?"

"I don't know," Emily said. "I couldn't pay for a flight, and I still have to find an apartment or somewhere to live, since my lease is up. I signed my teaching contract for next year, so I'll have to find one in driving distance to Nashville, but I want to look in the suburbs—that'll take some time, and I'll need to move all my stuff."

"Maybe if the sun comes out, we could just tack a few extra days onto the end of our trip," Blair suggested.

Truth be told, a few extra days would be nice. The last thing Emily wanted to do was go home. She could always do her initial apartment search and wedding cancellations from the beach. The only other thing she had to do was decide whether or not to sign the form for the house. At the very least, she'd make Will sweat a while. Even with the rain, living in the lap of luxury was pretty great. That was how she'd like to keep it for as long as she could.

TWELVE

"Look!" Sienna pointed outside when Emily came downstairs the next morning. "A tiny break in the clouds! I'm going to take a long walk on the beach. Want to come?" She was already in a pair of stretchy shorts, wearing sunglasses and flip-flops.

Emily yawned. Her neck ached from sleeping on tight shoulders all night. "I think I'm going to have some coffee first, so I can wake up. And with Blair asleep, I should probably stay in case Patrick comes by to get his things." She nodded toward the pile of kitchen items, bags, and food containers.

"Okay. I'll be back in about an hour. A long stroll will do me some good."

"Be careful."

Sienna waved and let herself out the oversized glass doors leading to the pool. The furniture was still stacked against the house, and the pool cover was on. The house crew would probably be by later to set it all back up for them, and then they could lounge all day, drift off between cocktails, and finally get back to their girls' week.

Emily padded over to the counter, made herself a steaming cup of coffee, and took it to the living room. The playing cards, books, and magazines were still on the coffee table where Sienna had dropped them. With her coffee in one hand, Emily fanned out the magazines, deciding on what she felt like reading. But a single cover stood out from the others. She'd seen it before when they'd first arrived: the one with Patrick's feature. Had Sienna even realized what she'd picked up?

She set her mug on the table and immediately scanned the contents, looking for the article about Patrick. Page 32. She flipped as quickly as she could and then there he was. A glossy photo filled the page: a spruced-up version of Patrick in a dress-white uniform. His strong jawline was set in a slight smile, and his blue eyes sparkled as though they were looking into her very soul. She had to drag her line of sight from the image to the words beside it. The title of the article read, "From Battleships to Beachfronts: Life after the Navy." She scanned the quote highlighted in blue type on the side of the page:

"The military taught me discipline and humility. I spent years sailing the world with the navy, but nothing feels more like home than here."

She read more about his naval service. He'd served for eleven years—two deployments, a slew of awards for leadership under pressure, and a reputation for unshakable poise. A culinary officer, he was one of the navy's rising stars in food service management. Assigned to a Navy SEAL Team, on a top-secret mission in the Pacific, he oversaw a galley that fed twenty elite officers with tight supplies and tighter timelines.

She picked up her coffee, her eyes glued to the page.

He was a quiet man who loved order, his country, and his family, which included his sister Julia and her husband, Daniel Simpson. Daniel wasn't just his brother-in-law; he was also Patrick's best friend since high school. The two had joined the navy within months of each other and eventually found themselves on the same deployment. During a routine resupply maneuver, a fuel line ruptured in the ship's lower engine room. Patrick had just finished prepping the galley for the night's meal when alarms blared.

Daniel was on the first response team. Patrick left the galley and headed for the central command post. Minutes later, a flash erupted, and a section of the engine room buckled. Smoke rolled through the corridors. Daniel and two sailors were lost in the blast, killed instantly, leaving Patrick in shock, and Julia and her one-year-old son on their own.

After the incident, Patrick experienced unshakable grief, anxiety, and nightmares.

Emily gripped her coffee, her heart pounding. How terrible. Suddenly, Patrick's demeanor made a lot of sense. His stoic nature and jumpiness during the storm came into focus; there was so much more to the story now than a distant chef. Had she been able to somehow sense his hardship? Was that why she'd felt curious about him, wanting to have a conversation when her friends didn't seem as interested? She read on.

Eventually, Patrick was evaluated by a navy mental health officer and entered into counseling. After several months of treatment and no improvement in his operational capacity, Patrick applied for a discharge under navy guidelines for psychological hardship and family dependency.

"At my lowest point, I went home to help my sister, and it was the best thing that ever happened to me," he was quoted saying. "In the midst of tragedy, the love of family and shared grief kept me going. We came out of this together. I couldn't have done it without them."

It had been five years since the accident, and while Patrick still dealt with post-traumatic stress, he'd found solace in his family and took great honor in the duty of raising his nephew, Winston. Having to learn how to use his talents outside of the navy, Patrick began his company, Main Course. Word spread about his heroic return, and his skills were unmatched. Before long, his company was a full-blown success, catching the attention of celebrities vacationing in the area.

Main Course had earned a reputation as one of the most exclusive culinary establishments in the state, catering to celebrities, musicians, and Fortune 500 executives with seamless precision. His work was recognized in *Worldwide Traveler Magazine* as a "Top Private Dining Experience," and was praised for redefining luxury hospitality through its personalized menus and discreet service. Main Course had also been awarded the Blue Ribbon of Excellence for Innovation in Cuisine, solidifying its reputation and confirming that it had achieved the highest standard in culinary artistry. He became so incredibly popular that he was opening his highly anticipated restaurant, The Low Tide Supper Club, catering to high-end clientele with unique coastal cuisine. The restaurant's launch was expected next summer.

When asked what he did with all that notoriety, he offered a humble chuckle. "I keep to myself," he was quoted saying. "I enjoy the privacy."

While his company continued to thrive, Patrick retreated further into the secluded life of a civilian, letting the success of Main Course and the buzz of The Low Tide Supper Club be the sources of interest—not him.

The chime of the doorbell startled Emily. She wasn't expecting Patrick this early. She ran her hands through her unbrushed hair, and quickly closed the magazine, shoving it under a pile of others on the coffee table, and sprinted to the door.

"Hey," Patrick said on the other side. His voice was tight and controlled, a wild look on his face.

"Hi." She willed her heart to stop pounding to no avail.

The storm in his blue eyes made sense now, but something else was brewing. She took in the rugged lines on his forehead and the tightness of his jaw as she opened the door wider and ushered him into the house.

He side-eyed her as he entered and peered around. Then he looked at the stairway, and his brows pulled together, but he didn't say anything.

Emily followed, not sure what he was doing. Her mind was occupied with whether she should bring up the article, given his mention of staying out of the limelight. If he'd wanted her to know, he'd have mentioned it when she'd asked him questions about the restaurant. But didn't the fact that he'd agreed to a national article give her the go-ahead she needed? Why had he agreed to that?

She was still debating the idea when she got to the kitchen.

"Have you not heard?" he asked, almost exasperated.

"Heard what?"

"The tropical storm offshore is gaining speed." He wiped down the grill and packed it away in haste. He was moving with incredible swiftness.

An awkward hush fell between them, and she turned to the window.

"Oh no," she said, squinting at the menacing dark gray in the sky. "The clouds are rolling back in."

"Late last night, they were warning people to evacuate. I figured you all would be packed and heading home."

Emily's mouth dropped open. "Sienna took a walk down the beach. I hope she's turned back." She peered outside, but there was no sight of Sienna. "Let me run up and get my phone to call her."

"Yeah, you'd better."

She ran upstairs. On the way to her room, she knocked on Blair's door. "You might want to get up. A big storm's coming."

A groggy Blair opened the door as Emily rushed past, swiping her phone off the dresser and dialing Sienna's number. A phone rang down the hall.

"Shoot." Emily ended the call.

"What's going on?" Blair asked, padding into the hallway.

"Sienna went for a walk. She's nowhere to be found, her phone's here, and the storm that's been brewing is now a tropical storm."

Blair's shoulders jerked in panic. She followed as Emily rushed down the stairs.

"No luck?" Patrick asked as he packed his final few things.

"She left her phone here."

Blair got the remote and turned on the TV. On the screen, lines of cars, bumper-to-bumper, streamed out of town while newscasters discussed the impending storm.

Blair whirled around. "How quickly is it coming?"

Patrick remained focused on the screen. "Faster than I thought."

Outside, the palm trees bent in the high wind, the usually docile waves slamming onto the shore. Emily frantically looked outside again.

"Do you know which way your friend went?" Patrick asked, his tone direct and confident—controlled despite Emily's growing panic.

"I didn't pay attention." Emily's mouth dried out, her heart slamming in her chest.

"The wind could knock her down," Patrick said.

Emily rushed over to Patrick and took hold of his biceps. "She's pregnant."

The information visibly sank into his eyes, but he remained steady, not rushed in any way. "I'll go look for her. Stay here until I get back. Don't. Move."

As the first giant drops of rain began to plonk onto the decking, Patrick opened the French door and darted out.

"Should *we* do anything?" Blair asked, terror flashing across her face.

"He said not to move, so I'm not doing a thing. He knows better than we do." Helpless, Emily ran to the door to watch, but Patrick was already down on the beach and fading out of sight. "Let's pack up our stuff," she said as the forecasters chattered on. "If we can get Sienna back in time, we can try to get out of town."

"I'll pack for her," Blair suggested.

They both ran upstairs.

Emily ran to her room and wrestled her way out of her pajamas. She pulled a T-shirt and shorts from her suitcase and threw them on. She'd grown up in Virginia, and they'd had their share of tropical storms and hurricanes, but she'd never been this close to the shore before. If this thing hit, the devastation could be widespread. With trembling hands, she brushed her teeth, then jammed her toothbrush and a comb into her purse and lumped everything else in her suitcase, then zipped it up. She rushed around the room, gathering her phone charger and her jewelry off the nightstand.

Within minutes, she was ready to go. She pulled the covers up on the bed and rearranged the pillows to double-check that she hadn't left anything.

When she had her bags in the hallway, she ran over to help Blair. The click of a door and the sound of the wind over the balcony drew her attention.

Sienna and Patrick had just burst inside, both of them soaking wet.

"Thank goodness," Emily said from over the balcony, relief flooding her. "Are you okay?"

"Yeah," Sienna said, out of breath, pulling her soaked hair into a temporary ponytail and squeezing the water on the floor. "Patrick told me about the storm, but I was already on my way back with all the rain." She shook her wet hair.

Emily and Blair dashed downstairs.

"We were about to pack your stuff," Emily told her.

A breaking-news alert sounded, and they all turned toward the TV.

"In the last twenty-four hours, the tropical storm has intensified, and it's looking like it's going to hit land more quickly than expected. A last-minute shift has this storm headed straight for the Gulf Coast. If you have not begun your evacuation, we suggest you shelter in place. Do not go out unless it's an absolute emergency. You have about a half an hour before landfall."

"Well," Patrick said, "I hadn't planned for that."

THIRTEEN

Breathless, Emily looked up at the beams in the mansion's vaulted ceiling. *Is this house strong enough to survive this storm, sitting right on the coast? Surely it had made it through others, right?*

As if reading her mind, Patrick spoke up. "The house is equipped with extra power and electric hurricane shutters. The owner and I had a conversation about it once. I'll find the smart system and see if I can figure out how to initiate the storm protection. If not, the glass is hurricane resistant, so a tropical storm should be no problem."

Emily took a step toward him, trying to remain strong but trembling. "Will we be safe here?"

He turned to the now-raging wind outside and then looked down at her. She didn't like the deliberation on his face.

His jaw clenched. "Are you all packed up?"

"All but a few things of Sienna's," Blair said from behind her.

His entire focus locked on Emily, and then softened, as if he wanted to ease her worry. "Get your bags, and I'll take you all to my sister's. I've gotten her house and mine secure for a storm already, and she lives farthest inland—about twenty minutes away."

"They said we only have thirty," Emily said, frightened.

"Should we just stay here and try to wait it out?" Sienna asked.

"The storm surge and coastal winds will be insane if this thing becomes a hurricane. *And* hurricanes can spin off tornadoes. They're worse the closer you are to the shore. You'll be safest inland."

"Do we need to do anything here?" She peered outside. The grounds crew had already stacked the outside chairs, the wind pushing against them. "They could fly through the air," Emily said.

"I'm sure they've secured the furniture as best they can, but there aren't any guarantees when Mother Nature is involved. Get your things." Patrick flew out of the room, rushing through the house, looking for the system. When he found it, he searched the buttons.

As Emily, Sienna, and Blair retrieved their suitcases from upstairs, the hum of the shutters rolling down the windows made Emily's stomach drop. Suddenly, the house was dark. A couple of emergency lights popped on along the stairs, giving the house an eerie feeling.

They dragged their bags to the front door as Patrick met them. Through the wild wind and rain, he loaded his cooking equipment and supplies into his truck. When he'd finished, he grabbed their suitcases, lumped them into the bed of the vehicle, and pulled a retractable cover over them to keep them dry. Sienna locked up.

He opened the door to a roomy backseat and Blair and Sienna climbed inside. Emily opened the front door and jumped in to ride shotgun. She brushed her soaking clothes, not making any headway in getting rid of the water.

The trees swayed precariously over them, the wind rocking the vehicle. Emily looked back at her friends' terrified faces.

Patrick started the engine, put the truck in gear, and then flew down the drive.

At the end, the road was jam-packed with cars weaving in and out of line, all frantically trying to get to safety in the short amount of time before the storm hit. Patrick's hand tightened around the steering wheel.

"The main roads are jammed," he said. "If we want to outrun the storm, we're going to have to take back roads." His voice was still cool and calm, despite his assessment of the calamity outside. "Y'all make sure your seatbelts are on."

He pushed the front bumper of his truck out into traffic, causing a few horns to sound in response. Ignoring their warning, he pushed into the mass and maneuvered around the cars, inching through several lanes. Emily closed her eyes. They did not need to get into a fender bender in this. But she opened them when he took a wide turn, bumped over the curb, and headed down a dirt path on the other side of the road at top speed.

Emily grabbed the door handle to steady herself as they bounded through the woods like an off-road speed-racer. Had anyone driven on this before? It looked more like a bike path. "This is a back road?" she asked.

Patrick swerved to miss a tree stump and then hit the gas. "It is today."

Through the blur of sheeting rain, an eerie green cast had fallen over everything. The truck jolted over debris, the woods on either side a blur through the deluge. They were all completely silent under the howling of the wind and the hammering rain. The windshield wipers smacked back and forth, but did little to clear the view.

Patrick moved with agile speed, taking turns with ease, as if he drove through the woods in a tropical storm on a regular basis. How the rain managed to still douse them through the thick canopy of swaying trees, Emily had no idea. The limbs arched and bent over the truck and then away like a nimble stalk of sea grass. The trees looked as though they could fall over at any minute, pinning the truck to the path. Twigs dropped onto the windshield, but the wipers brushed them away. Emily's shoulders tightened in response.

Sienna's weather alerts pinged from her phone in her handbag, but no one paid any attention to the updates. The branches cracking around them sounded like gunshots from all angles. The truck splashed through pooled water in low-lying areas, but just as Emily would worry that they were too deep, they'd bump up to higher ground again.

Through it all, she stole glances at Patrick. He was laser-focused on the path ahead of them, his face showing neither fear nor ease. He just drove, his large hands gripping the wheel, the whites of his knuckles the only indication that he was anything other than calm.

Thumps from debris hitting the top of the truck made Emily jump.

When he finally pulled onto an actual road, they were the only ones out there—at least it seemed like it. The pavement ahead of them was barely visible from all the precipitation. Emily couldn't tell where the sky ended and the ground began. How could Patrick even see where he was going?

He pulled out his phone and voice texted his sister. "I've got three people with me. Have the door ready." He dropped the phone into the console and grabbed hold of the steering wheel once more.

They finally reached a rustic-brown clapboard rancher in the woods. The windows were stormproofed with plywood, the front porch stripped bare. Through the gray haze, a faint yellow glow from inside was the only indication the front door was ajar.

Patrick pulled right up to the front. With the engine still running, he slid open the cover on the bed of his truck, and darted back and forth, throwing suitcases and cooking equipment onto the porch. "Go inside," he called.

Emily, Blair, and Sienna ran up to the door as he drove into the tightly packed garage.

A petite blonde with Patrick's eyes leaned out the doorway while she yanked Sienna's suitcase into the house. "Y'all get in!"

They clawed at their bags, tugging and pushing them to safety. What they didn't get in the first trip, Patrick snatched, along with his cooking equipment, in one haul, shutting the door and locking it behind him. Another crack of a limb outside had them all on edge.

Inside, the small house smelled of sage and vanilla.

"Uncle Patrick!" Winston ran over and wrapped his little arms around Patrick's soaking shirt.

Patrick tickled the boy's sides as if he hadn't just rescued Emily and her friends.

"This is Emily, Blair, and Sienna," he said.

Julia slipped her hands into the back pockets of her denim shorts and smiled curiously at Blair before addressing them. "Hi, y'all." She turned to Winston. "Let's get everybody towels."

"I got 'em!" Winston ran out of the room.

Patrick went into the kitchen.

Emily, Blair, and Sienna tried to move their suitcases out of the way, but they struggled to find a good spot for them in the tight space.

Patrick returned with a handful of dish towels and started wiping down his equipment and checking things over, his hands steady and strong. Then he wiped down their suitcases.

"Holy cow, Patrick," Julia said. "The storm came up on us fast. I was so worried."

"Yeah, it's chaos out there."

Winston came back in, handing each of them a fluffy bath towel.

"Thank you," Emily said.

The boy offered a proud puff of his chest.

"Y'all dry off, and I'll find you a place to put your stuff. I know you wanna get out of those wet clothes," Julia said. "Winston, why don't we let them stay on a couple air mattresses in your room? You can sleep with me, and Uncle Patrick can take the couch."

"Okay," Winston replied. "I'll show 'em."

Patrick pushed the last of his tools against the wall as the storm raged outside. "Where are the air mattresses?"

Julia nodded toward the hall. "In the closet."

"I should probably call the homeowner and let him know what's going on as a courtesy. Even if I just leave a message," Sienna said, digging in her handbag.

While Sienna dialed the owner's number, Winston took Emily's hand and led her and Blair down the short hallway to his room.

"Somebody can sleep here." He motioned under the wood-covered window, where a twin bed with a dinosaur comforter and shams was nestled between two green toy chests.

Patrick walked in, his arms full with two deflated mattresses, pillows, blankets, sheets, and an air pump. "We'd better get these blown up while we still have power. We're bound to lose it if this thing turns into a hurricane." He tossed the sheets over on the bed and dropped the mattresses. Then he picked up Winston's art table, folding the legs in and leaning it against the wall.

Winston stepped aside and stood next to a bookshelf filled with an assortment of Lego sets, puzzles, books, and action figures. He tugged on the heavy, folded air mattresses to help his uncle. Emily leaned in to assist him, grabbed a side of one of the mattresses, and handed the edge to Blair while Patrick plugged the air pump into the outlet.

"I put all our suitcases at the end of the hallway for now," Sienna said when she walked in.

Blair dropped the air mattress into place and put her hands on her hips. "You shouldn't be lifting anything."

Sienna tutted. "I'm fine. I rolled them most of the way."

Patrick inserted the air pump, and with a loud, mechanical whine, one of the mattresses began to fill with air.

Julia called Winston from the other room.

"Yeah?" the little boy called back.

"Breakfast!"

The boy ran down the hallway.

As the women stood idly, Blair tapped Sienna and said over the noise, "We need to call Tyson and Rocko and let them know what's going on, too, so they don't try to make the trip down here tomorrow until we have more information about the roads. We can always delay their coming and stay a few days extra if it works for everyone's schedule."

"Yeah." Sienna leaned over to Emily. "We'll be back." Then she and Blair left for a quieter spot to make their calls.

After Patrick capped the second air mattress, he

unplugged the pump. Emily divided the sheet sets onto each of the beds.

"I'll make sure you have some flashlights tonight. You might need them," he said.

She nodded and then fluffed out one of the fitted sheets. Patrick grabbed the other end and they wrapped it around the corners of the air mattress. Emily shook out the flat sheet and laid it neatly across the makeshift bed before adding a quilt on top and arranging the pillow at one end. They repeated the process with the second mattress, soundlessly moving in unison. Once the air mattresses were done, they changed Winston's dinosaur sheets to a set with satin trim.

Patrick's quiet behavior no longer seemed standoffish now that she knew a little of his story. The distance in his eyes was riddled with loss, and she couldn't unsee it.

She dropped the last pillow onto the bed. They stood together and surveyed her new sleeping quarters. A crack of thunder went off like a cannon, but Patrick didn't flinch this time. Instead, he offered her a half smile.

"The coffee pot's full, and Julia baked a sausage casserole, and cinnamon rolls, if you're hungry."

Only then did she realize that she was. "That sounds delicious."

He nodded toward the door.

In the living room, the weather forecast was chirping on the television. A newscaster stood in the downpour, his raincoat tightly bundled around him, the hood cinched around his wet face as he braced himself against the wind, chattering on about the current conditions. Sienna waved from the sofa, the phone to her ear. Blair was at a foldout desk in the back corner of the room, talking to Rocko.

Patrick led Emily through to the kitchen, with a round

table at one end and an L-shaped row of counter and cabinets at the other. Julia brought the breakfast casserole to the table with a pair of plaid oven mitts and set it on a trivet next to a windup radio. Patrick pulled out a chair for Emily, and she sat down.

"Dig in, y'all. No formalities in my house. Eat when you're hungry." Julia returned with a stack of plates and some cutlery. "Winston, get some sausage and eggs into ya. You need some protein or you're gonna be climbing the walls with all that sugar."

Winston was already chowing down on a cinnamon roll. He took a drink of milk from his glass, leaving a ring of white above his lip as he grabbed the serving spoon and lobbed a lump of casserole onto his plate.

Patrick went to the cabinet and retrieved two mugs. He was barefoot, and that tattoo on his round bicep peeked out from under his sleeve when he closed the cabinet door. His back was to Emily as he filled the mugs with coffee, and she struggled to take her eyes off his broad shoulders and the lean taper down to his waist. He turned around, and she quickly studied the casserole as he set a mug in front of her.

"Thank you."

Julia brought her coffee to the table, along with a serving spoon for the cinnamon rolls. Then, she scooted the casserole Emily's way. Steam rose above it, carrying the scents of cheddar, maple, and black pepper into the air.

Patrick left the room and returned with two more chairs, squeezing them around the table, and Blair and Sienna came in after him. They took a seat while Patrick made more coffee.

"Patrick, grab them a couple of mugs from the cabinet," Julia said as she handed out the plates, her attention lingering on Blair.

"I'll just have water," Sienna said.

Patrick filled a glass and handed it to Sienna. The lights flickered, and the house groaned from the force of the wind.

"If the power goes out, don't worry," he said. "I'm charging the portable power station. I can hook it up to the fridge. It'll run a few appliances."

"Ooh, if the power does go out, can I help you?" Winston asked.

"Of course." Patrick wrinkled his nose good-naturedly at his nephew.

Julia's attention returned to Blair. "I'm sorry," she said, leaning on the table. "Are you Blair Andrews?"

Blair paled. "Yes."

Julia seemed as if she wanted to spout a million questions, but she said, "I thought you looked familiar since the minute you walked in. I follow you on social media."

Sienna sat up protectively, but didn't say anything.

Patrick eyed them over his mug of black coffee.

Blair's smile wobbled awkwardly. "That's great."

Julia glanced at Blair's stomach, but she blinked as if she wanted to cover up her inquisitiveness. She scooted the casserole dish over to her.

Winston wriggled onto his knees, slicing through the moment. "We should play board games. It would be fun with all the people."

"That *would* be fun," Blair agreed.

"What's your favorite board game?" he asked them. "We have lots."

"I like Monopoly," Sienna chimed in.

Winston's head rolled back. "That game is loooong."

Patrick chuckled. "I made him try to play it once on vacation in the mountains. We were stuck inside during a snowstorm. We had nothing but time, and it was the only board game in the whole condo."

"It was too confusing," Winston said.

"How about Candy Land?" Blair offered, seemingly unaffected by Julia's recognition.

Emily was bursting with excitement for her friend. She'd made it through her first hurdle.

Winston brightened. "I love that one! I have it!"

Emily grinned at him, but then sobered when she noticed the indecipherable thoughts on Sienna's face. She caught Sienna's eye, but Sienna shrugged it off, pressed a smile across her face, and took a drink from her glass.

"Maybe we can play it after breakfast, once everyone gets settled," Julia offered.

Winston gave a little fist pump.

After breakfast, they offered to help Julia clean up, but she'd shooed them away. "Y'all should unpack what you need in case the power goes out. With the windows boarded up, it'll get pretty dark."

So they left her, Winston, and Patrick and headed to gather their necessities.

"Are you okay?" Emily asked Sienna, as they unzipped their suitcases in the hallway and carried their things into Winston's room. She'd been quiet since breakfast, which wasn't like her. "Something was bothering you at the table."

Sienna shook her head. "Nothing new."

"What's that supposed to mean?" Blair said, holding an armful of toiletries.

"I'm fine. Really." She bent down and set her pajamas next to the air mattress.

Blair leaned into her view. "You're not denying that Emily saw something, so you'd better just come out with it. We'll eventually pull it out of you anyway. Why wait?"

Sienna shook her head. "I don't know how to relate to kids. So why am I the one having one? I'm going to fail this child."

Blair put her arm around Sienna. "That's not true."

"Yes, it is. I offered a game suggestion to Winston, and he hated it. I haven't even heard of Candy Land."

Emily pulled a face. "What did you *do* during your childhood?" she teased.

Blair giggled.

"But, seriously," Emily continued, "you offered a suggestion that Patrick also tried. Was it perfect for Winston? No. But all anyone does is trial and error."

"That's right," Blair added. "The child's own likes and dislikes will guide you. *Your* job is just to love them and be a moral compass for them."

Sienna sat on the edge of Winston's bed and slumped. "Blair is far better suited to motherhood. How cruel is the irony?"

Emily lowered herself next to her. "Or maybe this is a wake-up call to the person you were meant to be."

For the first time in the entirety of their relationship, fear showed on Sienna's face. Tears glistened in her eyes. She tipped her head back and blinked. "I've been all over the place emotionally. I can't cry. I have to go back out there, and I can't have puffy eyes."

"Maybe we can stay in here and say we're tired," Blair said with a consoling grin as she took a seat on the other side of Emily.

"No." Sienna shook her head. "I won't make you stay shut up for me."

"It's not entirely for you. Julia knows who I am, remember? She didn't say anything more during breakfast, but I'm wondering when she'll ask the big question. I'd kind of like to hide out."

Emily's phone went off, interrupting their talk. She took it out of her pocket and paused before answering. "It's Will."

Sienna made a face.

With a sigh, Emily answered. "Hello?"

"Hey, I ran into Rocko at the gym, and he said there's a bad storm where you are. I was just checking on you."

So he was being chivalrous now? It was a little late for that. Had his conscience caught up with him? And what would his new flame think of him checking in on his ex?

"I'm fine."

A loaded silence filled the line, but she didn't bother asking what he needed. She didn't care what it was. She just wanted off the phone.

"Okay, well, I just wanted to be sure you were all right. I'll go."

"Bye." She hung up.

Blair grimaced. "That was weird."

"I don't think he has a clue what to do now. He's screwed everything up so much," Emily said. "There might be a side of him that still worries about me, but checking in isn't his place anymore." Emily fell over onto them, amusement bubbling up out of nowhere.

"What's wrong with *you*?" Sienna asked.

She waved her hands around. "The Broken Hearts Beach Club—still brokenhearted and now coming to you from Winston's room—in a tropical storm."

The wind howled outside.

"It's so us, isn't it?" Blair asked.

Sienna let out a laugh. "The vacation will go up from here, right?"

Emily put one arm around Sienna and the other around Blair. "I can't imagine it wouldn't."

FOURTEEN

By midafternoon, as the storm raged on, they'd all had enough small talk. They'd played Candy Land, tic-tac-toe, and The Game of Life with Winston; Emily had colored with him in his coloring book; and Blair had tested the obstacle courses he'd built with blocks for his Matchbox cars while Julia finished the laundry, taking advantage of the power still being on.

"I'm bored," Winston said, climbing into Patrick's lap on the sofa.

Patrick had been on the phone for quite a while, checking in with his crew. He'd called the building team to be sure they'd safely dismantled the remaining scaffolding and secured the dumpsters; then he'd jumped right on another call, asking if they'd sandbagged all the low-entry points, telling them he'd gotten all the furniture and equipment to higher ground himself. Once the restaurant was taken care of, he alerted a couple of clients that he'd have to reschedule their events due to the storm. It was clear the locals had all been through this sort of thing before, every move seemingly done like clockwork.

After his calls, Patrick had clicked between baseball games and The Weather Channel all day. He turned away from the third inning of the Phillies and Reds to respond to Winston.

"Sorry, bud. There's not much we can do with all of us stuck in the house. Wanna draw or something?"

"I already did that."

"What about your Legos?" Julia offered, walking through the room with a laundry basket full of folded clothes.

Winston made a face.

They were going to have to get creative. Emily stood up. "I've got an idea. Want to play a game?"

Winston brightened.

"I'll need some supplies from your room. Is that okay?"

He nodded.

"Be right back."

She went into Winston's room and looked through his shelves and toyboxes, collecting small toys. In a few minutes, she'd gathered another Matchbox car, an action figure, a small parachute man, a large marble, a bouncy ball, and a slew of other items. She came back into the living room and dumped them on the table.

"What's all that?" Winston asked, catching the runaway marble.

"It's going to be part of your scavenger hunt."

He gasped. "Scavenger hunt?"

"Yep. All I need to make it is a piece of paper and a pen. Know where I can get those?"

Winston scrambled off Patrick's lap and ran over to the desk at the back of the living room. He retrieved a pad and pen from the middle drawer and ran back over to her, holding them out.

"Now, you can't look at what I'm writing," she said. "It's a surprise."

Winston giggled with anticipation. He went back over to Patrick and sat next to him. "This is gonna be fun!" he told his uncle.

Patrick chuckled.

As Emily wrote, she glanced at Patrick. His attention was on her with an interest she hadn't seen before. She dared not meet his eyes again because when he looked at her like that, it sent her heart pattering.

She created the scavenger hunt, and Patrick made small talk with Winston about the baseball game, explaining the different pitches and why one of the players stole second base. Sienna looked on curiously while Blair's attention moved from Emily to scrolling on her phone.

Emily finished. "Now, Winston, you'll have to leave while I hide these. Want to go into your bedroom?"

"Okay!" Winston ran into his room. The door smacked shut.

"He's excited about this," Julia said, sitting next to Patrick when Emily got up to hide the items.

She wagged the action figure in front of Patrick. "I need to hide this in the sofa. Could I use your pillow?"

He leaned away from it, and Emily reached around him, burying the toy in the pillowcase. She was close enough to catch his woodsy, spicy scent. It was more masculine than Will's, and her breath suddenly became shallow so as not to breathe it in. Too much of that and her heart might beat right out of her chest.

She righted herself. That thoughtfulness flickered on Patrick's face again, but he didn't say anything. His sister seemed to notice, though, her attention moving between him and Emily. Sienna and Blair weren't any better. Emily cleared her throat and went into the kitchen to hide the bouncy ball.

When all the items had been hidden, she called for Winston.

He raced out of his room.

"Ready for the first clue?" she asked.

The boy nodded excitedly.

"I'm quick and small, and I zoom on the floor, but right now, I'm hiding near the door."

He ran over to the front door, lifting Patrick's boots, and running his hand under the mat. He put his little hands on his hips and surveyed the area. "This door, right?"

"Yep," Emily said.

Winston ran his fingers around the flowerpot on the shelf by the door, pulling the ball out from the back. "Found it!"

"Yay! That's awesome. And quick," Emily said. "Ready for the next one?"

Winston jumped around. "Yes!"

"I'm a tiny hero who's taking a nap in a place where soft pillows fill in the gap."

Winston ran down the hall and into Julia's bedroom, making Sienna and Blair laugh.

"His enthusiasm is contagious," Blair said.

"And look at Emily," Sienna added. "Totally in her element and making us look like bumps on a log. The best I had for Winston was hangman."

"She's right," Julia said. "I wouldn't have thought of this."

"I'm used to keeping kiddos busy," Emily replied.

"You're good at it," Patrick said, his deep voice sailing across the room.

Emily swallowed. There went her pulse, racing. "Thanks."

Winston ran back in, holding a bed pillow. He pushed it into Julia's arms. "Nothing's in there. You check."

"Are those the only pillows in the house?" Emily asked.

"No, but I was in my room while you hid it, so it can't be in *there*."

Emily looked around dramatically.

Winston gasped and dove over to Patrick, sinking his hand under the pillow.

"You think it's that easy? You're gonna have to find this one while fighting off the Tickle Monster." And with that, Patrick bombarded him with tickles.

Winston flailed around, giggling and wrestling Patrick while trying to find the action figure. He heaved with laughter, grasping Patrick's wrists with his hands.

The sight of them made Emily's chest bubble with affection. That brooding man she'd first encountered at the mansion was actually a lighthearted, affectionate guy under the right circumstances. She couldn't take her eyes off him.

Then, suddenly, Winston raised his little fist in the air with the action figure.

Patrick let him go. "That's skill," he said playfully.

Winston doubled over, hooting with laughter and out of breath from wrestling.

Patrick glanced over at Emily, and she locked eyes with him. She smiled, and the soft lift of his lips in return gave her a rush she wasn't sure what to do with.

THAT NIGHT, while Patrick cleaned up a crab-leg dinner worthy of a five-star restaurant, and they finished their final round of Candy Land, a call came through on his phone. His tone was serious while he wiped parsley bits off the counter, the phone tucked between his ear and shoulder. "I hear you, but I'm done. After the last thing, I'm *done...* Look, there's a storm raging right now. Let's talk about promotion opportunities once we get through this. I'll call you tomorrow."

"Okay, buddy," Julia said to Winston, standing from the kitchen table. "Time to get into your jammies and hit the sack."

"One more game," Winston whined, clutching his purple Candy Land game piece.

"That was the last game, remember? I think everyone's tired," she said, winking at Emily. "We've been going strong all day."

"Maybe we can play again over breakfast," Blair offered.

Just then, the lights flickered, and they were plunged into darkness. Until that moment, it had been pretty uneventful inside, once Emily got used to the smack of branches hitting the house, the loud shush of the rain against the roof, and the house creaking from the high winds.

There was a faint pop and a fizzle, and then a soft light bathed the immediate space. Julia sunk a match into a jar candle and set it in the center of the table, sending a gold light onto their faces.

They followed the storm on the radio, and while it was still wreaking havoc, it seemed to be turning out to sea again.

"It looks as if we're going to get the back side of it," Sienna said, "and the worst will be out in the Gulf."

Patrick reached over to the counter and clicked on a

flashlight, the white beam cutting through the buttery glow. "It's still too early to know for sure. But for now, I'll go get the power station."

He opened the door between the kitchen and the garage and disappeared. Minutes later, he emerged with a contraption the size of a carry-on suitcase.

Winston clambered down from the chair. "You said I could help."

"All right, bud, but then you need to get some sleep. It's late."

"Okay," he said, already crouched down, pawing at the machine. "What's this?"

"That's the LED display," Patrick said, unbothered, his large biceps flexing in the dim light as he maneuvered the refrigerator away from the wall. He handed Winston the flashlight.

"How about this?" The little boy shone the beam onto what looked like a cigarette lighter.

"DC ports," Patrick said over his shoulder while creating a wedge of space between the back corner of the fridge and the wall. "Hey, can you come over with that light? I need your help."

Winston jumped to his feet and ran to him excitedly.

Blair and Sienna looked on with interest. But a new kind of curiosity had taken hold of Emily. She couldn't shake how safe she felt under Patrick's composed watch. Did he always have all the answers? She'd yet to see him falter. Clearly, he had his issues, but when it came to taking care of people, he'd been incredible. He'd managed to secure his house and his sister's, take care of that massive restaurant, and save three women from a storm, and yet he was completely relaxed. It was as if doing for others fueled him. It was such an interesting juxtaposition to his quiet nature. He seemed almost flustered whenever he had to talk to people, but he was fine caring for them. Emily wanted to peel back his layers like an onion and get to the soft underbelly of who he was. She'd gotten glimpses of it through his interactions with Winston, but she wanted nothing more than to see that same openness directed at her. The thought surprised her.

"Shine that back here so I can see the outlet," he said to Winston, who did as he was told. "Perfect." Patrick unplugged the fridge. "Turn the light around now and let me see the power station."

The two worked in tandem, while Patrick connected the plug to the device. He opened the fridge and the light came on.

"There we go," he said, shutting the door. "That oughta give us about twenty to thirty hours before we need to recharge."

Julia gave him a squeeze. "You saved the day." She grabbed hold of Winston spiritedly, making him giggle. "You too."

The gentleness in Patrick's eyes revealed his affection for his sister.

"Okay." Julia clapped her hands. "Winston. Bedtime."

Sienna yawned. "I should probably turn in too."

"Same," Blair said.

Julia took the flashlight over to a cabinet, pulled out two more jar candles, and lit them. "There's not much else we can do but sleep, is there?" She handed Emily a candle. "Use this to get to your room. Extra towels are under the sink in the bathroom across the hall if you need them. Patrick, I'll set this candle in the living room for you."

Emily, Blair, and Sienna said their good nights and headed to bed.

In Winston's room, Emily put the candle on the dresser. Before she could do anything else, her phone lit up. She had a text from Will.

> Have you signed the quitclaim deed yet, by chance?

Sienna looked over her shoulder and gave an annoyed groan.

Blair leaned in to have a look at the message. "Are you going to sign it?"

Emily's throat closed up with emotion. "I battle myself," she said with a wobbly voice. "Part of me hopes if I stall, that he'll eventually come to his senses. But another part of me isn't sure anymore if I want my old life back."

"Would you even want to take him back?" Sienna asked.

Emily shrugged. "Sometimes I think that I want the him I had before everything happened. I want my old life." Patrick's grin floated into her mind, bringing with it a wave of confusion. "I don't know how to be anyone other than Will's fiancée. Who am I if I'm not Will-and-Emily?"

"Don't sign it yet. Make him sweat." Sienna plucked the phone out of her hand and set it on the dresser. "Em, you take the bathroom first."

Pushing Will out of her mind, Emily picked her phone back up and turned on its light. Then she rummaged around for her pajamas, facial cleanser, and toothbrush. Once she had everything, she made her way to the bathroom. The rain sounded like a band relentlessly playing maracas. Now that it was quiet in the house, the torrent was all she could hear. The amount of rain that could make that much noise might sweep them away at any minute.

She splashed her face with warm water and lathered up a washcloth with facial cleanser. In the dark room, all by herself, exhaustion finally set in. Her eyes stung. She rinsed out the washcloth, folded it, and draped it over the edge of the sink. Then she changed out of her clothes and into her pajamas. Bundling her laundry in her arms, she opened the door to make her way back to the bedroom and slammed into a rock-hard chest.

"Oh!" She dropped her clothes in a heap at her feet.

"Sorry," Patrick said.

They both leaned down to get the clothes and nearly collided once more. He stood up and let her gather her things, stepping out of the way, a blanket under his arm.

The two lingered awkwardly in the dark hallway, illuminated by the tiny light on her phone.

"Got everything you need?" he asked.

"Yeah. Thank you."

"Sure."

He turned, and she caught his arm, stopping him.

"And thank you for letting us stay over tonight. I don't know what we would've done if you hadn't come by."

He seemed startled by her gesture, but it was hard to tell in the low light. "It's no problem."

"Well, good night," she said.

He looked down at her, a tick of silence falling between them. "Good night."

Just then, her phone rang. In case Winston had already fallen asleep, she quickly answered it to avoid the noise.

"Em. Have you signed the form or not?" Will's voice pierced her ear.

"I'm in the middle of a major storm right now," she said, trying to keep her voice down.

"Uncle Patrick?" Winston called from the doorway down the hall.

"Yeah, buddy." Patrick made his way to the boy.

"Who's there?" Will asked.

Emily recoiled. "I'm sorry, *what?*"

"I heard someone. That didn't sound like Sienna or Blair."

"I don't have to answer that." A mixture of indignation and emptiness welled up suddenly as tears, and a lump formed in Emily's throat. "If anyone owes answers, it's you, not me. I'll get to your form when I get to it." She hung up on him.

Patrick strode toward her as Emily wiped at a runaway tear, hoping it was dark enough that he wouldn't see. But by his pause when he reached her, he'd noticed the sudden change in her demeanor.

"Sorry. Julia's in the bathroom getting ready for bed, and Winston wanted to know how long the storm would last."

"Oh." She tried to huff out amusement, but it fizzled between them.

"Everything okay?" he asked.

"Yeah," she said, even though nothing was okay.

He searched her face. "Want to talk about it?" He nodded down the hallway to the living room.

She was dog-tired, she didn't want to talk about Will at all, but her curiosity won out. Why had Patrick invited her into a conversation? Didn't he say that he preferred silence? She poked her head in to let her friends know the bathroom was open.

"I'm gonna hang out a little longer with Patrick," she

said, dumping her clothes in the room and setting her phone on silent mode.

Sienna's brows rose in interest.

"I'll be back in a few, I'm sure," Emily whispered, turning on her phone's light. Then she went down the hallway to find Patrick.

FIFTEEN

The candle Julia had given Patrick flickered in the center of the coffee table. He put the folded blanket he'd been holding at the end of the sofa and sat down next to it.

"The guy who prefers to be left alone asked *me* to talk?" Emily took a seat next to him.

He offered a small smile, but something lurked behind it. "I'm not tired, and you look upset."

"I'm not sure you really want to hear my drama," she said.

The corner of his mouth twitched upward. "I've been in the navy. Throw it at me. I can take it."

She liked him. And there was an electricity between them that she'd never experienced. For a split second, she wondered if telling him everything would turn him off. They hadn't known each other long enough for her to spill her life to him. She'd rather start over. But something in his honest gaze made her want to strip away the pretense and tell him her deepest thoughts. She gave him the rundown on Will and what she'd been dealing with.

"The craziest thing is...I keep beating myself up,

thinking I should've seen it coming. The whole ordeal made me realize that I didn't really know him like I thought I did. I should've spent more time with him, asked him the hard questions, to really understand who I was marrying, but I was so busy trying to make a life for myself that I didn't stop to consider what I wanted in all of it."

"What had you so busy?"

"First, it was finishing college. After that, I had to find a job. My friends were getting married, so I had to cross that off the list. The next step was we needed a house... I got caught up in building a life and didn't stop to pay attention to who I was building that life with. And then it all came tumbling down."

"Maybe it was God's way of putting a stop to it before things got too heavy," he said. "Before you had kids in the mix. You know?"

"I hadn't thought of it like that."

His demeanor was soft tonight, his undivided attention intoxicating.

"What would you do differently next time?" he asked.

His question surprised her. Until this moment, she hadn't considered there would even be a next time. "I'd slow down, I'd ask questions, have more meaningful conversations."

"Like what?"

Emily thought for a minute, considering what she thought meaningful. "Like, where do you see yourself in five years?"

The slight lift in his features dropped.

"What?" Had she said something wrong? Had he thought she meant *him*?

"I don't know the answer to that."

"You don't have to answer it. It was just a hypothetical question for my hypothetical next boyfriend," she said.

"Regardless, I should be able to, but my life has started to move so quickly that I don't know what I want my future to look like. I originally moved here to help Julia and take care of Winston. I had to make money, so I started cooking for people under my company, Main Course. I gained a pretty prominent client out of Nashville through word of mouth and that spread my reputation from Nashville to LA." He stopped as if he couldn't believe it. "People were bombarding me from every direction, wanting to know how to get my cooking. Some suggested catering, but I can't be in two places at once. My schedule was already full with private clients. So it occurred to me that I could build the recipes and hire chefs to cook them. Before I knew it, I was in the planning stages of The Low Tide Supper Club.

"But I'll be the first to tell you that all the great success in the world can fall in an instant. I have no idea what my career will look like in five years. I worry that I'll lose my personal life, miss major events in Winston's childhood... I've been incredibly intentional about including him, but I'm worked to the bone. I've just been trying to survive each day." He frowned.

"I've noticed how you react under pressure, and I have no doubt you'll find a way to fit everything in. You won't miss out on a thing. You'll make sure of it."

He searched her face, so many unsaid thoughts behind those blue eyes. "How about you? Can you answer the question of where you'll be in five years?"

"Definitely not. The future I'd planned is gone, so I haven't quite mapped out the next five years. I guess I'll be in an apartment somewhere around Nashville, teaching, having coffee with Sienna and Blair on the weekends."

"Is that what you want?" he asked.

"Is that not a good enough answer?"

He shot back quickly, "I wasn't criticizing it. I was legitimately curious. Is that the life you want?"

"Regardless, it's what I'll have, given the situation."

His expression crumbled. "Says who?"

"Me?"

"You could've said, 'With everything I've been through, I'm selling it all and moving to Paris, or I'm buying a boat and sailing around the world; I'm living off-grid...' It's your life. You get to choose."

"So, what kept you from doing those things?" she asked.

"Originally, I didn't want to do any of that. I wanted to live in a little house in the woods, visit my sister and her kid, and disappear. But when I was presented with a successful business, I had to regroup, change plans."

His vulnerability gave her courage. "I read the article about you in that magazine. I know what happened to Winston's dad."

He visibly clammed up. His shoulders rose and his jaw clenched. "The allure of a private chef to the rich and famous opening a restaurant was pretty strong, and I had people calling me left and right to do interviews. I wasn't sure how to manage all that, so I hired a PR person one of my clients suggested, Tabitha Reynolds. She's been relentless about 'putting me out there,'" he said with air quotes. "She says that emotion sells, and the more people know about me, the more they'll want to visit the restaurant, so I agreed to the interview, thinking it would be about my cooking. But they didn't put any of that in there. Instead, they made it a sob story about my life—something I never felt comfortable sharing with everyone. It's too painful. I've regretted that interview ever since."

He shook his head. "And she wants to do more promotion. She's got a national morning-news show on standby, but I'm not doing it."

"I wanted to read the article," Emily admitted.

He made eye contact. "In print, it's an inspirational story. But it was real life for me. I heard him scream; I carried his casket..."

"I'm so sorry," was all she could manage. Seeing his anguish, she regretted mentioning the article. What a stupid idea that was. But she was only trying to learn more and be honest with him.

"It's not your fault," he said. "But it's why I do better when I keep to myself."

"Have you talked to anyone about it?"

He scoffed. "Please. None of that 'deep breath, get in touch with your feelings' mumbo jumbo is going to help. My best friend is gone, and it's my fault."

"Your fault? How? You didn't cause the explosion."

"I talked Daniel into joining the navy. He'd waffled, wanting to continue his father's general contracting business. But I wouldn't let up. I kept trying to convince him of how great it would be... Until he finally relented."

She put her hand on his arm, and he flinched. "You couldn't have known what would happen."

"I bugged him and bugged him about it. I was young and stupid. I wanted to have all these great adventures with my best friend. My mind was on port cities overseas and nights in the bar at the officers' club on base. He'd already told his dad he was carrying on the company, and he'd been spending long nights learning the business side of it when I finally convinced him. I wrecked that too. Without Daniel to carry on his legacy, his dad had to sell the business. Now Winston, who has an affinity for building already—if he grows up and wants to do something like that, I'll have taken his birthright from him too."

"Patrick, there was no way to know," she said again. "One changed decision by anyone in your past, and he'd be sitting right here with you."

"Right. And that decision was the one I had in asking him to enlist."

"He could've been assigned to a different ship," she offered.

But he shook his head. "I went up to Navy Personnel Command and had a talk with one of the detailers. He and I'd had a couple of beers a few nights prior. I asked him to put Daniel on the same ship."

"What about the fact that had Daniel wanted to continue in his father's footsteps, he could've told you no? But he didn't."

Patrick's eyes glistened and his jaw clenched. "I'm sorry. I don't want to talk about this anymore." He shut down. "I don't know how to do this." He waggled a finger between them. "I'm no good for anyone."

"If you ever do want to talk more about it, you can talk to me," Emily offered. "I'm not sure I can say the right things, but I can listen."

"Thank you," he said, his voice gentle and his tense muscles visibly softening.

Silence floated between them. He wasn't the only person who'd experienced tragedy, but it was clear his wounds were still fresh. The best thing she could do was to give him space.

She stood up. "I'm getting really tired, so I should head to bed."

He watched her as she took a step toward the hallway.

In a strange way, she hoped he'd ask her to stay. If he did, she'd spend the whole night talking to him.

"Good night," she said.

"Night."

She turned toward the hallway and, using the light on her phone, headed for bed.

PANICKED VOICES ROUSED Emily out of her sleep. She strained to hear, but in the haze of slumber, she couldn't make out what was being said. From the tones, however, something was terribly wrong.

Emily quietly got out of bed and opened the door. She followed the voices and rustling to the living room where she found Patrick—white as a ghost—frantically lacing up his boots, and Julia standing next to him, sobbing into her trembling hands.

He flung the door open, and rain blew in with the force of a bomb, debris littering the hardwood floor.

"I'm going!" Julia cried.

"No! Stay here." His words were like daggers, a fire in them that terrified Emily. He shot out the door and into the storm.

Emily rushed over to Julia. "What's going on? Are you okay?"

Julia looked up, terror in her wet, red eyes. "Winston's out there!"

"What?!" Out of instinct, Emily turned to the window, but every one of them was boarded up. "Why?"

"I don't know!" Julia paced, trembling, crying. She leaned over her knees and hung her head. "I got up to get a glass of water and the floor by the back door was soaking wet. His boots were gone. He'll be swept away!"

"Patrick will find him," Emily said, hoping her words would weave their way into the atmosphere and save Winston. Even Patrick would have a hard time coming back safely, given what she'd seen of the storm just now. The floor by the door was puddled, and there was so much debris, she could hardly see the floorboards.

"I'm so scared," Julia said, before wailing into her hands once more.

Sienna and Blair came out of Winston's room.

Emily could hardly get the words out through her fright. "Winston's outside, and Patrick just went after him."

Blair turned sharply to Sienna in alarm.

"Why is he outside?" Sienna asked.

"We don't know," Emily said.

Emily wasn't sure what to do, so she put her arms around Julia and held her tight. Julia's whole body shuddered.

"I can't lose him. He's my entire world," she croaked. She grabbed Emily's nightshirt in her fists. "I don't know how long he's been gone."

"If anyone can find him, it's Patrick," Emily said, trying again to ease her mind.

The door flew open, and they jumped. But it was only the wind, sending more rain into the house. Julia rushed over to it and could hardly get it shut on her own, so Emily, Sienna, and Blair assisted her, the four of them shutting the door and pushing against it until it latched.

Emily didn't want to allow the fear to overtake her, and she didn't want to think about how utterly devastating it would be if anything happened to Winston.

They huddled together in the living room, all eyes on

the front door. The storm thundered behind it, every snap and crack putting them on edge. Minutes went by. The door did not move, the knob remained still. With every tick of the clock, Emily's heart pounded, her fears overtaking her. If Patrick got hurt, no one in that house was strong enough to help get him and Winston inside, nor would they be able to find them. This wasn't like him running out to find Sienna. This was the middle of a tropical storm, with wind speeds that could knock down trees.

Emily closed her eyes and prayed over and over, begging God to save Patrick and Winston.

Eight minutes passed. Then ten. Then thirteen.

Suddenly, Patrick burst through the door, soaking wet, looking utterly exhausted, and holding Winston and an animal. The wind nearly knocked him off his feet, but he regained control, wobbling the precious cargo in his arms.

Julia screamed and ran over to them, throwing herself around them, sobs filling the room.

Emily pushed against the door to shut it and then locked it to keep it from blowing open again. Relief filled her and tears spilled down her cheeks.

"Why did you go outside?!" Julia shrieked, grabbing a soaking Winston and kissing his face.

"I heard a dog barking," he said, crying.

Patrick set a black lab puppy on the floor. The dog shook the water from its fur and then cowered next to Patrick's leg. The poor thing seemed utterly traumatized.

Julia visibly tried to pull herself together. She picked up Winston with trembling hands and squeezed him tightly. "You could've been swept away!"

"I didn't know," he cried. "I thought I could run out and back in again."

She wiped his wet hair off his forehead. "God had you."

She closed her eyes and her chest filled with a long, slow breath. "Are you okay? Does anything hurt?"

"No," he whimpered. "It was scary, Mama."

"I'll bet."

"We should get dried off," Patrick said, his face expressionless. He scooped up the distressed little puppy and left the room.

Julia kept him in her line of vision as she cradled Winston, worry still etched on her face.

Patrick returned with the puppy swaddled in a towel. He handed another to Julia. She took it and rubbed Winston's hair before wrapping him in it.

"Let's go change you out of these wet clothes," she said, still gripping the boy, carrying him down the hallway.

"We can wipe up the floor," Emily offered.

Julia waved her off, her voice trailing back to them. "It's okay. I don't care about the floor."

"I'll take care of it," Patrick said. From his jagged breaths, he was still getting himself together. He ran his hand through his soaking-wet hair. From the look on his face, he didn't seem as if he was in any mood to talk to anyone.

"Well, you'll probably want to get into dry clothes," Sienna said. "We'll leave you to it." She patted Blair and Emily on the shoulders. "Let us know if you need anything."

Emily nodded.

The three of them went back into the room and got in their respective beds. No one spoke. Emily was still in shock from what she'd just witnessed. Her eyes stung and her heart pounded. Things could've gone so terribly wrong tonight, but they hadn't, thank God. She sent up a little thank-you prayer and then tried to get back to sleep.

SIXTEEN

Emily awakened to complete silence. Sometime during the night, the storm had ended. She'd lain in bed as it raged, thinking about everything. Who was this new version of herself and what did she want in life? What would her future look like? She'd shed her old life like a worn blanket, but now she wasn't so sure what she needed to stay warm. Her wide-open future sent a chill down her spine.

She kicked off the covers; her bare legs holding a thin film of perspiration. The room was muggy and hot. With no electricity, any cold air had dissipated overnight. She turned quietly on the twin-sized mattress. Blair was already awake, staring at the ceiling, and Sienna stirred.

"Morning," Emily whispered.

"Morning." Blair ran her fingers through her long hair and piled it on top of her head, twisting it into a knot. "Can you believe what went down last night?" She rolled onto her belly and faced Emily. "It feels like some sort of nightmare." She put a hand over her mouth and shook her head.

"I know," Sienna agreed. "It took me ages to relax

enough to fall back to sleep. Between that and the heat, I'm exhausted."

Emily rubbed her aching shoulder. "I finally did fall asleep, but I slept on edge. And I woke up again in the middle of the night. I think Patrick might have actually had a nightmare. Did you hear him?"

They shook their heads, frowning.

"I heard him call out and say something indecipherable," Emily said. "His voice was so loud I almost shot out of bed."

"I slept through it. Did you go out there?" Blair asked.

Emily shook her head. "I listened for a while, but there was no other noise after that. In my groggy, sleep-deprived mind, I guessed he was talking in his sleep. He looked really unnerved last night when he came in, though."

"I noticed too," Sienna said, rolling over.

Emily chewed on her lip, thinking. Breakfast might be interesting. Did they need time as a family? "Should I check to see if the coast is clear before we all descend upon them? They might want a quiet morning."

Sienna repositioned her pillow. "We could hang out in here and talk for a while. Then we could all go out together."

"Maybe we should," Emily agreed.

"I'm afraid to go out, honestly," Sienna said. "Patrick looked pretty rattled. And he seemed contemplative even before that."

Blair propped her chin on her hands, leaning on her elbows. "What did he say when you went out to talk to him earlier last night?"

"Yeah, I'd like to know too. I went to the bathroom to brush my teeth, and you two were so deep in conversation you didn't even notice. You sure are chummy." Sienna's last few words came out slowly, suggesting more than just "chummy."

"I assure you, it was nothing," Emily said.

Sienna wadded her sheets and balled them under her, propping herself up farther. "That's not what it looked like. The two of you were lost in each other's eyes by candlelight." She threw a dreamy look at Blair, making her laugh.

"During a tropical storm." Emily laughed, too, but then sobered. "It wasn't at all like that. He actually told me something pretty heavy." She filled them in on the highlights regarding Daniel's accident, figuring it was safe to tell them anything that had already been published.

"Oh wow," Blair said, her features dropping in alarm. "That's so sad."

Emily stood and pulled the blankets up on her bed. "Yeah. He's still struggling with it."

Sienna pushed herself into a sitting position. "Can you imagine if something happened to one of us?"

Emily bit her lip. "No, I can't." Her friends were her support system. She couldn't fathom going through what she was going through without Blair and Sienna.

The loud whine of a drill silenced them, and then the wood covering fell off their window. Sunlight poured into the room.

Emily squinted, trying to acclimate to the brightness. Patrick caught her gaze through the glass. He paused for a second, but his expression didn't offer any insight into whether his state of mind had improved. He just disappeared, and the drill started back up again.

She barely knew him, but she worried about him.

"Well, we made it through the storm," Sienna said.

But by the look in Patrick's eyes just now, Emily thought, he hadn't yet made it through.

JULIA WAS HUNCHED over the kitchen sink, yawning, when Emily finally entered with Blair and Sienna. Sunlight streamed into the room, and Emily could finally see the wooded view out the back window. Trees were down, branches everywhere. The yard had so many leaves in it that it looked more like fall than summer.

"Good morning," Julia said in a bleary voice, contorting her face to a less-exhausted expression for their benefit. "Careful on your way to the table." She pointed to the floor where an extension cord stretched from the counter to the portable power station. "Coffee's going, although I know the heat isn't conducive for it. But I needed the caffeine." She handed each of them a mug. "Help yourselves."

Emily joined her at the counter. "Thank you."

Sienna filled hers with water and took it to the table.

"Of course. Patrick brought in the small stove. I thought I'd make some eggs for everyone."

"Where's the puppy?" Sienna asked.

Julia yawned again, covering her mouth with her forearm. "Asleep in the bed with Winston. I doubt it's house trained, so I'll have to check on him soon. Both of them were out for the count all night—not a peep." She grabbed her coffee from the counter and took a long drink.

"Did Winston say anything more about what led him outside during the storm?" Emily asked, twisting her hair into a knot to keep cool.

Julia set her mug on the counter, steam rising into the air, sending a nutty aroma Emily's way. Then she took a stack of plates from the cabinet and put them on the table, along with a wad of forks from the silverware drawer. "He and Patrick look for strays whenever they do their little hikes together. Winston knew if he could get the dog, he could keep it."

"How did he hear it in the storm?"

"It was crying pretty loudly, according to Winston. It had its foot stuck in the fence, and the wind was whipping the poor thing everywhere. I checked his legs and they feel okay—no crying or whimpering when I touch them. But I'm going to take him to the vet to get him checked over—*if* it's open."

"It was just the one puppy?" Sienna asked. "No owner or mother to be found?"

Julia shook her head. "He didn't see anything else. Although, it's kind of difficult in a tropical storm. Patrick went outside and looked this morning, but there was no trace of any other animal out there. It might have wandered away from the litter. I'm planning to put some photos online in case he belongs to anyone."

The garage door opened, and Patrick walked in. His temples glistened with perspiration, and his shirt had a V of sweat on the front and back. After setting the drill and a small radio on the table, he nodded hello.

"Everything good out there?" Julia asked him.

He wiped his brow with his dirt-speckled forearm. "The storm ended up turning out to sea like they thought, and we got the tail end—we were lucky. We've got a couple big trees down. We're fortunate they didn't hit the house."

Julia's chest filled with a deep breath. "Wow."

"I'll get them chopped up tomorrow. You'll have no shortage of firewood this winter."

"Want some eggs?" Julia asked him.

"I'm good, thanks," he said. "It's too hot. I'm gonna try to survive a cold shower." He clicked on the radio to a staticky station. "Listen to this and see if they say how the roads into town are. I need to get to the restaurant to assess any damage."

"The storm came up so quickly," Sienna said after he'd left the room. "I hope everyone got to where they were going before the worst of it."

"Yeah, me too." Blair, who'd been pouring coffee, came to the table with her mug.

Julia took a carton of eggs out of the fridge. "Who wants breakfast?"

When they all nodded she unhooked the coffee maker from the extension cord and then plugged in the electric stove. After cracking eggs into a bowl, she warmed a pan on the burner.

Without turning from the pan, she called over, "Blair, may I ask you something?"

Blair visibly stiffened. She wrapped her thin fingers around her mug. "Of course."

"What happened with your social media accounts?" She whisked the eggs in the bowl.

Blair's face lost its color.

There it was: the moment when Blair had to face the one thing she'd been avoiding since she'd lost the baby. How would she handle it? What would she say? They'd had conversations, but as far as Emily knew, Blair had never come up with an answer for her fans.

"I...uh. There was a family emergency that pulled me away, and I haven't quite figured out how to get back into the swing of things without being forced to explain it."

Julia left the eggs. "You could always just say *that*."

"She worries everyone will want a reason," Sienna said.

Julia poured the eggs into the pan, a loud sizzle filling the silence. Then she turned around. "Mother to mother, I can guess by your body language, and what I've seen since you got here, what that reason might be. And I understand."

Blair's eyes filled with tears. "How did you know?"

"Since you've been here, you haven't called anyone about your baby. Anyone with an infant would have. You haven't doted over a little one, showing photos and telling stories, which I'm sure you would. You weren't outwardly worried about your own fate in the storm last night. A mother with a small child to raise would be a basket case if she had to endure that without her baby."

A tear slipped down Blair's cheek, and her bottom lip wobbled. "If I put it online, I'll have to relive it. It'll be there forever," she explained.

Julia slid the eggs onto a platter and brought them to the table. She put her arms around Blair. "It'll be there forever regardless. That loss will remain with you. I get it. I lost a baby a couple years before I had Winston."

Wetness gathered along Blair's lower lashes. "You did?"

"Yeah. It was awful. Daniel and I had tried for months, and the test was finally positive. We were so excited. We did one of those cake reveals and everything. It was pink." Julia swallowed, compassion in her eyes. "I named her Abbey Michelle."

A sob escaped Blair's lips, and she quickly covered her mouth with her hand, but she couldn't hold in the emotion.

"What was your baby's name?" Julia asked.

"We didn't know what we were having. We wanted to see the baby first and then decide, but we'd chosen Chase, Joseph, Callie, or Willa." Her voice broke on the words. "We named her Willa. I've never told anyone her name or gender till now." Tears streamed down Blair's face.

She was being truthful. This was the first time she'd shared that—even her closest friends didn't know. It was also the first time Emily had seen her really cry without hiding it. It was as if she could be vulnerable with Julia because of their shared experience.

"How did you ever try again?" Blair said. "Weren't you afraid?"

"Terrified." Julia put her hand on her heart. "But I'm so glad we did because I have Winston. And losing Daniel, he's all I have of the man I love."

Understanding visibly dawned on Blair. "Oh my goodness. You're so right."

"Am I?"

"Yes. I'm wasting all these perfect days being scared—days I could be moving forward, but I'm stuck in limbo because of a past I can't change."

"You *are* allowed to grieve. It hasn't been that long," Julia said.

Blair nodded. "I know, but I haven't allowed myself to *live* since I lost the baby. It's hard to do."

A creak in the doorframe drew their attention. Patrick had been listening. He lingered in the doorway, clean-shaven with wet hair, and then stepped into the kitchen. He glanced at Emily. Then he reached around the corner, brought in a large box fan, and plugged it into the power station. With a twist of the knob, it whirred to life.

Air gusted Emily's way, immediately cooling her skin. Strands of hair that had escaped her makeshift bun blew into her face as Julia offered her a plate of eggs. Emily salted the dish, her tummy rumbling.

The radio squawked between Emily and the others, making them jump. Patrick crossed the kitchen and reached past them, grabbing the radio. He turned it up and went out of the room.

Julia ate quietly, their original chat dwindling.

"Is he okay?" Sienna asked, nodding toward Patrick's exit.

"Winston scared him last night," she said. "He scared me too, but Patrick has a harder time getting over things that make him anxious."

Sienna nodded.

"He puts a lot of pressure on himself," Julia said.

Just then, Patrick came back in, and the conversation hushed.

"The roads are blocked, but I think I can get you all home the way we came if you want to pack up after breakfast." He clicked off the radio. "I can take you on my way into town."

"I'm sure you'll want to get back to your luxurious accommodations, instead of hanging out here," Julia added.

"I should probably return to see if there's any damage to report to the homeowner anyway," Sienna said.

While Emily understood what they were all saying, she couldn't help but feel that Patrick had an ulterior motive. By his inability to look directly at her, her gut told her he wanted them to go, but she wasn't sure why. He was more distant than he had been before the storm, keeping himself busy—not sitting or having breakfast. It was as if he was avoiding them. Perhaps it was best they leave.

SEVENTEEN

The ride into town was both surreal and sobering. The woods were eerily quiet as they drove through them—a stark contrast to the day before's journey. The only sounds were the engine and the crackle of the tires through the terrain. The air was saturated with a heavy dampness that carried a thick scent of mud and seaweed. When they finally got onto the roads, they were layered with sand and debris. Patrick didn't flinch as his truck bumped over splintered boards, shingles, and palm fronds scattered in haphazard piles.

On the main route, heading toward the beach house, Emily gasped. Storefronts and cottages were visibly battered, some with broken windows, shutters hanging loose, and siding peeled back by the storm's force. They were all dark, clearly without electricity. Patrick maneuvered slowly around the power lines that drooped low, some tangled in their leaning poles.

In his truck, they were as quiet as the calm after the storm. Both Blair and Sienna pulled out their phones to text their significant others an update, but once they'd finished, their phones sat silent in their laps.

Patrick drove past his restaurant, craning his neck to view the property. The glass was boarded up, the coming-soon signs all removed, and the scaffolding hauled away. "Looks okay from the outside," he said, rolling slowly past. "No flooding or anything that I can see—that's encouraging." He pulled up to the stoplight.

"Hopefully, it will all be okay," Emily said.

"Our grand opening is in a little less than a year. This storm wasn't on the schedule. I'm going right over to check as soon as I drop you off."

"Let me know if you get in there and need any help. If there's anything I can take off your plate, it would be the least I could do after all you've done for us."

They turned onto the road with the beach house. Piles of ruined furniture, mattresses, and soggy belongings were already pushed to the curbs, waiting for cleanup crews; other items—clearly not there on purpose—had been shoved sideways and deposited in unusual places by the storm surge, such as a boat resting clumsily in the middle of a side street.

Emily turned away, the reality of what they'd made it through hitting her. They'd been tucked away, sheltered from this. She looked over at Patrick with a newfound respect and adoration for saving them.

The whole town was caught between ruin and resilience; when only a day or two ago it had been buzzing with life, it had now been muted with destruction. But within that, it was alive with the first signs of recovery, as people dotted the streets, talking with one another, pointing, lifting debris. It was as if the whole community were holding its breath, waiting for regular life to return.

When they arrived at the mansion, the gates were still standing strong, although palm branches were wedged between their iron rods. Patrick entered the code and, miraculously, the gates opened.

"Does that mean the house has power?" Emily asked.

"The owner told me last night it has a pretty substantial generator," Sienna replied, "so we should have power no matter what. And the grounds crew were able to secure everything pretty well."

Patrick pulled to a stop in front of the house, and they all climbed out. The beach itself was scarred from the storm, the dunes moved around, a boardwalk down the coast snapped in two as if it were a twig. Seagulls circled low, picking through the wreckage. But the palms on the property were all standing, surprisingly, and the house looked unscathed.

Patrick pulled their suitcases from the back of the truck and began taking them up the stairs to the front door.

Sienna let them in.

The hallways were dark from the electric shutters that had protected the glass from the storm. A small line of emergency lights running along the edges of the entryway illuminated the floors. Sienna clicked on the wall switch, the chandelier above them sending beams shimmering across the marble floor.

Patrick set their suitcases inside the door, then walked past them and into the other room. In a few minutes, there was a snap and then a hum as the metal shutters retreated to their cases above each window. Sunlight poured through the house, the bright-blue skies a stark contrast to the wreckage in town.

"Everything looks fine here," Blair said, dragging her suitcase to the elevator. "How lucky, compared to the rest of the area."

Sienna walked over to the French doors leading to the

pool. "The outdoor patio needs a good sweep, but the pool's still covered," she said, pulling out her phone. "I'll do a final check of the property and call the owner." She opened the door and stepped outside.

"It must take forever to clean everything up," Blair said.

"Yeah. It's always a tough climb back to normal, but we've experienced worse." Patrick strode in. "The owner usually has things put back together pretty quickly, and if it's just clearing the patio, consider yourselves fortunate. The storm turning saved us. One move in the other direction and you'd be digging the swimming pool out from under a few tons of sand."

A lull fell between them.

"Will we be okay here on our own with everything around us in shambles?" Having never been through a storm of that magnitude, Emily wasn't sure what to do next.

Patrick pulled out his cell phone. "Emily, what's your number?"

She rattled it off, and he typed it in. Her phone pinged in her pocket.

"Text me if you need anything." He fell silent for a moment with thoughts he didn't divulge. "If I don't hear from you, I'll be back later with lunch and groceries."

Though he said the words, it didn't look as if he wanted to say them. He was wrestling with something.

Emily fluttered her hands in the air. "Oh, you don't have to."

"What will you eat if I don't?" he asked.

"We can figure it out. There are leftovers, right?"

"Probably not enough for as long as you need. Nothing will be open for a while," he countered.

"Then how will you get us food?" she asked.

"This isn't my first rodeo. I'm prepared. *And* I'm a chef,

remember? I've got an entire freezer full of food in my garage."

"I'm sure you've got a lot of things to do. You should really help your family." The last thing she wanted to be was a burden.

"I can make something quick," he said. "I'll be cooking for Julia and Winston anyway. And I have tons of supplies at home. I can bring you basic necessities."

"Okay," she relented. "Thank you."

"I'll be back around noon." He slipped his phone into his back pocket. "I'll let myself out."

After he left, Blair returned to her suitcase by the elevator. "I'm going up to unpack. Again." She flashed a small smile at Emily.

"Sounds good."

Emily flopped onto the sofa and exhaled, the last twenty-four hours a blur. She rubbed her aching temples and leaned back against the cushion. Just then, her phone pinged. She fished it out of her pocket and opened the screen. Her stomach dropped.

Another text from Will to call him.

He had no empathy whatsoever. Everything was about him. How had she not seen this before? She clicked off her phone and closed her eyes.

"Since it was bolted down, the main furniture managed to make it through the storm," Sienna said as she came inside. She plopped down on the sofa next to Emily. "The grounds crew has extra cushions in storage. They also have dry tables and loungers. They'll be out in the next day or so. And the cleaning crew was scheduled to come at the end of the week, but with the storm, they didn't, so I told the owner to maybe just wait until we leave."

"Must be nice to have so much money you can stockpile deck furniture," Emily said.

"I know, right?"

"I'm not sure what furniture *I'll* come home to in Nashville, but that's due to a different storm." Emily blew a loud breath through her lips. "Will texted again."

Sienna offered a soft laugh with no warmth at all. "Do *not* text him back."

"Part of me wants to just get it over with, but the other part of me wants to make him wait because that's all I have to hold over him for what he's done."

"I say that you're in the right to do whatever you feel like doing, and he has to deal with it." She stood up and reached for Emily's hands. "Let's get our stuff back to our rooms and resume our vacation as best we can."

"That sounds like the perfect plan."

LATER THAT AFTERNOON, while the grounds crew hauled debris off the beach, the three women huddled together on the sofa, watching the aftermath of the storm on TV.

"Luckily people can still get in and out of town for the most part," Sienna said. "But I'm not sure Tyson and Rocko will want to come now."

"Maybe the storm is a message that we should call it a week and head home," Blair suggested.

Emily understood the sentiment, but she wasn't ready to get back to regular life yet. She clicked off the TV. "We have to stay. I haven't planned my day for the three of us yet."

Sienna and Blair gawked at her.

"I think we can give you a pass, given the circumstances," Sienna said.

"I'm creative; I can manage. We should do something here in the house together. And I'm going to plan it."

"You do know we just endured a major storm," Blair said. "Like Sienna said, I think you're off the hook for that."

"I know," Emily said, standing up. "But I'd hate for us to leave on this note. It's too late to drive home today, and we probably couldn't get down our road yet anyway in Sienna's car. You saw how Patrick's truck had to drive over debris."

"What do you have in mind?" Blair asked.

Emily tapped her chin. "Hm. Well, the tub in my bathroom is the size of a hot tub. We could get our swimsuits on and take a bubble bath. Light some candles... Have our own little spa day?"

Blair scooted to the edge of the sofa. "That's a great idea. I brought my cucumber-green-tea-face-mask cream. We could hydrate while we soak."

"I'll make drinks," Sienna added. "We had some club soda and a lime in the fridge after our last dinner. Do we have pineapple juice?"

"I think I saw some. Didn't Patrick use it to make the salad dressing the other night?"

Sienna stood up. "If not, I'll find something. Go draw the water."

The next thing Emily knew, she'd texted Patrick to hold off until dinner, and was in her bikini, with a green face mask tightening on her skin as it dried, soaking in a bubble bath with Sienna and Blair.

"Now, this is the life," Sienna said, taking two sliced cucumbers from the silver tray next to them and placing them on her eyes. "Great idea, Em."

A pair of lavender candles flickered on either side of the

tub, and the crisp white tile shimmered under the glow of the chandelier.

"Sitting in this beautiful place, it's hard to believe there's such a mess outside," Emily said, running her hands in and out of the bubbles.

"I got some cool photos of it before we came in," Blair said. "I've been thinking I might post something, but I'd need your okay."

"What are you going to post?" Emily asked.

"I've been thinking about how our lives are like that storm, and how at some point it all ended and the sun came out."

"That's a great point," Emily said. "I hope we see the sun in our lives soon."

Blair twisted her hair into a clip. "Well, after talking with Julia, I decided that I should push myself to see it. I'll never find the sun if I stay in the storm."

Those words hit Emily right in the heart, giving her hope.

"I thought I might make a slideshow of some of our photos and use Sienna's idea of The Broken Hearts Beach Club. I'd tell my story and how great my friends have been in getting me through it."

Sienna took the cucumber slices from her eyes. "I love that idea."

Emily agreed.

"Maybe you all can help me with it tonight," Blair said.

Emily glanced at Sienna, smiling. "We'd be happy to."

Maybe, Emily thought, she could take a page out of Blair's book. Could she somehow find sunshine in her storm too?

EIGHTEEN

That evening, while they were scrolling through Blair's photos, there was movement out the back window. *Must be the grounds crew finishing up.* Emily leaned in to see what they were doing. But it wasn't the grounds crew. Patrick was clomping down to the beach, his muscles bulging as he carried a metal container to the sand. With a thud, he dropped it at his feet. When he turned toward the house, Emily took a step back to stay out of his view.

A few minutes later, he reappeared with his arms full of logs and dumped them into the metal container. Blair and Sienna joined her at the window.

"What's he doing?" Sienna asked over Emily's shoulder.

Blair squinted. "I have no idea."

Emily stepped away. "I'll go see."

She slipped on her flip-flops and padded onto the deck just as he came around the side of the house with an armful of folding chairs.

"Hey," she called, stepping into the warm sand. "What's going on?"

"With everything closed, I thought you all might be

bored, so I planned dinner out here for a change of scenery."

"You shouldn't worry about us. You have other things you could be doing."

"The restaurant only had minor cosmetic damage—absolutely incredible."

"Oh, that's wonderful," she said, relieved more than she should be. It wasn't even her problem, but she felt as if she'd been holding her breath over it.

"Indeed," he said. "And it gave me time to take care of all Julia's trees. We were able to keep most of the wood, but she already had this stacked in the garage." He waved a hand at the pile of wood and then opened the chairs and set them around what she now realized was a fire pit. He clapped the dirt off his hands and reached into his pocket, retrieving a lighter.

"What are you cooking?" she asked, contemplating what he could manage to prepare over an open fire.

"I brought seafood skewers and a simple dough with herbs and cheese." He lit the logs, a golden flame rising and licking the air.

Emily's stomach rumbled. "That sounds delicious. Do you need any help bringing the supplies down?"

"I'll be fine. Why don't you ask your friends if they want to settle in by the fire?"

"Okay. Be right back." Emily jogged up to the house, an odd sort of happiness tingling in her chest.

"I went upstairs to comb my hair and heard your phone chirping, so I brought it down," Blair said when Emily walked in, handing it across.

A missed text from Will.

"He's being weird." Emily glared at the screen. "He asked what I was up to. As if we're chummy."

"He's relentless," Sienna said. "Isn't your silence enough? You're on a girls' trip."

Every time she started to move on mentally, Will sucked her back into their drama. And she didn't want to deal with it anymore. She'd tell him soon enough, but tonight she wanted to enjoy her friends. She clicked off the phone screen and put it into her pocket. Then she filled in Sienna and Blair on the plans, and they went out to meet Patrick.

Emily kicked off her flip-flops and sat in the chair nearest the water. The sand had started to cool beneath her feet, and it was damp from the old tide line. Her hair tickled her face, the coastal wind light. She pushed the strands out of her eyes to view the fiery oranges, pinks, and purples that had begun to overtake the daytime blue in the sky. The wind carried a mist of sea spray that settled on her skin.

With a deep breath, she pushed Will right out of her mind.

"It's almost room temperature with that breeze," Sienna said, wriggling into her chair.

Blair and Emily agreed.

Patrick returned with a soft cooler slung over his shoulder, a radio in his hand, and a long grate under his arm. He dropped the bag next to Emily, sending sand onto her feet. She wiggled them clean. He noticed and a lightness filled his eyes as he looked at her. He clicked on the radio to beach music, and set it in the sand. Then he unzipped the cooler and pulled out a bowl with a towel over it.

Emily peeked under to find a lump of dough, the scent of butter and rosemary tickling her nose.

"No peeking," he teased. His voice was gentle tonight, as if he'd come down from the stress of the storm.

While the dough rested, he put the grate on the campfire that had already burned down to glowing embers due to the small logs he'd used.

"How's the puppy?" Emily asked.

"Busy," he said with a grin. "So far, no one's claimed him, but I know a lot of people are without power. I hope Winston doesn't get too attached."

"And you never found the mother or any other puppies?"

He shook his head. "I spent a good few hours today searching the property to be sure, but there was no trace. I wonder if he got scared by the storm and ran off."

"No collar?" Sienna chimed in.

"Nope. I checked for that too. There was nothing by the fence or anywhere in the yard." He adjusted the large grate on top of the fire pit. "We're gonna bake the bread on this while the fire's low. The embers will provide steady, even heat so we don't burn it."

He set a cast-iron skillet on the surface of the grate. Then he reached into his bag and took out a bottle of olive oil, pouring in a thin layer on the cooking surface. With the beach behind him and his T-shirt rippling in the wind, Patrick looked completely different from the man she'd first met. He took the bowl from beside Emily, his spicy scent mixing with the briny air, and added the dough to the makeshift grill. Emily, Sienna, and Blair looked on, silently enthralled.

"I've never seen anyone cook an actual meal on an open fire before," Sienna said. "It's like you're some sort of culinary caveman. Very rugged."

The corner of Patrick's mouth turned upward, but he didn't reply.

The dough sizzled. Patrick opened a container of seafood skewers, loaded with a mix of shrimp, scallops, chunks of salmon, bell peppers, red onion, pineapple, and cherry tomatoes, then set them on the side of the grate. Before grilling them, he brushed the metal with more oil and then positioned each one in a neat line above the heat.

Emily peered into the cooler. "What are those?" she asked, pointing to two juice containers of white, icy liquid.

He finally allowed a wise smile and her stomach squeezed.

"The appetizers." He dug around in the bag and pulled out four cups, filling them with ice, handing one to each of them, and setting his on the sand near where he was working. He flipped the skewers and then took the bottles from the cooler. "Piña coladas," he said, shaking the bottles. "I've got alcoholic and non-alcoholic—pick your preference." He popped the lid off the first bottle. "Who's up for rum?"

Emily raised her cup. He poured the icy-cold concoction into it. Then he topped it with a pineapple wedge and a curly straw.

As he fixed the other drinks, Emily took a swig of the sweet cocktail. When the drink touched her lips, the rich sweetness of coconut cream glided across her tongue, followed by the bright, tangy sharpness of pineapple juice and a soft, warming finish of rum. It was cold enough to send a pleasant chill through her body, yet the alcohol and the summer heat brought a gentle warmth that balanced the temperature.

With each sip, Emily's shoulders relaxed, her thoughts slowed, and a sense of ease began to settle in. The savory aroma of seafood and coastal salt, the combination warm and smoky, was a smell she'd relate to summer by the Gulf from this point on. It was irresistible and unmistakable, and it gave her a dreamy sense of calm. Under the tinkling sounds of steel drums coming from the radio and the shush of the water, the world felt far away.

The only thing that brought her halfway into reality was Blair, who'd begun taking photos of the food, the waves, and her drink in the sand. They hadn't actually posted anything yet, but it was clear she was planning to, and the color that had filled her cheeks because of it was more than just the glow of the sun.

"This is delicious," Sienna said after taking a drink from her cup.

Patrick acknowledged her comment with a nod, then flipped the flatbread and continued working in his usual silence.

While Blair got up and moseyed down the beach to get a few more shots, Sienna sunned her face, wriggling her toes in the sand. Emily turned toward the turquoise Gulf, its waves still struggling for tranquility after the storm. The tide bubbled rhythmically at the shore. The rum and the sound made her eyelids heavy. She dragged her bare feet through the cool sand. In the quiet, her thoughts drifted, unwelcome and persistent, to Will—his sudden change in personality, the hollow explanations, the glint of guilt that hadn't quite matched the ease with which he'd left. For Lanie.

Wait. She thought she remembered her. An electric shock pinged through her limbs. She'd gone to the gym with him once for a trial membership, and the woman who'd helped her was named Lanie. Had that been her? The woman at the gym with the sculpted arms and manufactured laughter?

Emily clenched her drink tightly as the wind picked up, blowing sand onto her skin. She tried to sweep it off but was unsuccessful, just like a memory she couldn't erase.

She hated that buried part of her that still missed him, but hated more the small voice that asked if he came back, if he said it was a mistake, could she forgive him? She took another icy drink, fixated on the surf. The sea gave no answers, only the pull of the tide, coming and going like her resolve.

Patrick called Blair over, breaking Emily from her thoughts. He got out a bowl of crisp salad, plated their dinner, and handed each of them a serving.

"I got some good shots," Blair said, picking up the skewer with her dainty fingers.

Emily grinned at Blair.

"That's great," Sienna said.

Patrick quietly nibbled his skewer across from them.

"What are Julia and Winston doing tonight?" Emily asked.

"Taking care of the puppy," he said. "They've named him Stormy, even though I warned them not to. He might have a different name."

A warmth for Winston bubbled up inside Emily. He'd only been trying to save the little pup. She recalled the fear in his tear-filled eyes when Patrick had burst through the door with him. She thought again what a blessing it was that they were all okay.

"You should've asked them to come," Emily said, tearing off a piece of flatbread.

"The skewers would've been in real jeopardy," he said with a chuckle. "Stormy's definitely not trained."

"I don't know if I could ever get a dog," Sienna said. "They're a lot of work."

Blair snorted.

"What?" Sienna's brows pulled together. "Oh. Yeah."

She looked down at her belly. "I'll probably be the most ill-equipped mother on the planet."

"No one really knows how to parent, do they?" Patrick asked. "I mean, Julia surely didn't. She kept calling me with questions like I knew something. But then we just settled in, and it's not too hard, apart from running out in storms."

They all laughed, and Patrick's eyes met Emily's with an interest she couldn't define. He smiled and then looked down at his plate, fiddling with his bread. She couldn't help but think she'd finally gotten through to him.

NINETEEN

The fire crackled as the last embers glowed, casting a warm, flickering light across Patrick, Blair, and Sienna's faces. The sky had turned to a velvet black, sprinkled with stars that glimmered behind the sporadic cloud cover. They sat together, their quiet conversation punctuated only by the rhythmic crashing of waves that had crept toward them and the occasional snap of a burning twig. In that intimate circle of light, the stress outside their little group felt nonexistent, leaving just the soft radiance of fire and the steady presence of this new bond between them all.

Sienna yawned and hoisted herself out of her chair. "I think I'm gonna head to bed."

"Me too," Blair said.

The last thing Emily wanted to do was try to sleep. The night hours tended to bring the heaviness of her life to the forefront again. If she allowed herself, she'd lie in bed, mind racing until her eyes stung for sleep, waiting for consciousness to leave her.

"I think I'm going to sit out here a little longer, if it's

okay?" she said to Patrick. "Do you need help to get the chairs folded up?"

"I've got time. Let me text Julia to make sure they're okay," he said. "I'll take the cooler and things to the truck, so if they need me, I can just help put the chairs back by the house and get the fire pit tomorrow." He gathered the supplies, slinging the bag over his shoulder.

"Okay." Her heart fluttered at the idea of the two of them around the fire. It was as if she'd been one person with Will and another with Patrick. Which one was the real her? Was this all some kind of dream she'd eventually rouse from? Would she get back into the classroom and just return to her old life, meeting up with Sienna and Blair at the coffee shop on weekends? Or was she someone different now? Someone who couldn't take her eyes off Patrick...

When he started making his way to the front of the house, Sienna turned around, her eyebrows bobbing.

"It's just too nice to go inside," Emily said. "That's all."

"If you say so." Sienna winked at her. Then she linked arms with Blair, and the two of them walked toward the house.

With the radio still softly playing against the lullaby of the surf, Emily consciously tried to feel this new version of herself. Had the breakup made her stronger or weaker? Was she always going to fear that anyone she met might leave, blindsiding her the way Will had? Would she ever have a restful night's sleep? When would that day come? Would she one day fall into slumber without a care in the world, the way she'd done before Will had shattered her heart? She couldn't imagine it.

The fact that her phone had sat silent in her pocket all night gave her an indication of how quickly Will had changed his tune. Why had he checked in that last time as if they were best friends and then nothing? She pulled out the phone and checked the screen. No calls or texts. As much as she loathed it when he broke into her personal time, a tiny part of her wished he had. Then she'd feel as if she was worth something, as if she hadn't just been discarded.

She shook the thought from her mind. What a stupid way to feel. She gritted her teeth, swallowing the tears that wanted to come. With determination, she opened her email, pulled up the quitclaim form, and signed it. Then she sent it off.

There. Stay far away from me now.

"Julia said Winston's already asleep," Patrick said, rounding a chair and plopping down into it. "Stormy's in bed with him."

She slipped the phone back into her pocket. "That's so sweet. I hope he gets to keep him."

"Me too. He's wanted a dog forever. If we can't find an owner, I'm going to have to help Julia with taking it to training classes, and it's going to be a lot with work, but Winston needs a buddy. He's always with adults. It would be good for him to have another friend to occupy his time at home."

She smiled. Patrick took her mind off Will, and somehow managed to lift the weight on her heart at the same time.

"I'm not keeping you from anything, am I?" she asked.

"Not with Winston asleep. And once the sun goes down, there's only so much cleanup I can do around her house and mine. The restaurant's in good shape. We haven't brought in much of the furniture yet because we're waiting on a custom hood and bar to be built and installed. Most of it's in a storage facility inland. I've been waiting until Julia's class is finished to bring it all over so Winston can play basketball while I work. It's the only thing that keeps him entertained."

"You help out with him a lot?" she asked.

"Yeah." He reached down, scooped up a fistful of sand, and let it fall slowly back to the ground like the soft stream of an hourglass.

"That's really nice of you."

He made eye contact. "Nice?" His jaw tightened. "It's my duty. Ever since Daniel died, it's felt like something heavy on my chest—a kind of responsibility I can't shake, no matter what goes on."

"While it's wonderful of you to offer your sister help, I wish you didn't have so much guilt over what happened. From a bystander's point of view, it was a case of wrong place, wrong time."

"Even still, it's become my obligation. The funeral was barely over before people started looking at me with a renewed sense of what my purpose was. Some offered sympathy, others offered suggestions, but the message was always the same: *You're the one now.* I was suddenly supposed to become something I'd never prepared for. A guardian. A father. A steady hand in a life that had just been torn apart—which I can't stop believing was my fault." He looked into the blackness of the Gulf.

Emily followed his line of sight, but the darkness was so vast it was as if someone had turned off her vision.

"When Winston went out in the storm, all I could think about was his safety and that Julia could lose a second family member on my watch. Already, I don't sleep well."

"I understand not sleeping well," she said, turning to face him.

She hadn't planned to say anything—he was almost a stranger, a quiet presence on an otherwise empty beach.

But as the flames danced, something inside her wanted to tell him how different he'd made her feel. So she started to.

Patrick said nothing, just listened, his face calm and open, the firelight casting gentle shadows across his features. It wasn't comfort she was seeking, just a place to unload the weight of it all while letting him know he'd made a difference. Somehow, with the quiet murmuring of the Gulf behind them, it felt safe to do just that.

She shrugged. "Maybe this change was God's way of shifting the path I'd set for myself. I've thought about it sometimes—usually when I'm lying in the dark." This would be her go-to answer, she'd decided, for when she went back to school next year and her colleagues wanted to know what had happened. "What's on your mind now that Winston's safe and sound?"

"Most nights I just lie there, staring at the ceiling, wondering how I'm supposed to do this. Winston will need me, but my career keeps growing, taking more and more of my time. But when I look at him, I see a kid who's looking back at me like I might be the last thing that makes sense. Raising my sister's kid doesn't come with a set of directions, and I want to do it right. I don't get a do-over."

"Given how much he loves you, I don't think you need any directions," Emily said.

"That's actually what terrifies me." His chest rose with his breath. "It's in the quiet moments—the way he waits for me to speak, the way he hangs on my words like what I say matters. And even though I don't feel ready, I'm trying. For him. Because ready or not, he needs someone. And I'm the closest thing to a father he's got."

Emily put her hand on his for an instant, sending his attention down to their fingers. She drew her hand back, worried the touch was too intimate.

"I'm honored you shared this with me," she said, "since I know how much you enjoy your silence."

He allowed a small smile to emerge.

"So, what *did* make you tell me? You barely know me."

"I don't know. You're easy to talk to."

"Well, that's good, I guess." But then she pressed him. "What, exactly, makes me easier to talk to than other people?"

He looked directly into her eyes, as if searching for something. Her heart pattered at the sincerity on his face.

"I don't really like silence, actually. It just makes things simpler for me. I don't have to dive into my feelings if no one is there to make me. But you walked in that day we met with your sincere smile and all your questions." He looked into the flickering flames in front of them. "I thought, 'If I don't cut her off now, she might be trouble.'"

"Trouble?"

His smile reached his eyes. "I'd rather not elaborate." A huff of laughter escaped with his words.

"No, seriously. Tell me. Do I look like a menace of some sort? Am I high maintenance or something?"

Fondness lifted his features. "Definitely not any of those." He swallowed, his Adam's apple bobbing in the weighted silence. "You're as kind inside as you are attractive."

Emily had to work to make her mouth move, but she didn't have a clue what to say. It had been a long time since she'd heard a compliment, and his candor floored her.

When she didn't say anything, he pursed his lips and bent forward, leaning on his knees.

"Sorry," she said, scrambling. "Your honesty took me off guard." Patrick didn't look at her, so she got off her chair and squatted in front of him. "I like what you said," she told him softly.

His eyes met hers.

"What are you doing tomorrow?" she asked. It was a forward question, but with him she felt like a different person—someone she'd been all along, but had never allowed herself to experience. Her adult life had been about chasing Will's dreams. She'd tagged along, following him to Nashville, eating dinner alone and saving him a plate because he had some meeting with another person he was sure would open doors for him. But Patrick hadn't asked her for anything.

"I've got a few calls to make for work and then I'm assisting with the town cleanup."

"Want a pair of extra hands?" she asked.

"I don't want to take you away from your friends."

"Maybe we could all go. What time?"

"Around ten," he said, a glimmer in his eye.

"Emily!" Blair's voice cut through the moment like a hot knife through butter. "I need you to come here!"

Patrick stood up. "I should pack all this and get going. It's late."

"I'll see you tomorrow?" she asked.

"Definitely." He began folding the chairs.

"Do you need any help?" she asked.

They stood opposite one another, every nerve in her body zinging.

"I'm fine. You should go see what Blair wants."

But she didn't have to. Coming toward her on the beach, through the soft light emanating from the grounds surrounding the house, were Blair and Sienna. But beside them were Tyson, Rocko, and...

Will?

TWENTY

Tonight, talking to Patrick, Emily had only just begun to loosen her grip on the life she'd thought she and Will were building. Her evening on the beach had given her a moment to catch her breath, a place to begin truly forgetting—but now, there was Will, cutting through the darkness with the others, like some ghost she wasn't ready to face.

Had he come to explain, to reclaim whatever was left of them, or to break her all over again? The ache stirred in her chest, sharp and familiar, but beneath it, a newer thread of resistance tugged gently.

"Hey." Will reached out for her arm, running his finger down it.

Anger boiled up that she'd allowed the gesture.

"Can we talk?" he asked.

She looked over at Patrick. His gaze moved from her to Will.

"I'll finish loading all this," he said. "You can go on inside with the others. I've got it."

"I'll help," she offered, taking a step away from Will.

"No." Patrick shooed her away. "You have visitors. I'm just the chef, and my work is done." His jaw clenched.

Emily felt vulnerable, as if the tide had gone out too far and left the disarray of her heart exposed. She wanted to make a good impression on Patrick, to let him know she wasn't a disaster. More than that, she wanted him to know how *good* he was. And Will's presence had just made him secondary. He couldn't compete with her and Will's past. She wanted to run after Patrick and tell him that none of that mattered.

Will stood just feet away—once the center of her world, now more like a stranger with shared history. She didn't know what he might say or do. Nothing about his responses was recognizable.

But Patrick was someone who had, in mere days, looked at her as if she mattered, with genuine interest, as if he actually saw her. It was confusing, almost absurd, to feel steadier beside a near stranger than the man she had promised to be with forever. Guilt flashed through her, followed quickly by defiance. She wasn't Will's to hurt anymore—he'd made that clear.

"Let's go inside," Sienna suggested.

Blair linked arms with her and offered an empathetic smile.

Emily shot a look of apology at Patrick. She'd have to explain it all to him, if he'd let her. But tonight, maybe she wouldn't crumble when facing Will. She would hear whatever it was he had to say—and stay standing.

"I'll see you tomorrow," she said to Patrick, but he'd turned toward the fire pit, throwing sand on the glowing embers. She caught his brief glance as she walked away.

"Sorry to get here so late," Tyson said, grabbing Sienna's

hand. "We were hoping to get into town more easily, but with that storm, it was tough going."

Emily took another step away from Will, moving to the other side of Blair and Rocko.

Is anyone going to tell me why my ex came along?

"Can I get anyone a drink?" Sienna asked as they entered the house. Discreetly, she widened her eyes at Emily as if to say, *I know you'll need one.*

"Why don't we get their things upstairs and then we can all settle in?" Blair suggested.

Rocko came up behind Blair and kissed her cheek. "Sounds like a plan." Then he shot Emily an apologetic look over his shoulder.

The two couples began to load their suitcases into the elevator, leaving Will and Emily in the living room.

"Why did you come?" she asked him.

"I feel like we haven't really had a chance to talk—just the two of us."

She gawked at him. "And whose fault is that?"

He tapped his chest. "Mine." His dark eyes were full of remorse, something she hadn't seen before now.

"Yes." She didn't know what else to say to him, her anger building like an inferno.

"Can we go somewhere we can talk?"

With a deep, steadying breath, she led him up the stairs to her room. She could hear Blair filling Rocko in on all the amenities of the place. Sienna and Tyson's muffled voices bounced down the hallway. But Emily hadn't uttered a word. Her hands trembled and her heart pounded.

"Wow, this is incredible," Will said, dropping down on her fluffy duvet-covered bed.

She shut the door.

Inside the quiet bedroom, the noise of the ocean and voices outside fell away, leaving the enormity of everything unsaid between them. She stood near the door, arms crossed, and Will got up again, uncertainty flashing across his face.

"You look different," he said finally, his voice softer than she expected.

Emily didn't answer right away. What was there to say to him? That being left had originally hollowed her out emotionally, then oddly freed her? That she was angry—not just at him for blindsiding her, but at herself for not noticing that things weren't good between them until it was too late?

"Why did you come?" she asked again.

He hesitated, then shrugged. "The storm freaked me out. I was worried for you. It got me thinking. I figured maybe we could have a conversation about us?"

"*Us?* Where's Lanie?"

The color drained from his face. "You know her name?"

"Well, if you hang out with my friends, I will, eventually, know her name. But even so, I met her the day I went with you to the gym. She tried to sell me a month of hot yoga."

He flinched.

So it is the same Lanie. Emily walked toward him. "Will, what do you want?"

He shook his head. "I don't know."

Emily scoffed.

"I'm not even sure how to start, but I'm going to try to get my feelings into words. Will you at least hear me out?"

She nodded slowly, not because she agreed, or was necessarily interested in his about-face, but because she knew this moment needed to happen. It was time. She didn't care about answers, but she yearned for an ending that didn't feel like absolute rejection.

Will took a step forward, invading her personal space. "I really messed things up."

She stared at him, her lips pressed together, waiting for at least a meager apology rather than a confession. It was clear he'd messed things up. Now, would he be a man and tell her how sorry he was?

"You and I met so young..." He paced. "I got to Nashville, found a few new friends, and began to make a name for myself. I didn't know who I was yet."

He looked over at her, but she didn't budge from her cautious stance.

"I couldn't be a good husband when I didn't know who I was."

"I'm the same age as you are, and *I* didn't stray," she said. Her limbs wobbled, but she stood firm, trying not to let the humiliation that had saturated her very being show.

He sat on the bed and put his face in his hands. "I know," he said, his words muffled. "I screwed up."

"I'm sorry. Have I missed something? The last real conversation we had was to get me to sign over the house I'd put all our hopes and dreams into, to give it away to the woman who stole my entire life. And now, suddenly you're here, without her. You've skipped a few steps. Want to catch me up?"

"I broke up with her."

"Why?" Emily asked, suspicious of his motives. She had every right to be guarded. She didn't know who he was anymore.

He patted the bed next to him, but she stood her ground.

"Come on, Em. At least sit down."

With a deep breath, she climbed onto the bed, but scooted up near the head, putting a pillow in her lap.

"You being here in the middle of a tropical storm freaked me out. I realized I didn't want to lose you."

She squinted at him in confusion. "You left me. I wasn't yours anymore, so you had nothing *to lose*."

He looked at his lap. "I don't know what I was thinking," he said in an exasperated whisper. "The thing with Lanie started as a minor flirtation. It exploded into more, and before I knew it, I was sneaking around behind your back. I felt awful about it, Em. I'd done the deed, so the only way to do the right thing was to break it off with you so you could find someone who would treat you better, and then I tried to make good on what I'd started with Lanie."

"I never realized you were such a weak individual," she said.

"I didn't either. But it happened. I thought if I acted awful to you that you'd leave, find someone else, and I could feel a smidge less horrible for having let you go."

Tears swelled in her eyes, and she cleared her throat.

"I figured Lanie and I deserved each other. But you didn't deserve any of it."

Look at him, acting as if he'd done some heroic feat in setting me free. Did he really think she was going to believe it? "You still haven't answered why you suddenly wanted me back when you thought I was in harm's way."

"Because I was with her for the wrong reasons. I liked the newness of the way she looked at me, how she didn't know all my little dark places yet. Things started to snowball. She got this big idea about living together, and I didn't know if I was ready for all that, but she kept on. I let things go too far, asking you to give up the house, trying to hold on to the thing that had been so important at the time that I'd ruined my upcoming marriage for it. But when it came down to it, I didn't love her. I had to put a stop to all of it, whether I get you back or not."

"I signed the documents, so the house belongs to you and whomever you choose," she said.

"You did?"

The drop in his voice almost made her falter.

"So now—what?—you're here all weekend with Rocko and Tyson?"

"Yeah," he said, looking as if he was about to be sick. "I imagined this going differently."

She tilted her head, shaking it in bafflement. "Why would you imagine anything other than this reaction from me?"

He blew air through his lips. "I don't know." His voice was shaky, unsure. His eyes glistened with emotion. "I always thought we could get through anything. I just didn't ever fathom that I'd be the cause of this kind of pain."

Her heart squeezed. He looked like the old Will, albeit battered and broken down. Her tense shoulders fell, but she forced herself not to comfort him. He'd hurt her in an incredible way, and even though he'd shown some remorse, she wasn't sure how to respond to it. She felt herself slipping back into the old version of Emily, but the new version was hanging on for dear life, pleading with her to stay the course. She liked who she was becoming without him, and while, originally, she'd wished for this very moment, she didn't know if she welcomed it anymore.

"Should we get ourselves together and go downstairs with the others?" she asked.

He stared at her. "They're going to want to know where we stand."

"We'll tell them. We are exactly as we were before you decided to come crash my vacation." With that, she pushed away any lingering affection she had for the man she'd thought he was. She stood up, straightened her T-shirt, walked out of the room, and headed downstairs.

TWENTY-ONE

The next morning, Emily woke with the weight of last night still lingering behind her eyes, the remnants of tears dried tight on her cheeks. After they'd all gone to bed—with Will in another guest room down the hall—she'd cried herself to sleep, the two sides of her battling for control.

The morning light felt too bright, almost intrusive, and her body was weary with an ache that hadn't faded with the nighttime hours. She recalled pieces of her conversation with Will, as well as good moments they'd had together over their lifetime that had unraveled her. Though the quiet of the room offered some peace, it did little to steady her busy mind. Everything felt distant, dulled, as if she were floating just outside of herself, trying to make sense of the aftermath.

But worse than all that was her worry about how the evening with Patrick had ended. She'd finally made him comfortable enough that he'd shared his thoughts with her, and allowed himself to be vulnerable. And now, Will could ruin anything she'd managed to build with Patrick.

She hadn't meant to have any opinion whatsoever about

the chef, but the thoughts had crept up on her, slipping in without her even trying to summon them.

Emily got up and moved to the upholstered chair by the window, the sun on her face. The grounds crew had completely cleared the remaining debris, and if she hadn't just experienced the tropical storm, she wouldn't have known, from this view, that it had ever happened.

The memory of her life with Will crept in once more—his laugh, the way he used to touch her back absentmindedly, the promises he'd made with eyes that, she realized now, seemed to always be scanning the room. She used to think it was his inability to attend to their relationship—a creative instability and need to chase inspiration rearing its head. But given recent events, she wondered if she hadn't been enough to keep his focus. And now, he was wrestling with that same pull of distraction.

She had loved Will unapologetically, blindly. And yet, last night, Patrick had simply smiled at her from across the fire, and something—something real and startling—had stirred in her chest. He'd asked about her, listened as if her words meant something, and in that brief moment, she'd seen no ghosts in his eyes. It wasn't love. Not yet. But it felt like hope. And that was something Will could no longer give her.

Was Patrick as stunned as she'd been to see Will appear? Did he have a restless sleep, full of questions? Had he second-guessed his decision to open up to her?

Now, she was stuck with Will in the house for the rest of their vacation. And she'd lost any chance she'd had to learn more about Patrick—he certainly wouldn't be divulging anything more with Will and all the others around.

Maybe it was for the best. Patrick lived in Florida, he

had a brand-new restaurant to run, and she'd signed her contract for the next school year in Nashville. There was no way they could even develop a strong friendship that many miles apart. One week with someone could never sustain indefinite long-term separation. But even her rationalization didn't stop her from thinking about it.

Emily got up from the chair, slipped on her jeans and a T-shirt, and quietly left her room to make herself a cup of coffee. But as she padded down to the kitchen, the scent of fresh grounds, robust and bitter, and the salty aroma of a cooked breakfast filled the air. Someone else was up. A quiet cough made her skin crawl. *That sounded like Will.*

She paused at the bottom of the stairs, her movement on the last step giving her away. He was already in the kitchen, barefoot, shirt wrinkled from sleep. He turned at the sound, his eyes meeting hers with a trace of hesitation, as if he wasn't sure whether to smile or apologize.

"Morning," he said in a low voice that was familiar in a way that made her chest tighten.

"Morning," she echoed, the word flat. She crossed her arms. It wasn't cold, exactly. But there was the iciness of the space between two people who used to be everything to one another.

"I made some scrambled eggs if you want some." He gestured toward a pan sitting on the stove. "I can make you toast."

He must have made eggs because he knew how much she liked them.

"I can do it."

She stepped up beside him, the two of them maneuvering around each other with the kind of silent choreography of people who used to know the steps. She reached for a mug just as he moved aside, neither speaking, both pretending it wasn't strange to be together again. So many mornings when he'd stopped by her apartment before work had been just like this. How could the same hands that once held her like something sacred now fumble around the kitchen? She hadn't known back then that one day those simple morning routines would cease, and she'd never again be the same.

The fridge and cabinet doors opened and closed with soft thuds, spoons clinked in their mugs—small sounds that felt too loud in the loaded silence. Emily kept her mind on the hum of a piece of machinery outside, which was probably part of the storm-cleanup efforts, in an attempt to detach from the thought that Will's hand used to brush her waist as he passed or he'd reach out and tickle her sides, making her squeal. Now, he kept a deliberate distance. *Good.*

The toast popped up and she scraped some butter on the surface. Then she set it beside her eggs, took her mug, and walked to the table.

"May I join you?" he asked.

She waved a hand at the open seat across from her and then looked out the window.

The bad weather had passed, but inside her the real storm that had been brewing since she got there was exploding. Her thoughts spun harder than any gale-force wind, circling the same questions with relentless power. The bright-blue sky outside was calm, almost smug in its stillness, but her mind crackled with unrest—grief, anger, longing for normalcy, all tangled like the power lines downed in the aftermath.

"Good morning," Sienna said, shattering the tension. She offered Emily a loaded glance before she retrieved the orange juice from the fridge, pouring herself a glass.

She approached the table, one hand resting on the small, still-flat curve of her stomach. There was something different about her today. Her face was softer than it had been, the kind of softness that follows a storm—not peace exactly, but surrender.

Emily held her coffee, eyebrows raised in question, but didn't speak. She didn't have to.

Sienna offered a small, breathy laugh, then said, "I told Tyson last night." Her voice cracked slightly, but it seemed to be more from release than fear. "He was okay." She sank into the chair as if the weight she'd been carrying had finally shifted. "Surprised, obviously, and not sure what to do next, but he didn't freak out like I thought he would. I'd been so worried for nothing."

Will looked on curiously. "What did you tell him?" he asked.

"That I'm pregnant."

Will's lips parted. "Oh wow. Congratulations."

"Thank you." She sipped her juice.

"How do you feel now that he knows?" Emily asked. "Is it a weight off your shoulders?"

"Yes. I feel a sense of purpose that I couldn't take hold of until Tyson was on board. I can't say for sure where it's coming from. And I still worry that I'm going to get so busy with the baby that I'll lose myself."

"I have to wonder if you might find yourself instead," Emily offered.

Sienna put her fingers to her smiling lips and shook her head.

"We should celebrate," Will said.

"Oh! That reminds me..." Emily checked her phone. No service. She turned to Sienna. "I offered to help Patrick with the town cleanup today at ten before I remembered everyone was coming. I thought maybe you, me, and Blair could help, but with your hubbies here, I'll go by myself. We can celebrate after."

"Who's Patrick?" Will asked.

"The guy you interrupted last night," Emily said.

His face crumpled. "The fire-pit guy? Didn't I hear him say he was a chef?"

"A chef who saved us from the worst of the storm. I'd like to repay his kindness."

"Was that the same guy I heard on the other end of your phone that night?" he asked, that tone she'd heard over the last few days creeping in.

Was that jealousy on his face? How dare he... Not only had she just met Patrick, but who she planned to see was none of Will's business. It struck her how different he seemed, how much she had overlooked during the bustle of their life together. Where once she saw kindness, she now noticed the edge in his smile, the way his laugh reached just a little bit too far. With distance and clarity, she saw him as others must have all along—not cruel, not evil, but small. Long ago, she'd put him on a pedestal as the man she loved. But sitting across from him in that moment was like adjusting the focus on a camera lens; suddenly, the image sharpened, and he didn't look the same.

When Emily surfaced from her thoughts, she found Sienna telling Will about how they'd stayed at Julia's, and with every word, his face grew paler and paler. He frowned and nodded, but didn't say anything else.

He didn't need to. He'd made his bed. Now he had to lie in it.

TWENTY-TWO

After a text to Patrick finally went through, he picked up Emily. She was glad to escape Will. A mix of guilt and relief swallowed her as she stepped into the truck, leaving her ex irritatingly standing in the driveway of the house.

As they rumbled down the drive, she glanced back once, catching a final glimpse of Will. With the fresh air rushing through the open window and Patrick's quiet composure, it felt as if she was finally moving forward, not just through the wreckage of the storm, but out of something that, looking back with a clear head, had long been broken.

Patrick didn't say anything about Will being in the driveway. He didn't say much at all, his expression unreadable. Was he only picking her up out of duty because they'd made plans? Did he want her there? From the way he reacted last night, it was pretty clear he didn't want to be in the middle of things.

In the quiet between them, Emily turned her attention to the scene through the window. In the aftermath of the terrible weather, the area still bore the scars of high winds and storm surge. Side streets remained littered with fallen branches, shattered glass, and remnants of homes and businesses.

"The cleanup crews have been working round the clock in the sweltering heat," Patrick finally said, rounding a corner. "I've got water bottles in the back to hand out, since they have limited access to clean water."

"Okay." Her elbow hung out the window as the warm breeze blew strands of hair across her face. While she wanted to explain what had happened between her and Will last night, she kept silent.

Patrick pulled to a stop along the side of the road. "We'll start here."

The air smelled of damp wood, salt, and gasoline. The constant hum of generators and chainsaws filled the background while workers moved methodically through neighborhoods, clearing debris and assessing damage. A few people stopped to wave at Patrick.

Despite the chaos, the crews operated as a tightly knit unit, each person understanding the urgency of their role, all of them working with the kind of precision that only comes from years of practice—they'd faced these storms before. Local contractors and volunteers labored alongside utility trucks with out-of-state insignias. Every action visibly contributed to restoring a sense of order and safety.

Emily hopped out of the truck and met Patrick at the tailgate. He opened his cooler, retrieved a couple of bottles from the ice, and handed them to her. Then he got his own.

"Anybody need free water?" he called, striding across the street toward a group clearing debris from a parking lot.

Emily followed his lead.

A couple of people stopped, clapped the debris off their hands, and met them happily. One of the men clapped Patrick on the back.

They continued passing out bottles. Once everyone there who wanted water had received one, they got back in Patrick's truck and drove until they found the next cluster of people, where they made the same offer.

"I'm surprised Winston isn't with us," Emily said, making conversation. "I could see him enjoying this."

"He wanted to come with me," Patrick said as they drove. "I thought, too, it'd be a good job for him."

"Why didn't he come?" Emily asked.

"Julia convinced him not to when I told her you were coming. She said she'd rather I have some time to talk to you when I wasn't preoccupied." When Emily didn't respond, Patrick continued. "How's the ex?"

Her chest tightened at the mention of Will. "Just as much of a disaster as ever."

Patrick nodded, his lips set in a pout, his wrist guiding the steering wheel as they made their way down the road. "I want to apologize for my...openness last night. I don't want to create any extra stress."

"You didn't."

"I know you've got a lot to deal with right now. You don't need me adding another layer."

"I don't have 'a lot' to deal with, apart from the fact that Will drove here in Tyson's car and is stuck here for the weekend."

"Maybe it's meant to be. You two will have time away from your lives to figure out what you really want to do."

"What I want to do is kick him out of the house. He cheated on me. I can't forgive him for that."

"Your emotions are raw right now. You might not forgive him. But you won't know until you two have some time."

His words hit her with a unique blend of truth and

discomfort, like someone gently pressing on a bruise she hadn't fully acknowledged. She wanted to believe she was done with Will, that her time here had removed any remaining attachment, but now doubt flickered at the edge of her certainty. She didn't want to forgive Will, didn't think he deserved it. But hearing Patrick's words unsettled her. Patrick was rational, thoughtful, and she trusted him. Was she rushing toward something new just to outpace the old— the dreaded rebound? Or was this the clarity she needed?

He stopped at the next group of people and got out, tossing a few bottles to the workers. Then he climbed back in and they were off once more. As the truck rolled forward and the landscape blurred past the windows, she wrestled with the quiet truth: Healing wasn't just about moving on. It was about understanding who she planned to be. In a very short time, her interactions with Patrick had begun to shape her. Without even trying, he'd shown her what she should expect from someone and the kind of person she wanted to spend time with. But just when she'd found him, she had to leave him.

Emily let the conversation go. Patrick didn't offer anything else, and she didn't bother to stand her ground—it wouldn't matter if she did say something, given the situation. Instead, she focused all her energy on the people who worked so hard to make a difference.

Despite the crews' obvious fatigue and the endless challenges she'd witnessed, there were moments of humanity that reminded her why the work mattered. A homeowner offering coffee to workers at a table in his front yard, children waving from porches, and, one time, it was the simple nod of appreciation from a wearied worker when she handed him water. This work wasn't just about the physical recovery of the town, it was about helping a community stand strong. And Patrick was right in the middle of it. She would've never guessed it early on.

When all the water was gone, Emily didn't want to return to the beach house.

"It's still early," she said. "Is there any other way I can help today?"

"You don't need to get back?"

She shook her head. That was the last thing she wanted.

Patrick eyed her, clearly thinking—debating? "How are your raking skills?"

"As good as they'll ever be."

He abruptly changed direction, the truck's tires grinding in protest. With a wide arc, he maneuvered past piles of windblown trash and debris and headed in a direction she'd never been before. The scenery evolved into a less-populated landscape, the beachy appeal of shops and vacation homes giving way to a more rural area.

Patrick took her down an extensive dirt road, into the woods. They bumped along until they arrived at a small cottage.

"Home sweet home," he said with a hint of sarcasm.

The roof had a tarp protecting a large portion of it where shingles must have been torn off, and the yard was indistinguishable from the woods, due to fallen debris. A few trees were uprooted, their exposed roots clawing at the earth like outstretched fingers. The path leading to the cottage, probably once quiet and shaded, was nearly impassable, buried under leaves, branches, and soggy debris. A portion of the fence enclosing the backyard was pinned to the ground by a large tree trunk, leaving a gaping hole.

"You're planning to fix all this with a rake?" she teased.

The corner of his mouth twitched upward in that

adorable way. "I'm giving *you* the rake. I've got bigger fish to fry."

"Sorry, but I'm not sure I can handle this with a rake."

"Sure you can." He pointed to a Bobcat bulldozer sitting at the edge of the property. "Just as soon as we clear it." He shut off the engine and got out.

As he slid the cooler out of the bed of his truck and dumped the ice onto the ground, Emily put her hands on her hips to survey the damage in front of her.

"Where do you even start?" she asked, bewildered.

"At the beginning." He tossed the cooler back into his truck and shut the tailgate. Then he nodded toward the Bobcat. "Follow me. I'll show you."

Before she knew it, she was climbing up into the small bulldozer. The metal steps were slippery with damp leaves. She gripped the side rail, and Patrick offered a steadying hand. His strong grip kept her stable as she entered the cab, which smelled faintly of diesel and the outdoors. The seat creaked beneath her.

Patrick turned the key in the ignition and the engine roared to life, vibrating beneath her feet. With practiced effortlessness, he moved the levers, guiding the machine into the tangle of branches and wreckage that had consumed the yard.

The heavy bucket scooped up broken limbs and crumpled siding, the machine cutting a path through the chaos as if it had a mind of its own. He filled the bucket with the remains of the storm and, with a jerk, moved it to the side of the property and dumped it out.

"What's that?" she called over the racket, pointing to a small shack of a building she couldn't believe had survived in the high winds.

"That's my fishing shed. It's got all my gear in it."

"You fish?"

"There's nothing better than catching your own dinner," he said loudly over the rattle of the engine.

"You look like the fishing type."

He downshifted, the machine groaning. "There's a type? What's the fishing type then?"

"I'm not sure, but if there was one, you'd be it. Maybe rugged?"

The corner of his mouth twitched in that adorable way of his. "I'm not sure. Winston fishes with me. I'm less cowboy and more babysitter, but we get some great dishes out of it."

She imagined him taking Winston into the shed, choosing just the right fishing pole, and their spending the day out on a boat together. The idea warmed her heart.

There was something calming in the rhythm of the task as he worked quietly beside her—destruction being undone, one load at a time. The machine was too loud for any real conversation, and Emily was glad about that because she still wasn't sure what she wanted to say to him. So she allowed herself this moment to be next to him, to see how easily he was able to plow through the chaos and give it a semblance of normalcy again. His mere presence doing the same thing for her.

TWENTY-THREE

When the last load of debris had been hauled away and dumped, revealing the torn-up yard that was in dire need of a green thumb, Patrick turned off the engine and looked at his watch.

"It's after lunchtime. You hungry?"

"Starving," Emily replied.

"Come on. Let's make some food." He helped her past a smattering of limbs, then onto the porch, and with a twist of the knob, he opened the front door and let her inside.

His cottage was the perfect balance between relaxed coastal charm and deliberate bachelor style. The uncluttered atmosphere, with natural light pouring in through wide, salt-sprayed windows at the back, gave her a sense of immediate calm. The thickly planked, weathered wood floors looked built to last, with a few well-placed woven rugs adding just the right amount of texture.

"Can I get you something to drink?" he asked. "I've got sweet tea and lemonade."

"I'd love some tea."

He offered her a seat on the sofa in the open-plan living

area attached to the kitchen, and she sat down while he went around the island, washed his hands, and opened the fridge.

His furniture was simple, manly, but looked carefully chosen. The deep couch in soft neutrals complemented a rugged wooden coffee table and a worn surfboard mounted on the wall like art.

"You surf too?" she called over to him.

"No. Definitely not. It was left by the previous owner, and I didn't know what to put there, so I left it."

She twisted around to see him. The kitchen was small, but neat and efficient, with open shelving and a few vintage touches that revealed his occupation: a French press, hand-made pottery mugs hanging from hooks, and a collection of spices intentionally arranged. It seemed he lived there with purpose, as if he found peace in order. She could totally relate.

Patrick brought over her glass, then sat across from her with his own. "I've got shrimp, oysters, flounder, crab, or steak," he said. "What sounds good to you?"

"Surprise me," she replied.

"All right." He got back up and handed her the TV remote. "Make yourself comfortable."

She set the remote on the coffee table, stood up, and followed him into the kitchen, taking a seat across from him on a wooden barstool. A glimmer of fondness shone in his eyes, and he quickly turned away, pulling covered containers out of the fridge. He worked quietly, as usual, busy with the cooking tasks.

"We're having crab cakes," he said, greasing a cast-iron pan and then chopping parsley on a wooden cutting board.

The small kitchen filled quickly with the scent of Old Bay and salty butter as he moved between the narrow counter and the stovetop. There was barely enough room for the mixing bowl, but he managed with precision, gently folding lump crab, breadcrumbs, filling, and the parsley with practiced hands.

The skillet hissed as the first crab cake hit the oil, golden edges forming almost instantly in the hot pan. Steam rose while he flipped each cake with care, mindful not to break their delicate shape. He turned down the heat and whipped together a vinaigrette before tossing some salad fixings together. He combined the vegetables with the dressing and plated them. Then he slid the spatula under each crab cake, adding it to their plates.

"Here you go." Patrick gestured to the bistro-sized dining set against the wall by the window and then brought their dishes over.

Emily followed him to the table.

Once she was settled, she tucked into her meal. The crab meat was seasoned just enough to enhance the flavor without overpowering it, with a fresh touch from seasonal herbs. The texture was crispy, and only after her first bite did she notice the hint of a tangy contrast to the sweet, buttery flavor of the crab from a sauce he'd hidden under the cake.

"I can't imagine being able to cook like this for every meal," she said, still delighting in the dish.

"Well, I don't usually. After cooking all day, most of the time I heat up a frozen pizza, if I'm lucky."

"But you're so talented. You don't treat yourself?"

"I only cook at home when I have someone to cook for. Which is rare, apart from Julia and Winston." He shook his head. "Speaking of cooking, he wants me to make home-made dog treats for Stormy. Dog food isn't in my repertoire. I'll have to look online for a recipe."

"I'd love to help you now if you have time."

"Do *you* have time?"

"I'm free until this evening. Sienna revealed the news to her husband Tyson that she's expecting, so we're celebrating tonight."

"Sounds better than my evening. I have to help my sister and Winston rearrange his bedroom for Stormy's crate."

"They got him a crate?"

"Yeah, no one's claimed him yet, so he needs somewhere to stay. I've got to unload Winston's giant bookshelf and get it to the other side of the room. But don't worry. I've already planned to bring dinner for you all. I'm preparing for six."

"Do we need to pay you for the additional people?"

"No, no. Don't worry about it. With the storm, you all won't eat unless I cook for everyone, and I've got tons of food between my private client stock and the early orders I've made for the restaurant. Do you want anything special for the celebration?"

"Please don't feel like you have to do all that. I think Sienna's more excited to sit back and relax than she is to have a big spread of food."

"I'll see what I've got and maybe I can whip up something extra."

Emily nodded, wondering how the night would go with both Patrick and Will there. It was unbelievable that Will had shown up and crashed her vacation. Trying not to let it put a damper on today, she scooped up a forkful of salad and took a bite.

After lunch, she and Patrick looked online for dog treat ideas. Emily came across simple homemade peanut butter treats and decided it would be the perfect recipe.

"I've got all those ingredients: whole wheat flour, oats, peanut butter, eggs, and water." He went over to his pantry and pulled everything out, setting it on the counter. With a click of a few buttons, he preheated the oven and then eyed the screen of his laptop.

"I think we should add a banana and pumpkin puree."

"You're the boss," she said. She grabbed the bowl he'd set out and read the directions on the screen. "In a large bowl, combine peanut butter, flour, oats, and egg. Stir to combine."

While he cracked the egg on the side of the dish, she measured the other ingredients.

"You should always crack your eggs first, so if there's anything wrong with them, you don't ruin your flour," he said.

She squinted at him. "Are you...chatting?" she teased.

The corners of his mouth twitched. He offered her a large spoon.

"I like it when you make conversation," she said.

"I could guess you'd like chatter."

"Why?" she asked suspiciously.

"Because you always want to talk when I'm cooking."

"And look at where it got me—in your kitchen, making dog treats. I'll bet you didn't see that coming when we met."

A grin emerged. "Is that what you were trying to do that day—get into my kitchen?"

Heat rushed over her cheeks. "No. I was just being friendly. What I meant was that if you actually talk to more people, you might find that they're enjoyable and your life might look different."

"It definitely does look different," he said, his voice slow and soft.

She liked his attention. Even when they were dating,

Will didn't flirt with her like this. There was something both youthful and yet very adult about the look in Patrick's eyes.

"Good," she finally said, her heart pattering.

With a soft chuckle, Patrick rooted around in a drawer and took out a circular cookie cutter and a wooden rolling pin. "This is all I've got. I'm not a baker." He handed her the cookie cutter.

"That'll do," she said.

Mixing the dough turned out to be easier than she'd expected. And the peanut butter gave off a warm, nutty aroma, which made her want to nibble it from the wooden spoon. She went over to the laptop. "Slowly add water, a tablespoon at a time, until the dough holds together but isn't sticky," she read.

Patrick chuckled as he filled a measuring cup with water and handed it to her. While she added it in, he floured the counter.

"What's so funny?" she asked, his slight smirk making her stomach do a little flip.

"You follow the recipe to the letter."

"And? Why wouldn't I? You're the chef, not me." Emily rolled the dough onto the dusted surface and used the cookie cutter to press out each treat.

Patrick lined them neatly on a baking sheet. "Cooking isn't about getting perfect amounts. You can improvise for taste. The unexpected brings more flavor most of the time."

"Yeah, but I might get it wrong and ruin it."

"I don't think you could ruin it."

What happened with Will and the way she'd happily planned her life, missing all the signs flashed through her mind. "You'd be surprised."

His head tilted slightly. "Are we still talking about cooking?"

"Maybe... Maybe not."

"Wanna let me in on your thoughts?" he asked.

They hadn't known each other long enough for her to start spouting her flaws. What if she turned him off too?

"Tell me," he encouraged her.

"I've wondered if I was lacking in something that caused my ex to stray. Was it something with *me*? Maybe I wasn't exciting enough, interesting enough."

"I'm willing to guess that you're the same person he proposed to, right?"

"Yeah."

"Then it wasn't you."

She leaned against the counter. "When he left me, I realized I didn't know him as well as I thought I did. And now, when I look at him, I don't feel the same way for him. Could the same have happened to him?"

"I'm willing to bet that your feelings for him changed because of his actions. They revealed to you who he was—a side of him he hadn't shown you before. Maybe he always would've strayed. I don't know him so I can't say."

There was a tangible shift in the air, and she bit her lip. While Patrick made her feel better, she was probably ruining this lovely moment by ruminating on a relationship that wasn't even worth the effort.

The click of a radio made her jump. She refocused on Patrick. He was twisting the volume up on a small radio next to the fridge.

"Let's put you to the test. We'll find out if you're the issue," he said.

"How?"

He took her hand, and her breath caught. Then he gave

her a spin, both of them knocking into the cabinets in the small galley kitchen.

"Hang on. I can do better than that." He led her into the living area and gave her another spin, his strong arm at her waist, making her laugh. He caught her, pulling her into him, the two of them staring into each other's eyes. "Test one, you passed."

"How did I pass?" she asked, breathless.

"You didn't fight me off or anything. So you're up for spontaneity. You were worried about that, right?"

She laughed. "You said 'Test one.' Is there another test?"

"You up for another?"

"Definitely."

"All right. You asked for it." He grabbed hold of her and threw her over his shoulder. Then he took off, flinging open the front door and running full speed toward the leaf pile. All of a sudden, they were both soaring through the air, landing with a puff of leaves all around them.

She giggled uncontrollably, still trying to catch her breath. "What was *that* testing?"

"You don't mind getting messy." He brushed a leaf from her hair, his finger trailing along her cheek. "You're definitely not too formal."

"Is there another test?" she asked, her heart drumming as she hoped he'd say yes.

His smile softened into seriousness. "You want the last test?"

"Mm hm."

Slowly, he leaned down and licked his lips.

She held her breath.

"The last test," he whispered, "is whether you're a romantic."

She willed her racing pulse to slow. "And how do we test that?" But she already knew the answer.

His lips hovered above hers, his breath tickling her skin. She closed her eyes and tipped her chin up slightly.

Then, suddenly, she was pulled to her feet.

"Yep. You passed."

She swallowed, still trying to get her bearings. "Are you sure?"

"Yep. I could definitely tell." He plucked a leaf off the back of her shirt. "We should probably go inside and see if the dog treats are ready."

Stunned and confused, Emily followed Patrick into the house. Why hadn't he kissed her? Wasn't that what he was going to do? Had she wanted him to? Yes, she decided. So, what happened?

He checked the biscuits.

Maybe he was only trying to gauge her reaction. Or perhaps he overthought it, and worried it was too soon to make a move like that. They hadn't known each other very long. She breathed into her hand and tried to smell her breath.

Patrick's loud laugh pulled her from her thoughts. "It wasn't you." He laughed again.

He'd caught her checking her breath. How embarrassing.

"The last test was actually whether you wanted to go slowly or not." He stepped toward her.

"Oh. I failed that one then." She looked up at him, drinking in the lingering amusement on his face.

With another chuckle, he stepped closer, took her face in his strong hands, and gently, carefully pressed his lips to hers. Everything faded, and it was just the two of them and the soft hum of the radio. It was as if his touch had pressed the pause button on her thoughts, and all she could manage was the sensation of him. All her questions about herself were answered at once. She didn't need to know anything more because, right now, this was enough.

He pulled back, fondness in his eyes. "You passed another test."

"What's that?" she asked.

"Are you irresistible? The answer is yes."

The oven timer went off.

Patrick cleared his throat. "Yeah, it was definitely your ex's fault," he said under his breath.

TWENTY-FOUR

"Is that a leaf in your hair?" Will asked from the sofa when Emily walked into the beach house at around 3:30 that afternoon.

Blair, Rocko, Sienna, and Tyson looked on curiously. A baseball game played on TV.

"Maybe," she said, self-consciously pawing at the back of her head.

Will propped his feet on the coffee table next to a half-eaten bowl of chips. "You were gone a long time."

"There was a lot to get done."

"Did you have fun?" Blair asked, blowing on a bright-pink nail she was painting. "By the smile on your face when you came in, it looks like you did."

"Yeah, I enjoyed it." Emily licked her lips, feeling as if she had an invisible banner above her head that gave away the fact that she'd not exactly been doing storm cleanup the whole time. Patrick's lips floated into her mind and she blinked them away.

Open beer bottles littered the table, and baseball highlights flashed across the TV until an update on the efforts in town came on.

Sienna unsuccessfully scrolled her phone. "Ugh. I've had no service all morning."

Rocko pointed at the TV. "They just said the lines were down, and they're working on it." Then he started telling a story about a hurricane he'd been in back in Virginia.

Blair smiled at him innocently, waving her wet nails.

The atmosphere felt too normal. No one looked at Emily as if anything had changed. But everything had. She'd left the beach house feeling lost and wounded, and she'd returned with hope for the future. She sat in the chair opposite them all as if there wasn't a tiny explosion ready to burst from inside her, as if she hadn't just kissed someone she hadn't planned to. She nodded along to Rocko's story, but part of her was still in that little kitchen, remembering how close Patrick's face had been, how the moment had slipped past *Why didn't he?* to *Did we really just cross an incredibly important line?*

The ride home had been comfortably quiet, their wounded souls finding solace in that brief exchange in the kitchen. When they arrived at the beach house, she hadn't wanted to say goodbye. But when Patrick said he'd see her tonight, that sent her into a wild back-and-forth with herself about whether or not she should've let things go where they had.

Why had Will come? This would've been so much easier if he weren't there. His presence was a constant reminder of her past, and Emily needed some time to figure out things without him getting in the way. But perhaps she needed the tether to real life. Without it, she could easily be whisked away to a false sense of reality where a handsome navy veteran swept her off her feet.

"Did Patrick say he's making dinner tonight?" Sienna asked, the question seemingly sucked right out of Emily's thoughts.

Her heart pounded. Just his name caused a flash of panic to overtake her. What was this feeling? She was anxious, restless. "Uh. He said...yes. He is," Emily replied.

Sienna shot her a look, loaded with questions. She could always tell something was up by the most infinitesimal changes in Emily's expression.

"So, what are we doing to celebrate tonight?" Emily asked in an attempt to divert Sienna's attention from her inner turmoil.

"After dinner, we thought we'd sit around the pool and make some cocktails," Blair said.

"That sounds nice," Emily said, still trying not to make eye contact with Sienna. "Patrick said he might try to whip up something special." His name sounded different off her tongue just then, and she hoped no one noticed.

"After all your hard work today, you should take some time for yourself, maybe have a nap and then get cleaned up," Sienna suggested. "I brought a new shampoo I could loan you. You've gotta try it."

Emily wanted to use the moment to escape them and flee to her room where she could regroup and figure out how to get through the evening.

Sienna stood up, came over to where she was sitting, and took her wrists, pulling her to a standing position. "I *definitely* want to show you that shampoo," she said, dragging Emily to the stairway. "I can't believe I haven't shown you yet."

When they were out of sight of the rest of them, Sienna gave her a once-over, but didn't say anything. It was clear, however, from her shifting eyes, that she was going to have a million questions when they got upstairs.

They got to Emily's room, and Sienna pushed them inside with a flourish, closing the door behind them.

"Spill."

"Spill what?" Emily asked, knowing her cheeks were flaming.

Sienna pursed her lips. "You can hide *nothing* from me. The minute I said 'Patrick' you looked like you were going to throw up. I need to know what's going on."

While Sienna was great at reading people, what she wasn't as great at was being quiet about things. How she'd managed to keep her pregnancy under wraps from Tyson for as long as she had was a complete mystery. The last thing Emily wanted was to admit what had happened between her and Patrick today. It would make everything awkward. She'd tell her eventually, but not before Patrick came over tonight. Sienna was sure to give away the secret to the others, and Patrick seemed to be a private person. She doubted he'd want Emily blabbing to her friends. And Will definitely didn't need to know; that was a headache waiting to happen.

When she emerged from her thoughts, Sienna was waggling a finger at her. "*That* look. That's the nauseous look you had." Then she sucked in a breath. "You and Patrick didn't..."

"What? We didn't what?" Emily asked, barely able to manage speaking.

"I don't know," Sienna said suggestively. "What's the *what* you're wanting me to guess?"

"I'm not asking you to guess anything."

"Then tell me."

Emily wasn't getting out of this. Not with Sienna. And even if she tried, she was a terrible liar.

"If I tell you, you *cannot* tell anyone, you hear me?"

Sienna flopped onto the bed with a wild smile on her face. She air-drew a cross over her heart.

"I'm serious."

"Me too."

Emily took in a steadying breath and swallowed. "He kissed me."

Sienna's mouth dropped open. When she recovered, she asked, "In the middle of the cleanup efforts?"

Emily laughed. "We went back to his house."

Sienna's eyes bulged with interest. "You did? What's his house like?"

"Unfussy and quiet. Like him."

"There's a sparkle in your eye when you talk about him."

Sienna's perception unleashed a mass of invisible butterflies in Emily's chest, which must have had an outward expression because Sienna clapped a hand over her mouth, stifling a laugh.

"You're smitten."

"I shouldn't be," Emily said, dropping down beside her.

"Why not?" There was an undefinable heaviness in her stare, as if everything depended on this answer.

It didn't make sense to Emily. "I don't know how to do flings. That's not who I am. But Patrick and I don't live anywhere near one another, so a fling is all it is. It's too early to know if what we feel is lasting, and I leave in a matter of days, so we'll never know." She folded her arms. "And I've got Will downstairs."

Sienna bit her lip, something flashing across her face.

"What's *that* look?" Emily asked.

"Uh... Man, I hate to get in the middle of things." She sighed.

Emily's skin turned cold. "You're already in the middle, so you'd better just come out with whatever *it* is."

Sienna's knee bounced. "You need to tell Patrick not to cook for us tonight."

"Nothing's open, and we don't have enough food for everyone. If he doesn't cook, we won't eat."

"You'd rather be hungry," Sienna said. "And the boys brought snacks. We can get through with whatever leftovers we have and the chips they brought."

"Why? What's going on?"

Uneasiness flooded Sienna's features, her chest rising and falling a little too quickly. "Let's just say that the celebration for my growing family might be a cover for something more. Tyson filled me in, and Will's planning something romantic for you—a big surprise gesture to show how sorry he is. That's why he came. My announcement was a happy distraction for something he'd already planned."

Emily frowned. "What?"

Sienna hung her head and groaned. "He didn't tell me what it was, but I think it's something grand."

"You're making me nervous," Emily said.

Sienna bit her lip. "You should be." She stood up and walked to the door. "I'm gonna go keep them busy, but I suggest you call Patrick right now and tell him we don't need dinner. You need to deal with Will and whatever this thing is without the added pressure of Patrick watching it all go down."

In a rush, Sienna exited the room, leaving Emily in a cloud of confusion.

TWENTY-FIVE

By evening, Emily had gotten ready undisturbed, but she hadn't really been able to come down after Sienna's news. She was showered, styled, and outfitted in a yellow sundress, something she'd packed to be summery, but wearing it tonight, she wanted to crawl into some sweats, and hide for the foreseeable future.

Emily looked at her reflection in the bathroom mirror. She appeared put together, but inside, she was a wreck. She'd tried to both call and text Patrick over the last couple of hours, but the cellular service was spotty again. What was she doing accepting his advances? She was letting him get a hold of her fragile emotions, knowing she'd have to deal with the aftermath when she got home. And now, her worlds were overlapping, creating more drama than she was ready to deal with.

There was a knock at the door. "It's Blair. May I come in?"

"Yep, it's open." Emily walked out of the en suite and into her room.

Blair came in cautiously. "You look so pretty," she said.

"Thanks." Emily brushed the front of her dress, smoothing it out. "Am I missing anything downstairs?"

Blair sat on the edge of the bed and grimaced. "Yeah... That's why I came up."

"What?" Emily asked, sitting down next to her. Did she really want to hear what Blair had to tell her? From the look on her face, she doubted it.

Blair leaned in. "Can I ask you a serious question?"

"Of course."

"How do you feel about Patrick? Sienna told me you're hitting it off."

Emily didn't want to get into this conversation because she didn't know herself how to feel about Patrick. It was probably better to nip it in the bud. "He's a nice guy. But I have to go back to my life."

Blair nodded.

"What's going on?" Emily asked, alarmed by the serious expression on Blair's face.

"Will has been making all of us guard the steps to let him know if you were coming down. He sent me to get you." She chewed on her lip. "And Patrick's here."

"Wait, 'guard the steps'—why?"

"He's been putting together this elaborate setup while Patrick has been cooking in the kitchen with a full view of it all. Sienna and Tyson tried to pull Will aside and talk some sense into him, and Rocko and I suggested he wait until you two were back home, but he refused to listen."

"What is he doing?"

"It's probably better for you to see for yourself." Blair got up and took her arm. She walked Emily over to the bedroom door and gestured down the hall.

At the top of the stairs, Emily peered down at silk-rose-petal-covered steps.

"What is this?" she whispered, her breath shallow.

But she didn't wait for an answer. She started down the stairs, her blood boiling. In his usual manner, Will was thinking entirely about himself. He'd selfishly pursued another woman, selfishly asked for his and Emily's home for his own purposes, and now, he was putting on this extravagant show—for who? Not her. He'd made it *sound* like all this was for her, but it wasn't. It was to save his own backside. He had realized he'd ruined what they had, and he was scared. Lanie wasn't who he expected, and he was going to be alone, so he'd come back with his tail between his legs.

The bottom of the steps wasn't any less infuriating. The trail continued into the living room. Emily rounded the corner to find Will, all spruced up, standing with a velvet box in his hands and the rest of her friends looking on with unease. That alone would've been enough to deal with. But the light rattle in the open kitchen drew her eye to Patrick, who was making dinner. His attention fluttered between her and Will as he fumbled with a piece of tin foil.

"What's going on?" Emily asked, turning back to Will.

Will loped toward her and took her hands, the velvet box wedged between her fingers and his. "I made a mess of things in a huge way," he said. "And there's no reason for you to take me back. But on the small chance that you might, I thought I'd try. I know we'd have a long way to go, and I'm willing to go to counseling—whatever I need to do. It took losing everything to realize how stupid I was. I love you, and I didn't fully appreciate how wonderful you are."

Emily stood on the precipice between her old life and her new one. A couple of weeks ago, she'd have fallen into Will's arms if he'd confessed like this, but now she didn't want to have anything to do with him. He'd wrecked her entire life and left her to pick up the pieces.

Will let go of her hands and opened the box to reveal an incredibly huge oval diamond surrounded by smaller diamonds cascading down the band. This new gem dwarfed her old one. She made eye contact with him for an explanation.

He grinned at her. "I sold a song. Let's just say that we don't have to worry about the bills for a while." He took the ring from the velvet cushion and held it out to her. "I know I can't buy you back, but I hope this shows my commitment. Let's start over. I want to date you again, take it slow." His face looked as if it wanted to crumple with emotion, but he held it together. For her or for himself?

A clatter in the kitchen cut through the moment. She turned, but Patrick had bent over, collecting whatever he'd dropped. A small celebratory cake sat on the counter. They certainly wouldn't be celebrating this. She prayed Patrick hadn't spent too long making it, given all his work at the restaurant that day.

Emily's hands trembled, and she was lightheaded, struggling to get a breath. The room felt like as if it was closing in on her, her vision tunneling. She looked over at Patrick again, but her vision was blurred.

She needed to get out of there.

"I want to be alone."

She turned around, ran out of the room, up the stairs, and sat on her bed. Gasping, she hung her head between her knees to regain her composure, but she only felt worse. She lay back on her bed, struggling to breathe. Only then did the tears slide down her temples. For what, she wasn't sure—the loss of who she was, the absolute mortification she'd just experienced, or the absolute fear she had knowing, once and for all, that she did not want to be with Will.

After some time, the modern iron chandelier in the

vaulted ceiling slowly came into focus through her tears. Her mind was a muddle. Everyone else had benefited from being here, but she'd only managed to make things worse by falling head over heels for a guy she'd never see again. And Patrick had just watched that entire exchange. Things would certainly be awkward now.

But that niggling thought came back with a vengeance: Perhaps it was for the best. Maybe this was meant to happen to keep her from falling too hard for this mysterious stranger. "Stranger" was the wrong word for him, though. He already felt like a friend, someone she got excited to see.

A knock at the door drew her attention.

"It's Will. Can I come in?"

She rolled onto her side and wiped her eyes. "I need some time," she said.

The silence on the other side of the door was heavy.

"Okay," he finally said. "Want me to send Sienna or Blair up?"

"No." She sniffled. The act of talking was too much in her state.

As Will's footsteps faded, she pulled up the covers around her and buried her head in her pillow.

The next thing she knew, she'd drifted off, her mind weary from all the back-and-forth. She wasn't sure how long she'd been asleep by the time she heard the second knock.

"Yes?" Emily croaked.

"May I come in?" a deep voice said from the other side of the door.

Emily sat up and dragged her fingers under her eyes. "Yeah."

The door opened, and Patrick took a tentative step inside the room. "Everyone's out at the pool," he said. "I've just finished packing my things. I can heat you up some dinner before I go."

"Thank you. I'm not hungry," she said, forcing a smile.

He gestured toward the bed. "May I?"

She nodded, and he sat on the edge, the mattress dipping with his weight.

He chewed on his lip and then, on an inhale, said, "Look, I didn't mean to—"

"I know," she jumped in, guessing what he was about to say.

His blue eyes found hers. "You have a lot to deal with. I don't want to make things more difficult. I can drop off cooked food each evening until you leave, so I don't get in the middle of things."

"You don't have to do that. I'm a big girl. I can handle this."

He leaned on his knees. "Had I known your situation with your ex wasn't resolved, I wouldn't have been so forward. I'm sorry."

She put a hand on his bicep. "It is resolved."

"I don't think it is. I think it feels like it is." Patrick stood up, and her hand dropped to the bed. He looked at her, something lingering on his lips.

His chest rising and falling steadily, he finally said, "I've got enough guilt without adding home-wrecker to the mix. I think it might be better to keep my distance." Then those eyes, heavy with thoughts, landed on her. "It would make it easier for you...and for me." With that, he turned and left her alone.

She wanted to stop him, to bury her head in his strong chest, but she knew better. He was right. Leaving would be hard enough. Better to make a clean break now before they got any deeper.

TWENTY-SIX

Emily wasn't sure when she'd fallen asleep for good. But she'd been out all night, the mental exhaustion pushing her into a deep sleep. She hadn't left her room the rest of the evening. As far as she knew, Will hadn't tried to come in again, nor had Sienna or Blair. She rolled over to see the slip of morning light peeking above the horizon and tried to decide if the heavy night's sleep had given her any better perspective, but she was still just as confused.

She pushed the covers off her legs and went into the bathroom. Smudges of makeup streaked her face, her sundress was wrinkled from sleeping in it all night, and her hair was knotted on one side. She stared at her unsightly reflection. With no clear answers still, she turned on the hot water in the shower, letting the steam fill the room.

She slipped off the sundress she'd never changed out of and stepped under the stream. As she lathered her hair with shampoo, her life with Will flashed before her like a slideshow. She recalled their better times together. He'd taken her out for a nice dinner in Nashville for Valentine's Day with Blair and Rocko, and they'd laughed so hard at something she couldn't remember now that she'd almost spit her wine all over the table.

The next slide was Rocko—a tall, broad, imposing man—looking on last night with quiet awkwardness, when he used to make her laugh whenever she and Will double-dated with him and Blair. Tyson hadn't been much better. He kept shifting, full of discomfort as Sienna squeezed his hand. Wanting to get their faces out of her mind, she rewound the clock, attempting to focus on better times.

She dipped her head under the water. The shampoo slid down her back as she ran her hands through the strands, the memories coming relentlessly.

Then she remembered when she and Will had gone out to a fancy restaurant because her twenty-sixth birthday had been on a Tuesday and, with their busy schedules, he'd forgotten, so he'd made it up to her the following Saturday.

As she applied conditioner, little things she hadn't picked up on before slowly came back to her. Like the Christmas she'd really wanted a charm bracelet. Nothing fancy, but she'd had her eye on it. She'd hinted like crazy, showing him the silver charms—a coffee mug, a little stack of books, and a tiny cross—and when the holiday came, he'd given her a couple new sweaters instead, confessing that he hadn't known what to get her.

And when she'd had presentations at the school board office a couple of times, he'd never asked how they went, even though she'd always asked him how his songwriting sessions had gone. She'd teased him—something about the creative brain and how he forgot things. But today, those little moments held more weight for her. Now they seemed like quiet disconnections that had eventually led to his final betrayal.

But her conversation with Patrick last night whispered to her:

"It is resolved."

"I don't think it is. I think it feels like it is."

Will had never been the type to spend all that money on a fancy ring. So why now? In her anger and pain, had she misread his attempt to woo her last night? Had something changed in him? Would he be a better man? Surely a big ring didn't ensure that he'd be more attentive, and she'd never wanted anything flashy. But was the gesture his way of saying he was ready to put her first? And even if it was, did she want the new-and-improved Will?

Emily finished her shower, toweled off, and got dressed, trying to squelch the panic that had risen. She'd wanted to divide her old life and her new one into nice, neat sides, but this morning, the two sides were interwoven and tangled, and she couldn't unwind them. She wasn't a new person as she'd thought, but rather a bit of the old and the new. And Patrick had been able to see that before she had. She tried to push it all out of her mind as she applied lotion and combed out her wet hair.

Her stomach rumbled. Having skipped dinner, she was definitely in need of sustenance.

Quietly, she opened the door and padded downstairs. She was the only one up. An orange glow hovered over the horizon through the kitchen window as she loaded the coffee pot and clicked it on. White light illuminated the dim kitchen when she opened the wide stainless-steel fridge to assess her breakfast options. She pulled out the carton of eggs and then dug around in the cabinets until she found a pan, spatula, and dishes to cook with.

With a pop of the gas stove, she lit the pilot light and set the pan on the burner to warm. The coffee pot gurgled behind her. She cracked two eggs into a bowl and whisked them with a fork. They hissed as she poured them into the pan. She turned down the heat, then poured herself a cup of coffee.

Emily stood barefoot on the cool tile, scrambling the eggs. There had been a time when mornings like this were part of her rhythm. She'd regularly asked Will to come over for breakfast before he went off to write. And she'd made breakfast according to his preferences, waiting to cook until he'd arrived at her apartment, never considering his silence while she prepared their food as he scrolled his phone, or the messes he never helped clean up, that she'd never mentioned, chalking it up to his mind being full of creative ideas. Then, he'd brush her cheek with a kiss and hurry off. But now, in this unfamiliar kitchen, with its fancy appliances and chef-grade tools, the morning was entirely hers. She didn't need anyone's approval to have eggs, to fill her coffee mug first. Will's state hadn't even occurred to her, even though he was right upstairs.

While she struggled to completely tease out the new version of herself, a different inner growth had been discreet and gone unnoticed, like something unfolding on its own schedule, only revealing itself this morning. As she continued to scramble the eggs, she realized she didn't *have* to worry about Will, Patrick, or anyone else. And she recognized a brand-new feeling of belonging—to herself. Her tether to her old expectations—her timeline for getting married and having kids—didn't matter anymore. And it was freeing.

She turned off the stove, plated her eggs, and took her coffee to the table. The warm, nutty flavor of the coffee soothed her as she sat with her hands around her mug looking out at the view of the Gulf. Seagulls dipped into the water as the orange sky turned pink before the electric-blue sky began to emerge.

"Hey." Blair's voice sailed over to her.

Emily set down her coffee. "Hi."

Watching Blair walk around with her phone again was a welcome sight. She'd been doing that more and more lately, and it was good to see her getting back into the swing of things.

"How are you?" Blair asked.

"Decent."

Blair offered a smile that looked like relief and moved to the coffee maker. "You sleep okay?"

"Despite the drama, like a rock. I can't believe I missed all the action last night. What did you all do after dinner?"

Blair poured a mug of coffee and came over to the table, setting her phone down beside her. "Well, we went out to the pool for a while and talked about how long the guys wanted to stay at the beach—I think they might stay through today and leave tomorrow. But the whole time the atmosphere was kind of weird." She leaned in and whispered, "Will had to clean up all the rose petals, and while he tried to participate in conversations, I can guess he was embarrassed by how things went. He hung around for a little bit and then went upstairs."

"He can't expect me to fall right back into our old life," Emily said, shaking her head.

"When he did talk, he asked a lot of questions about Patrick."

"I'm a grown—*single*—woman. I can do what I like." She didn't have to tell Blair that, but defensiveness swelled anyway.

Blair nodded in encouragement. "When he went to bed, Rocko and I hung out with Tyson and Sienna for an hour or so. It was clear we all wanted to discuss what had happened, but no one was going to with both of you upstairs to possibly overhear." She ran her teeth along her bottom lip as if deliberating something.

Emily offered a questioning look.

"Before Will went to bed, we heard him crying in the bathroom. He seems to really be struggling with this."

Unsure of how to respond, Emily busied herself with her coffee mug, taking a long, slow drink. She could go back to her regular life. Will would probably be incredible...for a while. But would things go back to the way they were? And if she did go back, would she be able to manage her wild thoughts every time he canceled their plans on short notice or decided to go to the gym? But then again, should she just give up on everything she'd built with him if he was truly sorry for what he'd done? The tangled sides of her were fumbling for a clear answer.

"What's going on in that head of yours?" Blair asked.

Emily set down her coffee and rubbed her forehead. "I don't even know."

"Wanna change the subject?"

"Please."

Blair picked up her phone. "Well... Rocko and I had a heart-to-heart last night, and I finally relaxed, and we..." Her eyebrows bobbed.

Emily let go of the other things she'd been thinking about and focused on her friend. "Oh, that's wonderful. You feel okay?"

"Yeah. I think I needed time, and then we were here, away from our real lives, no service on our phones, completely set apart from the world. It was just the two of us, and it was so nice."

"I'm thrilled for you two."

"Thanks," Blair said, her chest rising blissfully. She practically glowed. "I can't believe it. Sienna finally told Tyson they're expecting, and the same night, Rocko and I were able to connect like we used to. Maybe there's something magical here." She waved an arm toward the view.

Emily wanted to offer a cute comment to include herself in that magic, but when it came to The Broken Hearts Beach Club, she was the final surviving member, still racked with indecision and confusion.

"Maybe," she said, not wanting to get back into it.

"And..." Blair swiped open an app and turned her phone around. "I posted."

On the screen was a photo of all of them from behind, sitting together in their sundresses on the beach.

Emily reached out and took the phone to read the caption.

Introducing The Broken Hearts Beach Club, a small association with only one entry requirement: A shattered heart and an incredible sense of humor.

One of us lost a baby.
One of us is changing her perspective.
One of us is learning to live on her own terms.

But somehow, here we are! Sunburned, salty, and still managing to laugh. Grief brought us together, and storms ripped through us, but this spot is where we remembered that healing takes time, open hearts, and sandy feet. I'm doing okay. And I promise to post more soon.

#BrokenHeartsBeachClub #Grief #Healing #Salty-
AndStrong

Emily raised her eyebrows at the responses. "Twenty-
one thousand likes, 5,684 comments, and 432 shares? I'd
say your first step back into social media was a success." She
handed the phone to Blair. "Congratulations on a
wonderful returning post. How do you feel?"

"I feel amazing. You know, talking to Julia really
changed things for me."

Immediately, Emily's mind went back to her time with
Patrick on the sofa at Julia's that stormy night. She pushed
the thought away, not knowing what to do with the flutter in
her chest.

"I wish we could repay her for her kindness somehow,"
Emily said. "A gift seems too small for what she did. But I
don't know what would be a good gesture."

"Maybe we could offer to have them all come to Nashville sometime," Blair suggested.

"Maybe..." Her pulse quickened at the idea of Patrick
showing up on her turf.

"Good morning." Will's voice floated over to them.

It felt out of place.

He opened a few cabinets, found a mug, and poured
himself a cup of coffee. "Mind if I join you two?" he asked.

Emily shrugged, a pinch forming immediately in her
shoulder. She rubbed it, unsuccessfully managing the
tweak, and peered out the window.

Will took a seat next to her and nodded good morning to
Blair, who offered an uncomfortable smile in response.
Blair, too, had lost something in all this. She and Rocko had
been their best friends, and Will had ruined that as well. It

had to be weird for Blair to try to be kind to Will while also supporting Emily.

"I've been up for a while," he said. "I was looking online to see if anything was open. The boardwalk has been cleared for the public. I thought maybe we could all take a walk later."

"Sure," Emily said, completely disconnected.

In all honesty, she needed some fresh air. Sitting with Will felt oddly suffocating. With him next to her, she waffled between feeling sorry for herself and wondering if she was the crazy one for not accepting his apology and at least trying to move forward. A part of her felt bad for him. He seemed to be trying. But *he* was the one who'd put himself in this position. His actions had caused irrevocable changes, and she didn't know if they could ever be what they were again. But could they be something new?

Maybe it would be worth working through her feelings and spending some time with him to see if she could get a handle on things.

TWENTY-SEVEN

"Ready?" Sienna said, gathering everyone and ushering them outside the house so she could lock up.

Blair hooked her arm with Rocko's and gave him a kiss on the cheek. Tyson followed Sienna outside, telling her something in her ear that made her laugh. Emily went down the staircase and stood self-consciously next to Will. Sienna secured the house, and they all made their way off the pristine property to the boardwalk entrance down the road.

The air was heavy with salt and the scent of damp earth. The path to the boardwalk still bore the beating from the wind and water. Emily treaded carefully over scattered palm fronds and clumps of seaweed that had made it too far inland for the tide to return them to the Gulf. Will tried to help her, but—instinctively—she took a step away from him to manage on her own.

Some beachside cottages down the road still had boarded up windows, some with handwritten signs on them reading "Made it through another one!" or "Back soon." Along the dunes, broken fencing leaned at haphazard angles, whole sections partially swallowed by sand, while crews pounded in new slats.

They all stepped onto the walk that led around the edge of the town, paralleling the water. The boardwalk itself— that Emily had seen humming with music, vacationers, and the buzz of excitement when they'd first arrived—was quieter now, punctuated only by the creak of loose planks and the occasional hammer from someone doing repairs down the road. A few vendors had reopened their shops with limited offerings. Coolers were propped open with free water bottles. And yet, despite the mess, something about the light felt softer, as if the storm had rinsed it all clean. Emily couldn't help but draw a parallel between her time here and how she, too, felt washed, changed in some way.

Rocko turned around and walked backward, facing the group, casting his wide shadow onto the wood in front of them. "Was the storm terrifying this close to the shore?"

"We were cocooned inland," Blair replied, shielding her eyes to view two seagulls as they squawked overhead. "Luckily, we didn't have to endure too much."

"Remember that storm where we were stuck in the car?" Will asked Emily. "We were locked out, and we had to wait until it passed because the rain was coming down so hard we couldn't see to drive anywhere?"

A pang of nostalgia overtook her. They were so young then. Sitting in that car with him, she'd had no idea what heartbreak he'd bring her.

"Yeah," she replied. She turned into the wind, facing the Gulf to fight the prick of tears that had come out of nowhere, the last remnants of her grief still emptying out. The waves were calm now, barely lapping the shore.

They'd laughed until their sides hurt in the car that

night, as the rain pelted down. Soaking wet and naïve, they'd had their whole lives ahead of them. Now, as she walked next to Will, she didn't feel the lightness of the memory. He was trying to draw connections to better times, but his actions fell flat. The memory didn't hit the same way. It felt as if something was missing between them that she couldn't get back.

"I love who we were," she said, verbalizing the thought. "I don't think we're who we used to be anymore, though."

While she didn't have herself completely figured out, something was becoming increasingly clear in the mixture of emotions she'd been feeling: Will belonged to a version of herself that no longer existed entirely, someone she wasn't sure she could ever be again. And while the old her remained, it was now clear that it had been diluted by her new experiences. She wasn't the same person anymore.

He didn't talk after that. Sienna and Tyson filled the silence with chatter about the best vacation investment homes and how, if they ever took the plunge, they'd have to stormproof their investment, and Rocko and Blair stopped along the beach to build a sandcastle. The whole time, Will was contemplative, quiet. Emily didn't try to facilitate conversation. Truly, she didn't know what to say to him anymore.

They continued walking, and in the distance, the whine of a lone drill caught her attention. A boat slip was being repaired. Emily squinted at the guy working, his build familiar. As they got closer, she realized it was Patrick, sprawled across the top, shirtless, now pounding in something at an odd incline. Something stirred in her. She quickly assessed her companions, but no one had noticed him. He didn't stand out for them the way he did for her.

"Hey, look. The ice-cream shop is open," Sienna said. "We should get some to eat on the way back."

The others agreed.

They stopped outside the door to view the menus, all of them focused on the task at hand, but Emily was in her own world with Patrick in her peripheral vision. In this collection of couples, she didn't belong anymore. She was still their friend, but no longer able to pair off seamlessly. She felt out of place. Almost as if she were in the *wrong* place. She'd rather be over there, talking to Patrick.

Will held the door open, and they filed into the tiny space. They all got in line, Emily hanging back near the door, mindlessly taking each step, her attention elsewhere. Rocko, Tyson, and Will went up to the counter, Sienna following behind, and then Blair.

"I think I'm going to stay out for a while," Emily said to Blair.

Blair's brows pulled together and her lips parted to say something, but Emily cut her off.

"I'll catch up," she whispered. Then she slipped out the door once more, before anyone could protest.

She paced quickly down the boardwalk until she was out of view of the shop. Then she slowed, taking in the sunshine and generally enjoying shedding the burden of Will. She walked over to Patrick. "Whatcha doing?" she called up.

He stopped pounding and peered down at her, that crooked grin surfacing, sending a fizzle of excitement through her.

"Oh, just, you know, hanging around."

"So this is your idea of that? Manual labor and possible tetanus?"

Stormy was tied on a long leash in the shade. Her attention still on Patrick, Emily went over to the dog and rubbed his head, his tail beating the wooden boardwalk relentlessly, nearly knocking over his water bowl.

Patrick grinned without looking up. "Some people tan. I prefer hauling soaked planks to broken-down boat slips and praying I don't fall in while I'm fixing them."

"Very heroic of you. With the cute dog, it looks more like a shirtless calendar shoot."

His eyebrows raised suggestively and he chuckled.

"You getting any real work done or just working on your tan?"

Patrick paused and wiped beads of sweat off his forehead. "If all I'm doing is tanning, are you volunteering to take the pictures, or just critiquing my nail placement?" he shot back.

"Oh, definitely critiquing. I give you an A-plus for effort." She laughed.

"That teacher side of you coming out?" He gripped the side of the boat slip's roof and swung down to stand in front of her.

Stormy's entire hind end swung back and forth when Patrick came over. He bent down and played with the puppy, then refilled his water bowl with a cold bottle from his cooler. He offered her one, but she declined. Then he sunk his hand in the ice and got himself one, uncapping it and pouring it down his throat. His bare chest glistened in the sun, perspiration trailing down his bicep over his tattoo. Emily swallowed and tried to still her pattering heart.

He set the bottle down and took her left hand, inspecting it. "No ring today?"

She shook her head. "Definitely not."

He looked surprised, that now-familiar interest flooding his face.

"You said maybe I just *thought* things were resolved, but it only took me a night to realize that while things are messy, I've moved beyond it. I want better. And to get better, there's no way I'm going back to my old life."

His blue eyes searched her face, thoughtful. He nodded toward a nearby surf shop. "Let's get out of the heat. Follow me."

Inside, the shop was organized; colorful surfboards, skimboards, and paddleboards in varying sizes lined the walls.

"Remember the guy with me at the bar that night after you and I first met—Mark? This is his shop. He lives upstairs, but he evacuated before the storm and went to South Carolina to stay with his mom. I told him I'd take a look to see if there was any damage. He gets back tomorrow, so I thought I'd be nice and fix a few loose boards on his boat slip for him." He pulled a stool from behind the register and offered it to her. "Just for you."

"I'll bet you give all the vacationing girls a stool," she teased.

He chuckled quietly. "All one of them."

"We're headed back home in a couple of days," she said.

He didn't respond. Instead, he lifted another stool over his head, walked around the counter, set it down next to hers, and took a seat.

Her phone pinged with a text.

"Sienna's wondering where I am. I'll let her know that I'll find my own way back." She fired off a quick response that she'd found Patrick and she'd meet everyone at the house in a little bit. Then she turned off the ringer and slid the phone into her pocket.

"Any big plans when you get home to Nashville?" he asked, his words measured, careful.

"I don't have any plans at all. In fact, I have no idea what I'll do when I get back. I don't return to work until the end of August."

"I'm sure you'll have a lot to do."

"I have to look for an apartment and call everyone to cancel all the wedding plans. Then I'll need to move my things..." She rubbed the pinch in her shoulder that had returned, wishing she didn't have to leave so soon. "The owner of the beach house is gone all summer. Maybe Sienna would let me stay a few extra weeks until I've figured out my game plan."

There was a notable spark of interest in his look. "I'd make sure you were fed," he said. "The owner's paid up with me through September."

"I was only kidding. I couldn't stay," she said with a laugh. "I rode with Sienna. How would I get home? It's quite a walk back to Nashville."

His features fell, and he nodded. "I'd drive you to the airport if someone could pick you up in Nashville."

She hadn't planned to stay, but all of a sudden, not going home sounded like the best idea she'd had since her troubles had begun.

"I'd love nothing more than to have some quiet time to myself where no one else would bother me, so I could really sort through my life without emotional distractions. But I have the mess of a breakup to deal with. If I want to get on with my life, I need to get back, sell that house, and take care of my wedding cancellations." *If only...*

The surf shop was quiet. Outside, gulls called lazily to each other at the shore, and the Gulf babbled as if it was still catching its breath after the storm.

Emily ran her fingers along the edge of a longboard leaning against the wall next to her, admiring its bright design. "You ever think about how many waves this board will see?" she asked, almost to herself.

He eyed it, clearly not understanding her change in direction.

She smiled faintly, then let her hand drop. "It feels like everything has a story. Life is full of stories, isn't it?" She took in his honest, attentive expression. Unfortunately, she wouldn't get to know the ending of this particular story.

Patrick didn't say anything at first. Just watched her.

"You've had a massive change in a short amount of time," he finally said.

She leaned back against the wall. "There's a lot on my mind."

"I can imagine."

"Will isn't one of the things anymore, though," she said softly.

The air between them thickened with his name. Because, regardless of her feelings for Will, she wasn't in a position to move forward with anything other than her own life.

Outside, the wind blew, tinkling a wind chime, both of them quietly digesting the fact that this was the end.

"I keep trying to convince myself this is just a vacation," she said. "A weird, tropical-storm-interrupted vacation. And you're part of it. The sunsets, the weather, the way you looked at me when we were stuck in Julia's living room..." She trailed off and shook her head. "It's like my life paused, and this whole experience exists in a bubble." She got up and toyed with the edge of the surfboard.

"And the bubble's about to pop."

She glanced up at him. "Yeah."

He hopped off the stool, walking a few steps closer. Not too close. Just enough.

"I don't want to make promises I can't keep," he said. "And I don't want you to feel like this is something you have to walk away from just because a ride home says so."

She laughed softly, but there was tension in it. "You make this sound easy."

"I know it's not," he said. "But I also know that feelings don't just disappear when the location changes."

She looked at him then, her pulse quickening. His bare chest, a slight shadow beneath his eyes from nights spent without enough sleep during and after the storm.

"I didn't plan on you," she said.

They stood in the hush of the shop, the surfboards silent witnesses, the place still humming with an unexpected, raw energy—and maybe, the beginning of something else.

She stepped forward, slowly. "Whatever this is doesn't have to be forever," she said, challenging him, more to protect her heart. "It was good while it was." She wasn't sure yet what the two of them were, and she dared not put any pressure on him. The last thing she wanted was for him to pursue something from another state longer than he wanted to, out of duty, because he'd made her a promise today.

"But it doesn't have to be nothing either," he said, yearning on his face.

And this time, she didn't look away. She stared into his eyes, wanting to stay there forever.

"YOU DECIDED TO JUST DITCH US?" Will asked when Emily walked through the door of the beach house.

"I took a walk."

"I went looking for you. I couldn't find you. Where did you walk to?"

She threw her hands in the air, flustered. "Nowhere specific." He wasn't in a position to require a rundown of her every whereabouts just because *he'd* decided to try to make things work. She was tired of living *his* life, following *his* dreams, doing what *he* wanted. The truth was that *before* she'd thought, eventually, if she did, he'd let her have her time to shine, but she was wondering if that would have ever been the case.

Then it occurred to her that the others were outside in the pool, but he'd been in the house when she came in.

"Why are you inside, fully dressed?" she asked.

He pouted. "I didn't feel much like hanging out."

"What did you expect? To come here, unannounced, after turning my life upside down, woo me with a flashy ring, and I'd fall into your arms?"

"Em, I'm trying here. What can I do?"

"I don't think there's anything you *can* do."

"So even with all we've been through together, and the fact that I'm willing to work at this, you're giving up?"

"I'm not giving up," she said, folding her arms. "I'm realizing who I want to be and I'm making a choice about my future."

His forehead creased. "You're different."

She dropped her arms, her shoulders slouching. "Look, you decided you wanted something else, whether you meant for things to go that far or not. You wanted the attention of another woman—however briefly. And after I had time to digest that fact, I realized that maybe you were right —you and I were too young, too inexperienced for the long haul."

"But many people are inexperienced when they begin

their lives together. Are you saying none of them should be together?"

"That's not what I'm saying at all. I'm saying that at a time when we should've been leaning on one another to figure out life, you chose to lean on someone else. And for better or worse, your actions clicked a switch for me, and now, I can't go back. You're right. I've changed. I was so busy playing it safe that I didn't consider whether playing it safe was actually good for me."

"So I've lost you?"

"I don't know if either of us ever had one another to begin with."

He nodded, frowning in contemplation.

The old her would've been worried at this moment, fearful without a plan. But standing opposite Will, she felt free.

TWENTY-EIGHT

Emily had been hiding out in her room all morning. Instead of facing everyone, she'd decided to email Martha Rogers, her school principal, to ask about her contract. It was too late in the year—two months before school started—to try to get a teaching job in another location, so she wasn't really sure why she was emailing, but she wanted to know if, legally, she could get out of it.

Why? She had no idea. She had bills to pay, and she had to be able to afford rent for her apartment, provided it was still available. She still hadn't renewed her lease. But a tiny spark of hope inside her wondered if, perhaps, she looked for jobs in Florida, one would magically become available and she'd live happily ever after.

But then the rational side of her reminded her that she hadn't known Patrick long enough to make that kind of move. Giving up her whole life, leaving her two best friends, and moving to an entirely different state was a risky move for someone she'd met on vacation.

She kept the message to Martha open-ended and left her cell phone number in case Martha would rather call.

But her phone never rang, so Emily finally got out of bed, made herself presentable, and then went downstairs.

The house was quiet. Blair and Sienna were sitting in the living room. Blair sinking her spoon into a bowl of cereal.

Emily sat down in a chair near the window. "Where are the guys?"

"They went home," Blair said.

Alarm shot through Emily. Had her issues with Will been too uncomfortable to endure? "Why?"

"We told them to go," Sienna said.

"But they had more time to hang out. We could've all left together."

Sienna leaned forward, her forearms on her knees, and clasped her hands. "Will let us in on the details of your conversation last night."

"I told Rocko privately that they shouldn't have ambushed you by showing up with Will unannounced. They should've let Will figure things out on his own," Blair said. "Rocko agreed, and I suggested that maybe they should go home and give us girls one last day together so you can end your trip on a good note."

"I feel bad," Emily said.

"We'll see them when we get back. But with the storm, we never really had a chance to unwind, just us girls. And we still have one more broken heart to mend. How can we give you a chance to do that with Will lurking around?" Sienna pointed spiritedly at Emily.

"Thank you," Emily said.

"Of course." Sienna stood up. "You know what I was thinking?"

Emily and Blair looked over at her.

"The town is still recovering from the storm, so we're

pretty much stuck in this gorgeous mansion. Why don't we ask Julia, Winston, and Patrick over as a thank-you for their hospitality? We could grill some hot dogs or something, swim, and play with Winston. Maybe he could bring his dog."

"That sounds like a great idea," Blair said.

Emily agreed, happiness already bubbling up at the thought of seeing Patrick again.

"Text him," Blair suggested.

Emily grabbed a cup of coffee and a piece of toast, then went upstairs and got her phone. When she did, she realized she'd missed Martha's call and checked the message. Of course, Martha's voice was lively and full of promise for the school year ahead. Emily decided to call her back right away.

Martha answered with her principal's phone greeting.

"Hi, Martha, it's Emily. I'm glad I got you."

"Great to hear from you. How's your summer so far?" she asked, her voice chipper down the line.

"It's...interesting." She hemmed and hawed, unsure what she really wanted to ask. But in the silence, she very quickly came to the conclusion it wasn't that she didn't know *what* to ask, but rather what she'd do if she did ask it.

"So, what's up?" Martha's unsuspecting voice floated into her ear.

Emily took a steadying breath. "I was wondering..." She swallowed. Was she really going to ask this? She reminded herself that if she got out of her contract, she had no work lined up, and she wouldn't have Will to keep her afloat if she were unemployed. "I was wondering if we had any professional development days this summer? I didn't see any on the calendar before August."

"I thought you all would like the break," Martha said

with a laugh. "But I admire your dedication. Your contract hours don't start until August. Now go enjoy your summer."

"Okay, thanks." Emily hung up, her heart pounding. Was she having some sort of early midlife crisis? She'd actually considered walking away from a perfectly good job with benefits and regular paychecks. And why? Because she'd hung out with a handsome guy for a few days at the beach? What was she thinking? On paper, it made no sense, but she couldn't deny what her heart was telling her.

"What did he say?" Blair called up the stairs.

"Oh, sorry!" Emily opened the door. "I had another call. I'm texting him now."

She sat on the edge of the bed, chewing the inside of her lip as her toast and coffee got cold. Maybe she shouldn't text Patrick. She'd only fall harder for him if they spent time together, and look at where that had gotten her—nearly ready to quit her job. They lived over seven hours apart.

Emily dropped her phone onto her bed, picked up her uneaten breakfast, and went downstairs. Sienna and Blair watched her expectantly.

"I was going to text Patrick," Emily said, dropping her dishes on the island and then plopping down on the sofa, "but it occurred to me that the whole reason the guys went home was so we could have the girls' time we never got. Let's spend the day together."

Sienna clapped her hands and stood up, the flowy pink, floral-printed kimono she wore over her tank top billowing out behind her. "That's a great idea. Let's make beachy drinks and have a swim in the Gulf."

Blair clutched her phone. "My notifications are blowing up right now. People are waiting for content. I could definitely do with some photos of the house and the fun we get into."

"Perfect," Emily said, deciding then and there that she needed to spend her time healing instead of swooning over someone she'd never see again, no matter how much she wanted to.

They put on their swimsuits, made coconut-rum lemonades (non-alcoholic for Sienna), and walked through the powdery sand down to the water. The surf gurgled over Emily's painted toes while she sipped her drink. The alcohol warmed her throat, and the sun beat down on her bare shoulders, reminding her of how she'd felt when they'd first arrived.

Blair videoed her feet as she kicked the water, splashing white suds.

Sienna protectively placed her hands on her belly. Blair turned the camera toward Sienna's hands and snapped a shot.

"The idea of a baby feels so much more natural after telling Tyson," Sienna said before turning toward the wind, her long hair blowing out behind her. "I still don't know if I'll be any good at being a mother, but I'm getting excited to try."

"You'll be amazing. I'm sure of it," Emily said. Her friends' lives seemed to have gotten back on track easily, and yet she was still struggling. "So much has happened since we got here," she said, taking a step and submerging her feet and ankles in the cool current.

"It's incredible, isn't it?" Sienna said, shielding her eyes toward the view of a seagull on the horizon. She waded in deeper with tiny shrieks as the water reached her thighs, then her hips, and her waist.

"It is." Emily studied the surf, pensive.

Blair went back up the sand and dropped her phone into her beach bag. "I know what you need," she called to

Emily. Then, at full speed, she ran toward her, grabbing her arm as she splashed past, dragging her into the cold water.

"Agh, it's freezing!" Emily protested, falling backward and trying to get her footing.

With a splash, she was in the water, pawing at a laughing Blair.

"You're too serious," Blair said, pushing her wet hair away from her face. "You know what hit me the other day?" She raised her hands in the air and did a spin. "Look around. We made it through a tropical storm. And you know what? The sun is shining again. The world keeps going no matter what happens to us. If the sun can shine after a storm, so can we!" She pushed herself toward Emily and gave her a playful splash.

Sienna swam over to them. "She has a point." She lay back in the water, floating, and closed her eyes.

"You're so right," Emily said. She addressed Blair. "How did you manage at your lowest? How did you get to the other side?"

Blair moved her arms in a breaststroke through the ripples of the calm Gulf to reach Emily. "I managed by having you and Sienna. And we're going to get you to the other side too."

Fondness for her friends bubbled up. Until that moment, Emily hadn't really realized what being there for Blair had done. And now on the other end, as a recipient of that support, she knew she couldn't get through her own trials without them.

———

THEY'D FLOATED on the water for so long that Emily still felt the swish-swashing of the tide while she was in the shower. She took her time, lathering every inch of her skin and adding in extra conditioner, before she dried her hair, applied her peach lotion, and put on a light sundress. Her cheeks were pink from spending all day in the sun, so she only needed some moisturizer and lip gloss. This evening, she was getting spruced up for herself. They were leaving tomorrow, so she was ready to make the most of her last evening there.

She, Sienna, and Blair had spent the whole afternoon talking and planning out their final night together. Sienna suggested turning on the lights around the pool, lighting candles, and maybe playing a game or two of cards, since she'd bought them a deck that they'd yet to use. Blair had run out to the market that had reopened and bought fixings for piña coladas. And they were sure Patrick would show up with something delicious to eat.

That was what had been on Emily's mind most of the afternoon. She was going to have to tell him goodbye tonight.

It shouldn't be a problem, she'd told herself.

So why was this tug in her heart so strong?

TWENTY-NINE

Emily had realized that their idea to have Julia, Winston, and Stormy come over with Patrick was a good one. She texted Patrick to suggest it and, since it was a workday, asked him not to worry about dinner—maybe they could grill hot dogs or something. It would be good to see Winston and Julia again before she left, and having them there would ensure that she and Patrick weren't on their own. Because if they were left alone, and he had a chance to sway her with those blue eyes of his, she wasn't sure she'd be strong enough to resist.

Now, only minutes from their arrival, the anticipation of seeing Patrick bubbled up, mixed with the dread of having to return to her life back in Nashville. But when the doorbell chimed, eagerness won over, and Emily was the first to offer to let him in.

"Emily!" Winston wrapped his little arms around her waist as Stormy slipped past them into the house.

"Hi! Sorry, I'll get the dog." Julia anxiously rushed in after Stormy. "You can't run through the mansion..." she called out.

Winston dropped his arms. "I'll help!" He ran after his mom.

Patrick stood opposite Emily in the doorway. "Hi," he said with a chuckle, the weight of thoughts behind that single word.

"Hi," she returned.

A buzz of electricity shot between them.

"I didn't have hot dogs, so I'm making pizzas. Prosciutto and fig for the grown-ups, and cheese for Winston."

"Sounds fancy for us, given that we thought we were having hot dogs. We'd have been fine with cheese," she said.

"I'm trying to impress you with my ability to provide a culinary feast on the fly," he teased.

"I think you've achieved that already." She ushered him inside.

"You saying I've impressed you?"

She nodded playfully, the ache in her heart already forming. The night was just beginning, and she already didn't want it to end.

"After a day's work, you didn't need to do all that," she said. "How's the restaurant?"

"It's good, but busy. I've been choosing tile patterns with the crew doing the kitchen and bathrooms, I had three interviews with potential waitstaff, and I had a remote PR meeting that had been postponed due to the storm. I can't wait until we open next year so promotion doesn't fall entirely on my shoulders. It's not really my thing."

"It's tough being so talented." She winked at him, giving him a chuckle.

When they got to the kitchen, Sienna and Blair were on the floor with Julia and Winston—all of them working to keep Stormy's attention.

Julia stood up. "We're going to take Stormy to the

beach to run. He loves chasing the waves. Then he'll be exhausted by the time the pizza's ready, and we can all eat in peace."

"We'll go with you," Blair suggested, grabbing her phone. Sienna followed them out.

They hadn't been there five minutes, and Emily had already found herself alone with Patrick.

"Want to help?" he asked.

The memory of the last time she'd helped him floated into her mind. "Sure." She washed her hands and dried them on a towel. She didn't want to think about how this would be the last time she'd have an opportunity to be with him like this.

"Could you grab that container?" he asked.

She opened the glass dish to reveal a ball of pizza dough, while Patrick sprinkled the counter with flour.

He reached out to her, and she handed him the wad of dough, gritting her teeth at the ease in which they worked side by side. Being with him felt more normal than anything she'd felt before. She couldn't even remember when she and Will had cooked together—or done anything together for that matter. A normal night was sitting on the sofa after work until one of them got tired and went home. And she'd almost married him. Yet she was about to walk away from this person she already felt more of a connection with than she ever had with Will. Nashville wasn't an option for him. He had Julia and Winston, and his business was thriving here.

Patrick stretched the dough into a thin, even circle, his hands dusted lightly with flour, then brushed it with a delicate layer of olive oil. "What's on your mind?" he asked as he sprinkled mozzarella on top, creating a bed for the toppings. He layered ribbon-thin slices of prosciutto over it, scattered chunks of goat cheese, and arranged the fresh figs with precision.

"Tomorrow morning," she answered honestly.

He nodded, not saying anything, but thoughts were evident on his face.

"I have to go back. I have a job in Nashville. And I'm going to need to work to get on my feet again."

"You sound like you were considering staying," he said in a hopeful tone.

"I don't know *what* I was thinking." She picked up the laminated measurement-conversion chart with the navy insignia on it. How much had changed since the day she'd tried to decipher it.

"Why don't you keep that," he said.

She held up the chart. "This?"

"Yeah. It's handy."

And it will remind me of you. "Thank you."

As the pizzas baked in the wood-fired oven, the scent of toasted bread and tangy cheese filled the kitchen, mingling with the faint sweetness of figs. Through the window, her friends laughed as they sat at the table outside, the puppy running after a ball that Winston threw onto the sand. Pretty soon, Emily would have to face reality. She just wasn't sure what that reality would look like.

***

"TELL EMILY BYE," Patrick said after dinner, ruffling Winston's hair. "She and her friends are going home to Nashville tomorrow." He shut Stormy in the backseat of his idling truck as Julia climbed into the passenger side.

Winston looked up at Emily with big brown eyes. "You're going home?"

"Yeah, I am," she said, trying not to let the little boy's disappointed look pull on her already breaking heart. She might never see him again, and the thought caused a lump in her throat.

"It's been so wonderful to have you here," Julia said, leaning out of the truck window. She waved to Blair and Sienna, who were looking on from inside the house.

"Thank you for letting us stay during the storm," Emily offered.

"Of course. It was no problem at all. Come anytime. Do you have your phone? Let me give you my address."

"Thank you."

"I'll give her mine," Patrick said, that longing in his eyes.

The truck's window slid up, leaving Emily and Patrick outside. Emily got out her phone, and Patrick typed his address into her contacts. Then he handed it back and looked down at her.

"Well, I guess this is it," she said, sliding the phone into her pocket.

His fingers found hers. "You going to be okay?" he asked.

"I don't know yet, honestly. I'm still figuring things out."

He frowned. "Yeah... So am I."

She looked up at him, wishing she had an answer.

When he leaned down and gently kissed her lips, everything inside her screamed to throw caution to the wind and stay—even if she had to sleep in a tent while she job hunted. But she couldn't do that. And just as she'd anticipated, her heart felt as if it were being torn in two.

THIRTY

Emily's mind was still reeling with indecision while she packed her things and tidied her bedroom the next morning. In so many ways, she, Sienna, and Blair had healed there, and as they loaded Sienna's car and locked up the house, The Broken Hearts Beach Club was quietly dissolving. The bond she had with her friends was stronger than it had ever been, and she realized how much she still had to learn about herself.

Sienna started the engine, and they made their way down the drive. From the backseat, Emily took one final look at the pristine beach and the mansion. Then, they pulled away and headed for home.

They drove through town and passed The Low Tide Supper Club. Patrick's truck was parallel parked out front. She sucked in a breath, ready to ask Sienna to stop for a second so she could say goodbye once more, but the lump that formed in her throat changed her mind. The light turned green, and they carried on. But Sienna's glance at her in the rearview mirror gave away that the thought had crossed her mind as well.

Many businesses were still working around the clock to rebuild. The area was taking shape again—just like Emily's life would. She just had to pick up the pieces. And now was the time to do that.

The rest of the drive home, when service kicked in between rural areas, Blair worked her social media, posting and responding to comments, still putting old rumors to rest and beginning a new chapter in her online story. Sienna was headed back to finish a deal she'd started when they'd first arrived at the beach. And Emily was about to face the rest of her life—whatever that might be.

When Sienna pulled up to Emily's apartment, she got out with her and helped her get her suitcase, bags, and cooler out of the trunk.

"It was a blast," Emily said. "Thanks for letting us come."

"Of course." Sienna gave her a squeeze. "Maybe we can do it again next year."

"Yeah."

What would their next trip look like? Sienna would probably have a newborn, Blair would be super busy with social media again, and Emily? Where would she be in a year?

Blair hung out the window. "Need any help getting your bags upstairs?"

"I'm good." Emily slung one bag over her shoulder and picked up the cooler by its handle.

"I'll call you to schedule next week at The Brewing Bloom." Blair blew Emily a kiss.

"See you next week," Emily said.

Sienna put a hand on each of Emily's shoulders. "Call me if you need me."

"Okay."

Sienna got back into her car, and they drove away.

Emily rolled her suitcase to the door, keyed in her code, and let herself inside. She took the elevator to her floor. When she got inside her apartment, she clicked on the lights and set down her bags. The space looked different than it had when she'd left—smaller, less like her. Her things were there, but it was as if she didn't fit them quite right anymore.

She took her suitcase to her bedroom, lay it on its side, and unzipped it. Slowly, she began sorting her dirty laundry from clean, putting clothes into the washer and appropriate drawers and hanging some up in the closet. She reorganized her makeup and tucked it away in the bathroom. All her shoes and extras were returned to their normal spots. In the bottom of the suitcase was the navy measuring card Patrick had given her. She plucked it out and stared at it, those ever-present emotions lurking just under the surface.

She'd packed the laminated card in her luggage, purposely putting it in the trunk of the car because when she looked at it, tears welled up. She tried to convince herself how silly it was to feel so strongly about someone she'd only just met, but no amount of rationalization could stop the deluge of emotion. When it came down to it, getting to know Patrick had been effortless; she felt an ease with him that she hadn't felt with anyone else.

She pulled out her cell phone to see if he'd texted, but she had no new messages.

He was probably busy with the restaurant.

She'd give herself a month or so. Surely, the spell would end, and she could move forward with her life.

Emily took the card to her desk, where she still had a stack of returned RSVP cards for her wedding. Flipping through each one, the guest numbers flashed before her like an old movie, reminding her of how many people she'd have to call. She'd originally left the stack on her desk because she'd been too emotional to look through them, but now, she felt relief. All these people might have witnessed her marrying someone who, in the end, hadn't been right for her. She'd dodged a bullet.

THIRTY-ONE

When Emily roused, the summer sun was already beginning to shine outside. She rolled over and checked her phone. 6:45. Not wanting to emerge from the comfort of her cocoon, she opened her social media and browsed Blair's feed. Her heart squeezed when she saw all the photos.

With expert precision and artistic flair, Blair had posted a reel of incredible shots documenting their trip. Adoration filled her as she played it. Blair had caught Emily and Sienna laughing together by the water, their bare feet on the white sand, a slew of stunning dinners Patrick had cooked for them, the tub of bubbles on their spa day, the candles lit by the swimming pool, their time on the deck drinking cocktails...

But Emily's favorite was the shot they'd taken at the beginning of their journey—the one of the three of them sitting together on the beach. Blair in the center with her sun hat, Emily on her left, and Sienna on her right. In front of them was the wide, beautiful Gulf in all its glory.

The photos, of course, were the highlight reel of their

stay, but they did their job and whisked her away to the best moments of their vacation. Emily, Sienna, and Blair had brought more baggage than their suitcases, and they'd left with bonds that could never be broken. With her friends by her side, she'd get through her hard times just as she'd gotten her friends through theirs. This, too, shall pass, and her highlight reel would begin again.

Emily closed the app and climbed out of bed, the photos giving her the energy she needed to start her busy day.

When she opened the bedroom door, the silence was jarring after spending so many days with other people. She already missed her friends and wished she was still with them. She pulled her clothes out of the dryer, folded them, and returned them to her room, before making the bed and folding the nightshirt she'd worn, setting it on the edge. Then she slipped on a pair of jean shorts and a T-shirt and got ready for the day.

She dropped a bagel onto a plate, along with a dollop of cream cheese, and took them to her desk with a cup of coffee. On her laptop, she pulled up the number for the florist and made her first call. The caterer was next, followed by the officiant. She answered their questions and thanked them for their sympathy, although she felt oddly at peace. Will wasn't the one for her. Then, she called the photographer, the limo driver, and the cake baker. She canceled the rentals of tables, chairs, and linens.

What made it finally feel real was when she called the church to let them know.

"We're really sorry to hear that," the woman on the phone said. "I'll cancel your meeting with the preacher, and if you'll hold just a second, I'll patch you through to him."

"Okay, thank you," Emily said.

When the preacher came on the line, she explained briefly what had happened.

"I'm sorry to hear that," he said. "Even when a relationship ends for the right reasons, it hurts. I want you to know that God's grace is with you, and you don't walk through this alone."

"Thank you," she said, feeling more hopeful than she had in a long time.

Emily peered down at the names of the wedding guests she'd written in her planner; the thought of calling them all felt draining. No one would have expected her and Will to fall apart, and she'd certainly have a lot of questions to answer. This group would definitely be harder on her emotionally. She needed a break before she started that task.

Apartment hunting as a distraction had just crossed her mind when Blair called.

"Checking on you," she said happily down the line. "How are you this morning?"

"I'm good. I've been canceling my wedding. I've just got to call my friends and family who were coming, but I might do it later. I think I want to apartment shop to lift my spirits."

"Ooh, I could help, if you want. We could take my laptop to The Brewing Bloom and grab a coffee. I miss you already."

"I feel the same way! Coffee sounds perfect."

Blair squealed. "Want me to call Sienna and see if she'd like to join? She'll have all the details on real estate."

"I'll text her."

"Okay. What time should we shoot for?"

"How about ten?"

"Perfect. See you soon."

Emily ended the call and texted Sienna, who immediately said that she'd be there.

Next thing she knew, they were all around a table at their favorite coffee shop.

"This is where the seeds of The Broken Hearts Beach Club were first planted," Emily said, settling into her chair with a cinnamon latte.

"This place sure has seen our worst moments," Blair said.

Sienna raised her soda. "Cheers to that."

They lifted their drinks with a giggle.

Then Sienna addressed Emily. "Are you ready to get your future started so we can officially end our little broken hearts club once and for all?"

"I am," Emily replied, ignoring the big what-if she'd left back at the beach.

Blair opened her laptop and logged in. As they sipped their drinks, they perused the various apartment complexes within a thirty-mile radius. Sienna checked real estate listings and offered suggestions and amenities.

"Here's a list in Columbia. That's a little farther than you wanted to go, but not *too* bad."

Emily shook her head.

"What about this one?" Sienna pointed to a new building about a half hour from downtown. "Quartz countertops, oversized closets, and more..."

"Not that one," Blair said. "It's too far from my house."

"Yep, she's right," Emily said. Funny that not too long ago, she was considering living in a tent in Florida. Normalcy was taking hold.

OVER THE NEXT WEEK, Emily saw the five apartments the three friends had written down as contenders. Blair and Sienna went with her to check out each one. With Sienna's keen eye for real estate and Blair's knack for design potential, Emily finally found an apartment that seemed perfect—bright, open, and just a few blocks from her school. Every step toward her future strengthened her.

She submitted her application for the apartment, nervous but encouraged. Then, she spent the next couple of days calling all her friends and family to let them know about her and Will. Explaining things wasn't nearly as difficult as she'd thought. Enough time had passed that she had a level head about it all, and her emotions had subsided. She was comfortable with herself, and excited about the choices she had ahead of her.

Two days later, she'd been approved for the apartment. Before she signed the lease, she planned to go through it with Sienna one final time.

In all the busyness, she'd been able to push Patrick out of her mind. But when she went to her desk to throw the RSVP cards away and organize the papers she'd laid out while making various calls, the navy measurement card came into view, and a hollow ache of what could have been formed in her chest.

He hadn't texted or called. But neither had she.

Perhaps, like her, he'd gotten busy. Or maybe, just as she'd suspected, the spell had broken, and he'd gone back to his life. But she missed him. She'd missed him the whole time, but simply wouldn't allow her mind to consider it. Would she find herself, two years down the road, wondering about him? When they were together, she'd been able to tell him anything. Could she still? Even with a couple weeks between them, she wondered now. She wanted to hear his voice... Maybe she'd start with a text to break the ice.

She pulled out her phone, but as she got going, she typed that she missed him. Should she disclose that? He hadn't texted her—what if he didn't miss her? But if she was being honest, she wanted him to know. She hit send.

The three bubbles immediately appeared on her phone, sending heat through her neck and up to her cheeks.

> I've been dying over here waiting for this text.

She laughed, his words filling her with happiness. Her phone rang, and she answered.

"You trying to kill me or something? It's been eleven days," he teased.

"What have you been up to?" She had to fight the smile off her face to speak.

"Just working and doing some renovations around the house. Winston's been helping me with some painting."

"Oh, how nice of him! What are you painting?"

"Just some stuff outside. I miss you," he said out of nowhere.

Her heart skipped a beat.

"When are you coming back?"

A tingle spread through her. Talking to him, all she wanted to do was to go back. As exciting as her new apartment was, and as encouraging as her friends had been, she wanted to spend time with Patrick to see where things would lead. What would it be like to date him? She'd be able to enjoy him so much more now she'd gotten through the issues with Will. No more storms.

"As soon as I can."

School started in six weeks. Could she get back before

then? She still had to get the rest of the boxes out of the house she'd bought with Will, make sure he sold it, and possibly have a yard sale for everything that wouldn't fit into her apartment. Then, she'd have to move in, which would take some time. But she could squeeze in a week somewhere, right?

"I thought about driving to you," Patrick said, "but I'm inundated with preparations for the launch of the restaurant, and Winston and I enrolled Stormy in training classes. I promised to take him."

"It's easier for me to come to you."

"Come anytime you can. Sooner rather than later. Surprise me for all I care."

She laughed. "I'll check my calendar."

"Okay. Hey, a huge delivery just showed up at the restaurant. I've gotta go. I can call you later?"

"Of course."

A strange, sobering weight filled her chest when she hung up the phone. She paced around for a little while, her mind full. Unsure what to do next, she went into her bedroom. She'd been so busy that her suitcase was still against the wall, like a symbol of the place where she'd become the person she was now.

The only change from when she'd been at the beach house to this moment was that now, when she asked herself what she wanted, she knew.

THIRTY-TWO

The next morning, while tidying her apartment, Emily was unsettled. Patrick's excitement over her text, and their subsequent call, had put tiny fissures in the wall of her new life. Just when she thought she'd gotten everything worked out, they'd reconnected, making her doubt her choices. Was that new apartment right for her? Did she want to rope herself into another year-long lease? Yes, she needed to, she told herself.

She eyed the suitcase that was still against the bedroom wall. It was time to put it away. It had been long enough. Emily made to roll it down the hall and into the closet. But as she pushed it toward the door, a pull in her heart stopped her, and in a moment of total impulsiveness, she switched gears.

She turned her suitcase onto its side, unzipped it, and began putting new clothes in it. She darted to the bathroom and scooped up her toiletries, then ran back to her bag, lumping them in. When she had everything packed, she zipped up the case, took it to the door, and went into the apartment hallway, locking the door on her way out.

A ping and then the hum of the pulley's engine rang through the silence as the elevator made its way to her floor.

She stared at the suitcase. What was she doing? Could she just leave everything right now? But a little voice inside told her that she knew exactly what she was doing: She was choosing. Finally, a choice for herself. She knew what she really wanted. She just had to figure out how to get it.

The suitcase rolled behind her as she made her way to the parking deck. When she got to her car, she put the suitcase in the backseat and got in the driver's seat. She pulled up Patrick's address from her contacts and typed it into her navigation. With the directions chirping through the car, she began to drive.

On the way, Emily called her school on her hands-free and asked for Martha Rogers.

"Hi, Emily," Martha said in her usual friendly tone. "What's up?"

"Hi. I have a question for you." She turned the corner and followed the map to the second turn, leading to the highway.

"Of course. What is it?"

"Am I able to get out of my contract due to an unexpected life change?"

"Oh goodness, is everything okay?"

"It's better than okay. There's a possibility I might move to another state."

"Well, I'd hate to lose you, Emily. But it's still early enough in the summer that I could let you out of your contract. It's not something I like to do, but given the circumstances of an unforeseen move, I could do it for you."

"Okay, thank you. I'll let you know in the next few days." She ended the call and then used voice commands to call the apartment complex and back out of her lease application.

She had no idea what came next, but for once, the unknown wasn't terrifying. The one thing she knew for sure was that there was a boy by the coast who made her realize she could change her mind, and a part of herself that finally believed she didn't have to choose between loving someone and loving her own life. So she drove toward the horizon, toward the beach, toward whatever future was waiting.

EIGHT HOURS LATER, in the soft glow of early evening, Emily pulled onto the familiar drive in the woods. She prayed Patrick would be home from work by now, since she hadn't seen his truck outside the restaurant when she'd driven through town. Her heart pattered at the sight of it in the driveway. She hadn't even considered what she'd have done if he hadn't been home.

She came to a stop and her breath caught at the view. After she got out of the car, Emily walked around to the side of the house to get a better look.

A stone path led to the fishing shed. It had been completely repainted a bright white, with window boxes full of purple and blue flowers flanking the front door. A little mat on the stoop read "Welcome." What was this for? It was too big and beautiful to be a playhouse for Winston...

"Looking for a rental?" Patrick said from behind her.

Elation swelled, and it took everything Emily had to keep her composure. She faced him, her entire attention landing on him and locking in place. He had a day's growth of stubble, making him look less refined than she'd seen him before. That, and his thin T-shirt that barely hid his physique, gave him a ruggedly casual appearance that she wanted to drink in for the rest of her life.

"Rental?"

He put his hands in his pockets as if her being there were nothing new, but by the glimmer in his eye and the tiny smirk playing on his lips, he was just as excited as she was that they were standing opposite one another.

He walked toward her. "So when I bought the house, this was plumbed and outfitted as a mother-in-law suite. I haven't started the inside yet, but Winston helped me paint the exterior. I'm going to renovate it and see if I can rent it to help Julia with the cost of her classes."

"You have time for all that with work?"

"It's a lot, but the rent would offset the cost of her classes, and she could finish her degree debt-free, so I'm willing to spend nights on it for a while."

"I'm in the market for a rental," she said. "But I'd have to get a job first."

His eyes widened with surprise. He took a step toward her. "What about your teaching contract in Nashville?"

"They let me out of it."

His gaze swallowed her, and he took a step into her personal space, putting every one of her nerves on high alert. "And you want to live here?"

"There's this guy I'm kind of seeing," she ventured, her pulse racing.

"Oh really...? You like this guy?"

"Yeah. A lot."

He reached for her hand and intertwined his fingers with hers. His touch was intoxicating and validated every feeling she'd had about him since she left.

"I never guessed that you'd actually be my first tenant, but I have to admit that the hope of offering you somewhere to stay was enough to get me working on it." He let go of her fingers and put his hands on her waist, pulling her in. "I'd need a few months, but Julia has a sofa while you wait. That might give you some job-hunting time."

She looked up at him, his woodsy, spicy scent robbing her of any good sense. "I'll sign the lease immediately—sight unseen."

The corners of his mouth twitched upward. "Consider it signed." He leaned in and pressed his lips to hers.

With no plans at all, she wrapped her arms around the next step in her forever.

EPILOGUE
THE FOLLOWING JUNE

"How does it look out there?" Patrick called from the back of the building.

"It's getting busy outside," Emily said. She smoothed her powder-blue gown and checked her dangly earrings in her reflection at the bar. Then she opened the door just a crack to get a good look at the crowd.

Guests were arriving and filling the front walk. They lined up between velvet ropes dotted by lantern-lit palms. The sound of soft waves offshore mingled with the hum of conversation and the gentle jazz playing inside.

The staff took their positions.

"Ready or not, here we go," Patrick said into her ear, giving her goosebumps.

She turned to view him one final time in his tuxedo. The dark color brought out the blue in his eyes. "You look handsome." She straightened his bow tie and kissed his cheek, then removed the smudge her lip gloss had left.

"I'm glad you're here to do this with me," he said.

"I wouldn't want to be anywhere else."

He leaned down and whispered, "Everyone's watching or I'd kiss you right now. And you look incredible."

"Later," she said.

He gave her a wink and then opened the door to the cheer of the crowd. They walked outside to greet everyone.

A crisp coastal breeze swept across the Gulf as The Low Tide Supper Club opened its doors for the first time, the evening sun casting a pink-gold shimmer and bathing the restaurant's glass frontage in a warm, luminous glow.

Photographers snapped pictures of the elegantly dressed gathering—locals, visiting yacht owners, and a few quietly recognizable celebrities, each drawn by the promise of an indulgent coastal experience unlike anything the area had seen before.

Patrick's PR person, Tabitha, addressed the crowd with a microphone and then handed it to Patrick.

"Good evening, everyone," he said, sounding more professional than Emily had ever heard him sound, "and thank you for being here to celebrate this moment with us. The Low Tide Supper Club began as an idea fueled by a love for this coast and the desire to bring my personal chef business, Main Course, to the masses. Tonight, that dream becomes a reality because of all of you.

"So please, eat, drink, explore, and enjoy this evening. Thank you for trusting us, supporting us, and stepping into this new chapter with us. We're honored to welcome you to the very first night of The Low Tide Supper Club—may it be the start of many unforgettable nights to come."

The crowd clapped.

Patrick clicked off the microphone and handed it to Tabitha. Then, the host began seating people.

Emily scanned the patrons, quickly finding familiar faces. She ran over to Blair and Rocko, and Sienna and

Tyson with a baby stroller, and pulled them out of the line, giving them hugs.

"Thank you for coming all the way here," she said.

"We wouldn't miss this for the world." Blair, dressed in a loose-fitting drape of silver sequins that landed mid-thigh, gave her a big squeeze.

"Let me see little Addison!" Emily squealed, moving over to see Sienna and Tyson's baby girl.

She sat nestled comfortably in her stroller, taking in the world with wide, wondering eyes. The soft Gulf breeze fluttered the edges of her pastel bonnet, and tiny fingers curled around the strap of her cream-and-pink rattle. Though she was far too young to understand the celebration around her, she seemed captivated by the shifting lights, the gentle hum of voices, and the occasional sparkle of laughter floating her way. She let out a delighted coo, as if adding her own small note to the evening's excitement.

"She's got your face shape, Sienna," Emily said.

Sienna grinned at her little one.

"Let's go inside. Follow me and we'll bypass the line." Emily led them into the restaurant.

Blair snapped photos on her phone. "VIP access to the biggest launch on the Gulf will be a fun post," she said excitedly. She was back on her game.

Inside, the atmosphere felt both extravagant and intimate, polished by luxury. The interior blended driftwood textures with brushed-brass fixtures, creating a modern maritime elegance. They walked under a vaulted ceiling featuring suspended sculptures inspired by sea currents, their contours catching the flicker of candlelight from the tables. Servers flowed through the room, offering celebratory champagne flutes filled with citrus-infused bubbles for waiting customers, while the open kitchen emitted enticing aromas of poached snapper and smoked Gulf oysters—Patrick's recipes.

Emily found Patrick talking to Julia. Her hair was swept up tonight with spiral curls around her face, and Winston was at her side in a miniature tuxedo matching Patrick's.

Emily said hello and bent down to talk to Winston. "What do you think of all this?"

"I think it was more fun when there was room for basketball," he said with a grin as he tugged on the collar of his shirt.

"You're probably right," Patrick said, overhearing. "But I promise the cake you'll get tonight will be well worth losing the basketball court."

"It's gonna have to be a biiiig piece," Winston said, widening his arms and making them all laugh. "And one for Stormy."

"They kept Stormy?" Sienna asked.

"No one claimed him," Emily replied.

While they all greeted one another, making light conversation, a deep, low voice said, "Hello there," to Sienna and then, "Hey," to Patrick. The man swept past them and disappeared into the throngs of people near the bar before Emily could determine who it was. She craned her neck to find him, but couldn't get a good look.

"Wait, was that…?" Blair tipped her chin up to see over the crowd. "That was someone famous. I know by the two men with earpieces I saw pass." She waggled a finger at Sienna. "He said hi to you *and* Patrick. Who was that?"

No one answered.

"What was he wearing?" Emily asked.

Julia looked around. "I didn't see."

"Neither did I." Blair turned to Sienna. "The beach house owner is here, isn't he?"

With a grin, Sienna air-zipped her lips and threw the invisible key over her shoulder, she and Patrick sharing a smirk.

"You'll tell me who it is, won't you?" Emily batted her eyelashes playfully at Patrick.

Still grinning, he shook his head and swiped a champagne flute from one of the waiter's trays. "Can't. Nondisclosure agreement." He handed her the glass. "But maybe if you're lucky, and after a few of these, he'll come chat with me." Then he whispered in her ear, "And I get front-row tickets to all his concerts."

Emily gasped.

Patrick laughed. "In the meantime, let's eat."

As they walked to their table, Emily stepped next to Blair. "Your dress is stunning. So trendy."

"Thank you." Blair flashed a smile. "I thought so too, but I really got it because I liked the loose style." She ran her hands along her waist, revealing a bump on her abdomen. She sucked in her lips and gave Emily a suggestive look. "I'm due in five months, and so far, everything is going smoothly. I get extra checkups to keep an eye on the baby."

Emily sucked in a breath and then pulled her in for a hug. "I'm so excited for you."

"It was scary to try again, but Julia's story stuck with me. I don't want to miss out on a child because I'm scared."

"I want weekly updates," Emily said enthusiastically.

As the night deepened, the restaurant seemed to glow from within, its guests laughing over handcrafted cocktails and dishes arriving that looked like works of art. The Low Tide Supper Club was destined to become a Gulfside ritual, a place where time slowed just enough to savor it all. And savoring was what Emily did best these days.

As she held her glass of champagne, she couldn't help but admire the solitaire on her left ring finger, a promise Patrick had pledged he'd see through to the end. With her new teaching position, she'd be busy, but planning their intimate wedding would be the highlight of her evenings.

Emily, Sienna, and Blair had put an end to their regular Broken Hearts Beach Club meetings. While they were sure to still have ups and downs, they had each other, and the hope that, no matter what, things would work out. Emily couldn't wait to see what came next for all of them.

Hello!

Thank you so much for picking up my novel, *The Broken Hearts Beach Club*. I hope it got you into a beachy mood and whisked you away to a tropical destination—wild storms and all!

If you'd like to know when my next book is out, you can **sign up for new Harpeth Road release alerts for my novels here:**

www.itsjennyhale.com/email-signup

I won't share your information with anyone else, and I'll only email you a quick message whenever new books come out or go on sale.

If you enjoyed *The Broken Hearts Beach Club*, I'd be so thankful if you'd write a review of the book online at your favorite retailer site. Getting feedback from readers helps to persuade others to pick up my book for the first time. It's one of the biggest gifts you could give me.

Until next time,
    Jenny

ACKNOWLEDGMENTS

I cannot write a book without thanking Oliver Rhodes, who saw my potential and taught me everything I know about the business. His incredible example paved the way for my journey. This book would not be here without him. I am forever grateful.

To the editors of this novel: To Megan McKeever, I am so thankful to have had your input on the plotlines and building out this story. Lara Simpson, thank you for your always fabulous line edits—I'm so thankful to have found you. Kendra Olson, you are quickly becoming one of my favorite editors. I get giddy knowing your hand will be on my story. Lauren Finger, thank you for shining this book up and getting it ready for a crop of new readers. To my cover designer, Kristen Ingebretson, you are the best of the best! Thank you for all the creative discussion around branding my novels.

And last of all, a heartfelt thank-you must go out to my husband, Justin, and my kids for rolling with the ups and downs of my workday. They are an amazing support and my whole world.